WICKED LUST

(The Wicked Horse Series)

By
Sawyer Bennett

ISBN: 978-1-940883-42-7

Find Sawyer on the web!
www.sawyerbennett.com
www.twitter.com/bennettbooks
www.facebook.com/bennettbooks

Table of Contents

Prologue

Cain

I FOLLOW WOOLF out of his office at The Wicked Horse.

No… correction… that would now just be Bridger's office.

I cannot fucking believe Woolf sold out completely to Bridger. I mean… he seemed so invested in this club, and not just monetarily. As head of security and a longtime friend of Woolf's, they both wanted me to be the first to know. They apparently signed the purchase documents last week, but they had to get some other things in order before they made the announcement to everyone else. I got the news first, but they're going to have a staff meeting tomorrow to let everyone else know, and I suppose some type of email will go out to the sex club patrons.

Just… damn.

Woolf Jennings went all legit and vanilla on us.

I watch as he walks over to the bar and slips his arm around the waist of Callie Hayes. There's no shame in admitting it… they make a gorgeous fucking couple. I've known Woolf a long time. I've seen him at what I've thought was his pinnacle of happiness when we opened the doors to The Wicked Horse, but fuck, when I look at him right now... The way he looks at Callie with such unfettered love and reverence actually makes my chest constrict a bit with overt happiness for my friend. It's at this moment I realize he's doing the absolute right thing.

I smile to myself because ever since I caught Woolf fucking her outside The Silo and watched how he tried to protect her so I couldn't see... well, I just knew then he was a goner. And you know what? Good for him. Everyone deserves a chance at love, I suppose.

I mean... if that's your thing.

Woolf catches my gaze and lifts his chin up to me in acknowledgment. I give him another congratulatory smile, watching as he takes Callie by the hand and leads her out of the club. I expect the only time I'll be seeing him now is on the days I work out at the Double J ranch. I've been working there on and off since high school as it's a good way to make some extra cash. While Woolf— I mean Bridger, now—pays me well, I'm on a mission to become debt free as quickly as possible. That means I work my ass off and live frugally, because I can't stand being constricted by financial obligations.

Making my way out into the main nightclub, my eyes do a quick sweep around. I have between four and six security men on duty each night to keep everything under control and running smoothly. There's no mistaking them in their black BDUs and form-fitting black t-shirts with The Wicked Horse logo on the front and the word *Security* on the back. I want them to be obvious to the crowd, so they know I don't fuck around when it comes to the safety of the patrons here. It's obvious I don't tolerate any shit on my watch.

I've got my black BDUs on tonight too along with my combat boots—product leftover from my days in the Marine Corps. Instead of my Wicked Horse *Security* shirt, I'm wearing a long-sleeve, black athletic shirt that fits my skin like a second glove because my job tonight is a little different from the normal security oversight I usually provide.

As I walk through the club to the front door, I continually scan my eyes back and forth. Old habits—those where I'm waiting for an ambush by Taliban insurgents while sweeping the Zabul Province of Afghanistan—die hard, and I suppose that will never go away.

Except, my gaze slams in an abrupt halt on *her*.

This is the third night in a row she's come in, and I don't necessarily like how she rattles my focus at work. I wish I could tell you what it is about her that caught my attention, but I'm ashamed I can't. It's a blow to my ego that my intuition and street smarts are failing.

She's pretty, for sure.

Not gorgeous, but really pretty. Wavy, blonde hair that is midway between her chin and shoulders, with bright blue, eyes. On the petite side, but with plenty of curves. I noticed this when she dances with the three girls she comes in with.

She only dances with those girls. She's turned down

every man who asks her to dance. I'm also ashamed I notice this because I have better uses of my time than watching a pretty girl get hit on in a bar.

I suppose the reason she caught my eye is because it seems she's been trying to catch it. While she sits at a table, talking and laughing with her friends, her gaze will roam around The Wicked Horse. She'll watch the dancers or the band if we have one going. She'll sometimes focus in on other tables of people, but she never rests her gaze in one place very long.

Except when it lands on me. Then she'll hold my stare if I just happen to be watching her, which is often. Sometimes, she doesn't look away for an almost unbearably long time. She's always the one who breaks eye contact though, and it's always with a wistful smile.

She's never approached me though, even though women do that all the time despite the scary-as-fuck scar that slashes across my face and the menacing glare I seem to give off most of the time. It's true... I've been hit on more times than I could ever hope to remember, and I'd be lying if I didn't say this job wasn't without perks. While I'd never leave my post while on duty, I've taken plenty of those women home and fucked them after work hours.

Hell, sometimes, I just take them up against the side of the building after I lock everything up.

My security team always shakes their heads with amusement at the amount of female attention I get, and I assure them it's not because of my charm or good looks, but rather the rumor floating around—which just happens to be true—that I've got a massive cock and I'm a god in the bedroom with it.

They all tell me to fuck off when I point that out to them. Jealous pricks.

I've never approached the blonde woman; although, I get the sense she wants me to. Again, when I'm working, I'm working. I don't have time for flirting or fucking. But maybe I should come in on my next night off and possibly talk to her. Try to figure out what's going on underneath those pretty, pale curls because she fascinates me. While I get hit on all the time, women have a hard time holding my gaze the way this one does. They're content to stare at my feet while they try to flirt because my eyes are sometimes too cold and my scar is too angry looking.

But not this woman. She looks me dead in the eye, and it's a goddamn turn on as much as it is a mind fuck to me.

I think she senses my gaze, because hers slides away from one of the girls at her table who seems to be telling quite an animated story, and she locks irises with me. We engage in the same staring war for only a moment, but I'm the one who has to look away this time as I reach the front door of The Wicked Horse. Things to do... people to see.

I nod at Peter, one of the security detail, who opens the door for me, and I step out into a warm July Wyoming night.

I LOOK INSIDE the glass panes of the back door. The living room is empty. People are so stupid sometimes when it comes to their safety.

First, they have their porch light off and with my black clothing, I blend well into the night. Second, they have flimsy glass panes that would be easy for me to break and unlock the door with a quick flick of my wrist.

Morons. Haven't you ever heard of double dead bolts?

But what I find to be insanely more stupid is the fact that these idiots left the back door unlocked.

Turning the knob, I sneak stealthily inside.

I can hear noise from the bedroom down the short hall… late evening news. The harsh quality of blue, flickering light into the hallway tells me the occupants are in bed with the lights off.

Possibly asleep.

So fucking easy.

I hold the gun in my hand down at my side as I sidestep quietly down the hall. These new construction homes are solidly built and not a floorboard creaks. Just before I reach the door, I pull the black knit mask down over my face, assured that the holes cut out for my eyes and mouth will not reveal my identity.

I take a deep breath… and then I step into the bedroom.

Husband and wife, lying side by side on the bed, watching TV. Mid-forties, I suppose. The guy has a bit of a belly on him, but the woman isn't too bad on the eyes. Dark brown hair cut into a bob and long legs pouring out from a silky, pink nightgown that barely covers what I'm betting are matching panties.

I'm a sucker for lingerie, and I start to get hard.

Raising my gun, I hold it sideways in a gangster sort of pose, which is not the way you should ever handle a gun. I just find the sideways tilt is more menacing, and it lets them know I mean business.

The woman sees me first, and a tiny scream pops out of her mouth. The man comes flying out of the bed, wearing only a pair of white boxers, and stops the minute I swing the gun toward him. His hands come up in an immediate pose of surrender.

"Turn the light on," I rasp out to the man. He reaches a shaky hand back and flips on the bedside lamp, coating the room in a soft glow.

"TV off," I command. I don't want anything interfering with my concentration.

He turns the TV off with the remote control laying on the table.

The woman has sat up in bed and is breathing erratically. It draws my attention down to her breasts, which are large and obviously fake. I see her nipples are pebbled against the pink silk, and it makes my cock swell further.

I turn the gun on her and make a motion with it toward me. "You... get over here."

She looks to her husband with wide eyes, and he tries to give her reassurance. "It's okay, honey. Just do what he says and I'm sure everything will be fine."

He turns back to me. His voice quavers. "Please… we have money… jewels. Whatever you want?"

"What I want," I say darkly as I cock the gun, "is for your wife to get the fuck over here."

"Okay," the man all but shrieks and actually makes a shooing motion toward his wife. "Amy… darling… just do as he asks."

He turns those somber eyes my way and begs. "Please don't hurt her."

I chuckle and don't give him another thought as Amy stands from the bed and tentatively walks toward me. Her large breasts barely sway with the motion and the rounded edges definitely tell me they're fake, but fuck… they're nice.

Very nice.

When she's standing in front of me, lower lip trembling, I lower my gun and with my free hand, stroke her cheek. She flinches but otherwise lets me have my way with her.

I slide my fingers through her hair, to the back of her head, and I grip her tight. "Now, Amy… I want you to get on your knees and suck my cock for a bit."

She lets out a whimper as I start to push her down.

"And if you bite me, I'm going to blow your husband's head off," I add on as I raise the gun back at him. "Are we understood?"

She nods her head vigorously and tears pool in her eyes.

"Good girl," I say with a grim smile. "Now… get my cock out and get to work."

She fumbles with the button and zipper of my pants, but makes quick headway because I'm not wearing any underwear. My dick comes out locked and loaded, swollen hard and ready for action. My eyes cut quickly over to the husband, but he's not moved a muscle, I'm sure worried that I'll shoot him. I'm not sure what he thinks watching this, but he can't seem to tear his gaze away from his wife on her knees before me.

The minute those lips wrap around the head of my cock, my eyes flutter closed just for a moment and I groan. "Fuck yeah, baby. Just like that."

Apparently, Amy's got skills.

Mad, mad skills.

She bobs up and down on my cock, with a perfect amount of friction, and has this wiggle move with her tongue underneath the head that almost causes my knees to buckle. When I feel my balls start to tingle, I push her off, noting the faint spill of drool from her swollen lips.

"Panties off and get on the bed," I tell her curtly. "Spread your legs so I can see that pretty pussy."

Amy looks to her husband pleadingly, but he just nods his head.

She does as I ask, shimmying out of the tiny scrap of pink silk. She lies in the middle of the bed, and as instructed, spreads her legs wide for me. My cock actually bobs up and down in anticipation, but I got to suit up first.

Stepping forward, I lay my gun on the bed, right between her legs. I give her a devious smile and taunt her as I reach into my back pocket for a condom. "I dare you to go for the gun. Think you're faster than me?"

She squeezes her eyes shut and doesn't answer me. But I know she's also too chicken shit to make a grab for it. While I rip the foil packet open, I add some further shame to her situation. "Touch yourself, sweet Amy. Let me see if you're wet for me?"

Her eyes snap open, and she actually glares at me. "You go to hell."

I laugh at her as I roll the rubber on my cock and pick my gun back up. Rubbing the tip of it through her pussy lips, I bring it up to inspect. It's glistening with her juices, just as I knew it would be.

Fear doesn't stop the thrill of excitement.

I don't spare Amy's good husband a look as I lay the gun back down on the mattress, this time out of her reach. I'm getting ready to put some concentration into my work, and I can't risk her making a grab for it. As soon as my hands are free, I snatch her by the ankles and pull Amy roughly to the edge of the bed. I actually pull up hard on her legs, lifting her hips off the edge, and I slam my way inside of her.

She lets out a yip of pain, because even though she's wet as all get out, I've got a big fucking cock—which is truth, not rumor—and I know that hurt. I stay lodged in her deep, letting her get accustomed to my size. I wait for her to open her eyes and when she does, I start fucking her.

I go deep and steady, but no need to go too hard. I'm going to make sweet Amy come hard around me, and I hope it fucking shames her.

Damn… she's so fucking wet; I slide so easily in and out. Feels amazing.

My eyes cut over to her husband and widen with surprise when I see he's got an erection tenting his boxers. That's interesting. Apparently, Mr. Amy is a little turned on by me fucking his wife.

"Get over here," I rasp out at him, and he jerks his gaze toward me. It had previously been pinned on my dick ramming in and out of his wife.

He moves forward, his eyes sliding back down to watch what I'm doing, and his cock peeps right out of the hole in his boxers.

"Fuck, dude," I pant as I keep moving in and out of her. "You're turned on by me fucking your wife."

He flushes red over my statement, and Amy doesn't even bother to look at her husband. Her eyes are squeezed shut and her fingers are grasping onto the bed covers.

"Jack off," I tell him.

"What?" He gasps in astonishment.

"Get on the bed, kneel by your wife's head, and jack off while I fuck her."

He makes a choking sort of sound, but he doesn't argue. That's because he doesn't forget there's a gun on the bed only inches from my hand.

Amy's husband kneels beside his wife and without any further direction from me, pushes his boxers down and starts jerking at his dick, his eyes pinned on my cock claiming his wife the entire time.

Yeah... this is actually kind of hot. Wasn't what I imagined, but I'm digging it.

I start tunneling into Amy a bit faster, and now she's making mewling sounds. Reaching a hand down, I pluck at her clit lightly, then press down on it so she can feel me moving in and out of her just on the other side of that sweet bud.

She gasps.

Cries.

Then screams as she starts to come.

"Oh, fuck," her husband groans. He starts to come as well, shooting all over Amy's big, round breasts and soaking the lovely, pink silk.

As I pound harder inside of her, my balls tighten. I grit my teeth, my neck muscles straining, and I start to come. I slam into her hard... brutally actually, and she gives a startled yip as I grind against her pelvis, unloading buckets inside the condom.

"Fuck, that's good," I croak, and then praise my captive fuck. "Amy, of the sweet pussy."

When I've expelled every fucking drop I have, I pull out and pluck the condom off. Amy's husband sags down on the bed beside her, and she scrambles over so they can hold each other.

Awww... that's sweet.

I throw the condom on the floor, tuck my dick away, and snatch the gun from the bed. Giving them both a nod and a toothy smile, I say, "Not one word of this to anyone. I so much as hear you've told someone, and I'll come back and I won't be so nice. Are we clear?"

"Yes," they both simultaneously say. "We won't."

I stare at them, my eyes promising all kinds of retribution. When I'm satisfied we're good, I turn and walk out of their bedroom.

Down the hall, and right out the back door. As soon as my feet hit the ground, I pull the black knit mask off and take a deep breath of the fresh Wyoming air. I swivel my head, the cervical bones in my neck popping.

I feel loose and relaxed.

I actually sit on the bottom step and look up at the stars hanging low and heavy in the sky. Beautiful. The porch light flicks on, bathing me in a yellow glow. The door opens, and I turn my head to see Amy standing there.

She's holding a bottle of Hoback Hefeweizen out to me and gives me a smile. "That was excellent, Cain."

"I thought it was some of my better work," I say with a grin and hop up to accept the beer, which is my favorite from the Snake River Brewery.

Amy's husband appears over her shoulder and pulls the door open. "Want to come in while you drink that?"

"Sure," I say and trot back up the steps, walking back into one of the fantasy cabins that belong to The Wicked Horse. This wasn't the first fantasy I've played in involving Amy and Charles Mason, but this was a special one. It's their wedding anniversary and, as members of The Wicked Horse's sex club, Bridger wanted to do something special for them.

As the door closes behind me, I wonder if the blonde girl is still back at the club. I'm technically off duty, and I consider for a moment finishing my beer and going back to check it out.

But then Amy's hand is on my crotch and she's rubbing my cock, which is eagerly responding, and I know the party here isn't quite over yet.

Blonde woman is forgotten.

For now.

Chapter 1

Cain

I KNOCK ON Bridger's office door. Three solid raps and I hear his heavy bootsteps on the other side. There is no polite "Come in" as the door is locked with a passcode that no one enjoys except for Bridger himself. Well, probably Woolf, as I doubt someone changed the code since the announcement two days ago that ownership changed.

He opens the door and gives me a small smile. "Thanks for coming in on your day off."

"No problem," I assure him as I step in. "Didn't have anything better planned."

Which is the truth. If I had my way, I'd be doing some extra work out on the Double J or some part-time construction with Walt, but neither of those sources panned out. And Christ... I could use the extra work as I got in another fucking bill that doesn't belong to me, and yet, it does.

It's the story of my life. Working to pay off debt I didn't incur, but that I'm still obligated to settle under the eyes of the law. If Rachel wasn't already dead, sometimes I swear I could wring her scrawny neck out of frustration.

Bridger closes the door behind me and motions to the couch. "Have a seat."

As he walks to sit behind his desk, I plant my ass on the dark brown leather couch that has seen plenty of action in this office. I know this because I've personally fucked a few of the bartenders in here, though only by express invitation of Woolf or Bridger to join in a threesome when things were slow.

"We got a problem that I need you to take care of," Bridger says bluntly, and it causes me to move from slouched posture to ramrod straight. The tone of his voice has me tense.

"What is it?"

"Colton Stokes' membership to The Silo has been terminated," he says with little emotion, but I'm still shocked. To my knowledge, no one has been kicked out of the club before.

"I need to know why," I tell him.

Bridger nods because he knows I need to know. As head of security, if this is due to some type of breach, I need to fix it. It's why they pay me a handsome salary with generous quarterly bonuses. To not only keep the patrons of the Wicked Horse—the nightclub portion of this business—safe, but to ensure the secrecy of The Silo, the sex club portion of the empire.

"He told Governor Hayes about the sex club," Bridger says with a hard glint to his eye. "Told him his daughter was at an orgy in one of the cabins. Told him about Woolf's involvement."

And sudden understanding dawns on me. I mean, I knew Woolf got out because of Callie, but I just assumed it was because the poor fool went and fell in love and didn't need this lifestyle anymore. But I get it now. There's no way he could have been with Callie if that information was threatened to become public. Governor Hayes is coming into an election year, and he can't afford for it to be public knowledge that his daughter was dating the owner of a sex club and she attended an orgy there.

"Fucking douche," I mutter as I scrub a hand through my short hair.

"Exactly," Bridger agrees.

"And not a damn thing you or Woolf can do about the non-disclosure breach?"

"Yeah, that's a dead end."

Woolf and Bridger have a non-disclosure agreement that every member of the sex club has to sign, agreeing to absolute secrecy of the existence of the club and its members. A breach of that agreement sets a minimum limit on damages at a cool million. The only problem is, to enforce that agreement, Bridger—as the sole owner of the business now—would have to sue Colton. That would be public record, and there's no way in hell a legal document could be filed and made available for anyone to see that publicly accused him of outing the governor's daughter as a participant in an orgy.

The desire to keep the club secret wasn't borne of

any shame or embarrassment by Woolf or Bridger. On the contrary, they're extremely proud of what they created, which is a protected environment where people can indulge in their most wicked fantasies. Therefore, they were fully prepared to enforce any breach of the non-disclosure through legal means. Hell, they have an attorney on retainer just for such a problem. But with the governor's daughter now being involved, it requires a different sort of way to handle this.

"What's the plan then?" I ask as I stand, the menace clear in my tone, because there's no way this is going to be overlooked. Not by Bridger and certainly not by me. That fucker not only just threatened my friends, but he threatened my very livelihood. He'll have to pay.

"I want you to visit him today," Bridger says as he hands me an envelope across the deck. It's thick, and I instantly know it contains cash for me. A bonus, so to speak. "Deliver the notification that he's not welcome back on Double J property, and he will not so nicely be escorted out if he makes an appearance at The Wicked Horse or The Silo ever again. Also let him know I'm not pursuing the non-disclosure, but impress upon him that there will be ramifications if he opens his mouth again."

"Any limit to those ramifications?" I ask, my blood tingling with excitement. I never did like the prick and I like to fight. More importantly, I like the money in this envelope. I intend to earn it.

"Don't kill him," Bridger says with a chuckle. "But make it hurt."

"Gladly," I say as I tuck the envelope in my back pocket and start to turn for the door.

"One other thing," Bridger says. I halt, turning back around to face him. "Amy Mason called me this morning."

"Oh, sweet Amy," I say with a chuckle.

"She was very impressed with your performance the other night," Bridger says with a lewd smile. "She wants to arrange for an encore. At her house."

"When?" I ask, because it will have to be on one of my days off.

"Week after next. Her husband is out of town on business, and she wants a repeat type of fantasy. You 'break-in' to her house, but she wants you to be a little rougher on her this time. Make it a bit more realistic."

"Does Charles know she's doing that with him gone?" I ask hesitantly, because something about this doesn't sit right. Amy and Charles Mason always act out their fantasies together.

"No clue," Bridger says, pointedly looking at me. "Is that a problem?"

My brows furrow as I contemplate. "I don't know. Just seems a little off. And of course, there's always a risk doing something like that off property. Last thing I need is for some crazy bitch to actually claim I broke in and raped her when it's part of a fantasy she requested."

"I can cover that in a fantasy agreement," Bridger offers. "We'll type up the exact scenario, have her sign it in front of a notary, including that it be done at her house at her request."

"I guess," I say half-heartedly, the idea still not sitting right. And nothing against the scenario itself. I've had plenty of women want to act out a fantasy where they're being forced, but the fact she doesn't want to do this with Charles involved sort of makes me wary. This is due to the mere fact that a good chunk of The Silo's members are in committed, monogamous relationships. A good third of the club is married, and they enjoy indulging in the fantasy aspect with their spouses.

Amy and Charles Mason are just such a couple. In the few that I've done with them, there's definitely a tight bond between them. I mean, you have to have an amazing level of trust in your partner to engage in some of the debauchery that goes on in The Silo. I guess it just feels a little disloyal, but truthfully… that's not really my problem.

"Want me to tell her you'll do it?" Bridger asks with a raised eyebrow.

"Yeah," I say quickly before I can talk myself out of it. It won't earn me any extra immediate cash, but my quarterly bonuses are calculated with how often I'm requested as a fantasy maker, so I want to keep the customers happy. "Work up the agreement and get her to sign it, then have her get up with me via email to set a date. That way we'll have that in writing too."

"Sounds good," Bridger says as he stands up from the desk, indicating our time is over and he has a million other things to do. "Anything else you think we should do to help seal this leak Colton made?"

"Update the security code on The Silo. Right now, it's just a five-digit number. I'd scramble the password and give each member a remote security access fob that generates a new passcode each day."

"Good idea."

"Oh, and think about maybe requiring a damages deposit for all members. Make them deposit a chunk of change into a trust account, separate from their membership fee. It's automatically forfeit if they breach. Make it in addition to the million-dollar clause."

"Brilliant," Bridger says with a devious smile. "And we should make sure that it covers any guests they decide to bring in."

"Definitely," I agree. "Especially since we don't have time to run background checks on each guest since no notice is needed. But if you tie the member's purse strings to the liability of the guest, it will make them think twice over who they choose to bring into the club."

This is actually a major weak spot in my opinion, allowing members to bring in guests. I pointed this out to both Bridger and Woolf before we even opened the doors, but it was ultimately decided we needed to give some latitude to the members, especially since they paid a whopping fifty thousand per year to be members. In addition, most members were affluent and couldn't risk exposure, so we figured they would pick their kink partners with care. In fact, they probably had their own non-disclosure agreements in place for protection.

"I'll get legal to draft up amended non-disclosures, and we'll notify the patrons about a damages deposit. Any thought on the amount?"

I shrug. "The members of this club are multi-millionaires. The membership fee of fifty thousand is chump change for them. I'd make at least the same amount for a damages deposit, if not more."

"A hundred thousand it is," Bridger says with a nod.

I chuckle, knowing every fucking member will pay it without batting an eyelash. The totally filthy rich have no qualms about blowing that kind of money on their kink.

All I know is I'm extremely grateful to not only be a fantasy maker for the club, so I can frequently get my rocks off in the dirtiest of ways, but also my employment through The Wicked Horse earns me a platinum membership free of charge. Call it part of the perks package that comes with the job as head of security. While a few select employees at The Wicked Horse have silver memberships as part of their pay, earning them two visits per week, I was granted a full platinum membership because I've known Woolf just this side of forever since we grew up together. My position comes with built-in autonomy and authority.

The benefit of the platinum membership is that I can walk into The Silo any day of the week, and I'm guaranteed a mind-blowing fuck because it's a private club of many like-minded people. I enjoy this freedom from responsibility and commitment to another person, since the last such person managed to make my life a living hell and even though she's dead, she still manages to fuck up my existence on a daily basis.

"Alright, man," I say as I turn for the office door. "I'm headed to Stokes' house now. I'll give you a call later and let you know how it went."

"Make it hurt," Bridger reminds me, but I don't need it. I'm looking forward to doling out a little Cain Bonham justice on behalf of my friends and employer.

And then after, I might just come back to The Wicked Horse and see if the blonde woman shows up again. If so, it will be five nights in a row as she had her pretty ass parked there again last night when I came on duty. We played our little staring match with each other, but tonight, I'm not working. If she shows again and wants to take that flirting to another level, I'm ready.

Game on.

Chapter 2

Sloane

G OD, I CAN'T stand country music. You'd think a girl born and raised in the great state of Tennessee would thrive on this shit, but I don't. Never liked it growing up, leaning instead toward grunge and rock.

But despite the twangy, deep voice of some vintage Garth Brooks booming over the sound system, I'm finding that I really like The Wicked Horse. Its rough pine flooring and dark paneled walls give it that rustic feel, but the expensive, cowhide-covered seats, custom-carved bar, and specialty drink menu speaks more to a clientele who prefers western chic. It's an interesting combination but ordinarily not one that would keep me coming back.

No, I come back for another reason, and that is mainly because I'm interested in the head of security, Cain Bonham. I just found out his name yesterday, and if I'm lucky, he'll be here again tonight. I'll keep coming back, night after night, hoping to catch him off duty. I happen to know, for a fact, that he does not engage with customers while he's working. I know this not only from personal observation, but because my girl Jasmine, who sits directly opposite of me right now at our little table we've managed to sit at for the past five nights, hooked up with him a few months ago. She assured me he never looked at her twice until one night when he came into The Wicked Horse dressed in jeans, a pair of heavy, black biker boots that seemed out of place in a country-western nightclub, and a dark gray t-shirt. He was clearly off duty. Once he went up to the bar and ordered a beer, Jasmine told me she had set her sights on him.

Said she'd been lusting after him for a few weeks, but the word on the street was that he was crazy rigid about not mixing work and pleasure. She decided to come on to him that night, and it apparently earned a one-way ticket to his bed.

Well, she confessed they actually fucked in the parking lot up against the side of her car in between beers, but still… she claimed it was the best sex she'd ever had.

She relished in telling me the story because Cain Bonham is an intimidating dude. Women don't know whether to fawn or fear… and I suppose that's reasonable. I'm not scared of much in this life, so I would totally go for the fawn path, which wouldn't be hard given his dark brown hair, hazel eyes, and sharply angled cheekbones. He's tall and built like a brick wall, his tight, black *Security* t-shirts hugging those biceps perfectly. I'm not put off nor scared by the large scar that runs along the ridge of one such perfectly sculpted cheekbone. The scar suits him because otherwise, he'd just be a pretty boy.

Instead, he looks raw, edgy, and utterly gorgeous in my opinion.

See… easy to fawn.

Jasmine thinks my interest in Cain is amusing. She told me he doesn't go back for seconds, or so rumor says, so she's all for me getting my rocks off with him if I'm so inclined.

And I am inclined because Cain Bonham is a job to me at this point. If I have to engage in sex with him to further my interests, then so be it. I promise not to enjoy it… too much, but that's probably a lie. You can tell just looking at the man that it's going to be explosive.

Cain didn't start out as a job to me. When I first came in here with my new girlfriends, I was casing the joint, no doubt. He caught my eye almost immediately with his rough good looks, and I got sidetracked from my mission to engage in some crazy staring matches with him where I tried to allude with just the power of my gaze that I was interested. It was sort of a game, and because I'm a sexually active and liberated woman, I have no problem in random hookups or one-night stands. That's what I was interested in.

At first.

But after a few nights of hanging out at The Wicked Horse for some basic background research purposes, I started to realize that nothing was going to jump out at me that would help me reach my goals.

And my goals are pretty nefarious… at least to the owners of this establishment.

I intend to infiltrate a supposed secret sex club that is being operated through this nightclub, and in turn, connect Governor Hayes to it.

That's when I set my sights on Cain Bonham as more than just a personal interest. From what little I know of the sex club, and let's face it, it's not very much at all, I need someone on the inside to get me in. Now, I have no clue if Cain's obligations as the Head of Security extend to that avenue of the business, but the magazine shot me over a quick employment background check on him that revealed to me a few interesting things.

Cain often works part time at the owner, Woolf Jennings' ranch, the Double J.

Most importantly, Cain was employed for three years by SDE Enterprises, which is a corporation based out of Driggs, Idaho. SDE owns a lot of different ventures, but one in particular caught my eye.

A sex club named Scandalous.

This was all enough to lead me to believe that Cain is probably involved with it.

He's my "in," and I intend to sit my ass in this bar every night until I have the opportunity to make a connection with him. It's my hope that said connection is going to be memorable enough that it will keep him coming back for more, which will hopefully give me an inroad into the underbelly of the business.

My reasons for doing this are layered and complex, but at its most basic level, I'm a reporter for *Revealed* magazine, a publication based out of Washington, D.C., that works to expose corrupt politicians. At a deeper level, I'm avenging my mother every time I take a sleazeball down who thinks he or she can use their public office to walk on the backs of others.

Admittedly, Cain wasn't my immediate target when I moved here to Jackson, Wyoming just a week ago. And he's not really my target now, just a means to hopefully discover something print-worthy. I'm still not completely sold on whether there is, in fact, a story here. The "anonymous" tip the magazine received isn't very promising in my opinion. I spoke to the tipster via phone at the order of my editor, Brant Sweeney. I say "anonymous" with air quotes and sarcasm because I was able to find out the cell phone owner's name easy enough with our background resources.

So I spoke to some dude named Colton Stokes— who still thinks he's anonymous to me. He was fairly tight lipped and would only tell me three things.

First, that there's a private sex club that's owned, in part, by Woolf Jennings, president and CEO of JennCo. This is interesting in that Woolf Jennings is a billionaire with a massive cattle and oil empire, but it's not news-worthy for *Revealed* magazine.

Second, that Woolf Jennings is dating Callie Hayes, whose father is the governor of Wyoming.

Third, that Callie also is a member of the sex club.

Again, these tips aren't promising in my opinion. I wasn't quite sure what he wanted us to do with the information, so I pushed him on it. My money is on the supposition that this Colton Stokes guy is probably nursing some bruised feelings from a rebuff from the lovely Callie Hayes—yes, I researched her too—and he wants some payback.

He could not, however, tell me how any of this tied to Governor Hayes.

When I pushed him on this, he was at a loss too, except to say Callie would probably be his campaign manager, and that would only naturally lead him to suspect campaign finances were probably tied to the sex club. In addition and way more promising, I also learned through additional research that Woolf Jennings is a major contributor to the governor.

This had possibility. A very slight possibility, but it was one that Brant felt deserved some attention. He had told me in his nasally tone, "People don't want to read about politicians taking payments from lobbyists. They want sex. Dirty, filthy sex. Go find it for me."

And so I moved to Wyoming.

While I don't think there's much of a story here, I'm still here to do my job. If there's something to be found, I'll do it. Besides, this article is pure gold as far as I'm concerned. Plus, again… if Hayes is dirty and I help to bring him down, I can visit my mother and tell her all about it. Not sure she'll understand, but it will make me feel better.

Jasmine kicks me under the table, and my eyes shoot up to her. Garth Brooks is gone, replaced by Luke Bryan, and I realize I've drifted hard. I raise my eyebrows and shoot her a look.

She nods past my left shoulder, and I turn slowly in my chair.

Cain Bonham has just walked in, looking as sinful as ever. Dark brown hair cropped close on the sides but slightly longer on top. I found out he served in the Marine Corps and while it's not military buzzed, it's still pretty short. It only serves to highlight those damn fine chiseled looks, and the stubble he wears on his jawline also lends to his overall rough allure. He's wearing dark jeans and a lightweight black sweater with a crew collar. I can't see what's on his feet because of the crowd, but I'm guessing biker boots, since Jasmine mentioned them before. She loves the biker type of guys.

Cain doesn't look my way but heads straight to the bar, nodding and giving what could pass as a half-smile to some. I turn back in my seat, surprised to find my heart beating so fast.

"You need to get your ass up and go talk to him," Jasmine pointedly says. "I'll go with you if you want."

She's sweet. Really, she is.

As part of my cover, I fortuitously got a job at a small, leather retail store on the town square, courtesy of a favor called in by my editor through the network of publication favors that infiltrates the United States. The woman known as Sloane Preston became Sloane Meyers—in tribute to my mother as that was her maiden name. I then became a retail clerk at Jackson Hole Leather Emporium. Jasmine works there as well, and we hit it off. Especially after I asked her about The Wicked Horse and she got all excited... told me she goes there all the time. The other two girls, Marilyn and Samantha, are local girls, close friends of Jasmine, very sweet but trolling for husbands, and they don't know any other way to do it than to hang out in a bar every night.

The group was my perfect cover for hanging out at The Wicked Horse, and I've been with them here for the past five nights, engaging in some flirty staring with Cain and wondering when I'd get to make my move.

It looks like tonight is the night, but how to go about doing it? I have to be different because I need more than a one-night stand with him. He has to be interested in more than just sex, but from what I've been able to glean just from observing him, he seems more of a loner than anything else.

My choices are to engage his mind to make him interested in me as a person, or give him the absolute best, dirtiest, mind-blowing sex he can ever imagine, so he'll want to come back for more.

I take a sip of my beer and contemplate how to go about setting the hook.

Chapter 3

Cain

I NOTICED THE blonde woman the minute I opened the door to The Wicked Horse because my eyes involuntarily went to the table she sat at with her girl-friends for the past few nights. It's odd to me that I felt a weird sort of elation over seeing her there, and it made me realize how much I was looking forward to hopefully figuring out the mystery of this girl tonight.

My powers of observation are keen. No more than three steps inside the door and I saw her friend across the table raise her eyes my way and tilt her head toward me. The blonde woman started turning her head my way, and I immediately averted my eyes and headed toward the bar. No sense in letting her know right off the bat I'm here for her. Make her work for it a bit, I guess. Otherwise, where's the fun in that?

That little exchange also told me something im-portant. The blonde was waiting for me to come in, and she shared that with her friends. I saw her friend clearly get her attention and nod my way, so that tells me one very monumental piece of evidence.

I'm going to fuck that girl tonight.

It's odd I'm attracted to her, but I'm only talking about her superficial beauty. She's a well-put-together package no doubt, because what red-blooded man doesn't love a blonde with curves? But it's more the way she looks with her hair curled in loose waves down just below her chin, wide-set innocent eyes of baby blue, and dimples to the left and right of her mouth when she smiles.

She looks like a metaphorical piece of apple pie, all sweet and sugary.

That's usually not my thing. I like women who are aggressive and know what they want. With as much dirty fucking as I do on a regular basis, vanilla women are just a tad too boring. Doesn't mean I won't fuck them, but it does mean they're forgotten sooner than the others are. But I have to hand it to the blonde. She's not been handing me shy smiles and surreptitious looks. No, she stares at me like a woman who knows what she wants, and that's just so contradictory to her naive look.

That's what, in fact, makes her such a mystery. I wonder when she's crying out in pleasure, will it be in a wholesomely saccharine way or if she'll pull my hair out by the roots while screaming for me to make her come harder?

It will be interesting to find out.

Now, how to go about getting in her pants?

I decide to drink a beer and ponder the question, because it's still early and what I know about the blonde is that she'll hang here for a good chunk of the night. At least, that's been her modus operandi so far, so I feel confident I don't have to make a move soon. And besides, if I miss the opportunity with her, that's no skin off my back. I've got The Silo sitting twenty yards off the back of The Wicked Horse. I can bust a nut there just as easy.

"Beer?" Ted says from across the bar. Good dude and he's also a fantasy maker at The Silo. He and I have starred together in some group fantasies in the past. The guy will fuck anyone that has a willing orifice, so it makes him a more popular member of the club.

I nod at him as I take one of the few empty seats and watch as he pours my favorite. After he sets the Hefeweizen in front of me, I slide a ten-dollar bill his way and thus is the extent of our exchange. I'm not an overly chatty dude to begin with, but when I come here, I like to drink, people watch, and keep an eye on my crew.

My back stays turned to the blonde for a few sips of my beer, but then I turn casually around on the stool and gaze out over the club. For a Thursday night, it's fairly packed, although it's still early yet. Give it another hour and it will be standing room only. My eyes first connect on Angel, our DJ, as she sits in a glass booth with a pair of headphones over her glossy, red hair. She's probably the only woman in the world who intimidates me, and only because she enjoys degrading and defiling men. She's a fem-dom, hardcore to the extreme. No matter how much weird shit I've seen happen in The Silo, it still blows my mind the amount of people who will pay to receive pain and degradation as a way to get off.

But to each his own.

I take another sip of my beer and casually move my gaze over to the blonde woman's table. I see it's empty but for their purses and drinks, but then immediately see her and her three friends dancing just a few feet away. Her back is to me and I have to say, it's not a chore watching her dance. Tonight, she's wearing a green floral pattern skirt that comes to mid-thigh and hugs her curves, and damn... she's got a delicious-looking ass too. She's wearing a blue, denim shirt that she has tied near her hips, baring the tiniest sliver of the skin on her stomach. It's unbuttoned to reveal a shadow of her cleavage, and she finishes the ensemble off with a pair of brown cowgirl boots. It's a sweet and sexy look, adding to the dual nature of this woman who is already sweet and sexy by leaps and bounds.

I've watched her dance before, many times. She's damn good, but she's also particular. There's not been a man yet who has caught her eye as she's declined every offer. I hope to God she's not waiting on me to come ask her, because even though I've been told on more than one occasion I have incredible hip action, I do not swing them around on the dance floor.

She doesn't look my way, and in fact, keeps her back to me. Perhaps playing a little hard to get?

Makes me want to spank her ass, if so.

I go to take a sip of my beer as I pin my eyes to her rotating hips, wondering how long she could keep that motion up if she was riding me, when I see a guy move into position behind her on the dance floor. She has no clue he's there, but he's openly leering at her ass, bending his knees and thrusting his pelvis suggestively behind her. Must be drunk, because no woman would ever find that sexy.

Oddly, my first instinct is to stand from my stool and march across the room, right onto the dance floor, where I'll put him in a headlock and drag him off before he touches her, but that would just be silly. What I should do is motion to one of my guys on duty and point out the potential problem, but when I look over at Gary, who's one of two guys in charge of the dance floor, I see he's already well aware and watching.

I ease my posture and try to relax. He'll handle it if necessary.

And necessary apparently comes sooner than later, because the drunken, dancing fool moves right in behind the blonde and puts his hands on her hips. He does a weird, epileptic kind of move and pushes his pelvis into her ass.

I start to stand from my stool again.

Gary moves a step closer.

We both watch to see if the guy backs off, but then I'm sure Gary is as shocked as I am when the diminutive blonde turns around, pulls her arm back, and slaps the shit out of the guy so hard, I can hear the crack of it over the blaring music. I'm momentarily stunned to inaction by this, but then the guy reels around, fury all over his face as he holds a palm to his cheek. He winds his other arm across his chest, indicating a clear intention to backhand the blonde, and I'm flying off the stool toward the dance floor.

I see Gary make the same move, but we are both too far away.

However, I'm brought to a dead halt, right in my tracks, again stunned to inaction, when the blonde pulls her right leg back and, before the guy can even swing his arm, she kicks him square in the nuts.

Holy fuck!

When the guy doubles over, she's not done with him. She balls her little hand into a fist, really so tiny it could never do damage, and lands a right hook to his face. The guy falls over onto the floor, one hand clutching his balls and the other his mouth, which is now bleeding.

Gary is now on scene. Because apparently, the man on the floor needs protecting, he grabs the blonde from behind in a bear hold and pulls her back a few feet. She glares down at him and yells something, which prompts me to move.

The dancing crowd has all halted, pressing in a tight circle around the combatants.

Blonde girl—1.

Douchey drunk—0.

Won't be a second round.

The minute my foot hits the dance floor, the blonde's eyes raise to meet mine. She stares at me with challenge, her face flushed red with fury.

"Let her go," I tell Gary, who immediately releases her.

To my surprise, she bends over the dude, who is now cursing through bloody teeth, and says, "Bet you'll think twice before rubbing your dick on a girl's ass, won't you?"

The guy starts to push up from the floor, glaring daggers at the blonde. "You fucking cunt," he sputters with blood spraying. "You could have just said no."

This infuriates the blonde, who steps toward him menacingly, and the guy isn't a fool. He leans warily backward, holding a hand out to stave off her approach. I have to suppress a laugh as I reach out and take her by the upper arm. Looking at Gary, I jerk my head to the guy. "Get him out of here safely."

"Sure thing, boss," Gary says before grabbing the guy by the back of his collar and pulling him off the dance floor.

"I'm leaving," the blonde says as she tries to shrug out of my hold. "You don't need to throw me out too."

Throw her out? After that glorious display to all drunk men everywhere that they should heed hitting on the wrong woman? No way. I'm not throwing her out, but I am taking her out of here.

"Let's get you cleaned up," I tell her as I start pulling her along. "Your hand's bleeding."

Because I noticed that too. She must have scraped it on his teeth with that punch.

She follows along easily behind me. As we walk past the table, she picks up her purse and calls out to the girls over her shoulder, "I'll be back."

Yeah, that's not going to happen either.

I lead the woman through the bar and toward the main doors. We step out into a mild, mid-July evening, right on the heels of Gary escorting the guy whose ass she just kicked over to a waiting cab. There's usually one or two lurking about waiting to take tourists back into Jackson. I turn in the opposite direction, heading across the wooden, covered porch of the club toward where I parked my truck.

She pulls against me, and I turn to look at her in question.

"Wait," she says in confusion. "You said we were going to get my hand cleaned up."

"We are," I tell her as I turn back around and start walking toward my truck. "I'm taking you to your place, and I'll clean it up there. I'm thinking in your shower would be nice."

Even though you'd never know it by the easy sway of my shoulders or my confident walk, I hold my breath wondering what she'll do. It was a bold statement on my part, but I don't feel like dicking around.

Besides, I just don't flirt well.

I'm immediately relieved when she says, "Sounds good to me."

And I already start to get hard thinking about how easily she just capitulated.

Chapter 4

Sloane

CAIN HAS A beat-up, late 90's model Chevy truck. There's a dent in the front quarter panel, and it's covered in dirt. I'm surprised with his gallantry when he opens the passenger door for me and holds my non-punching hand in his while I navigate the running board.

We pull out and head south on Highway 191 after I tell Cain I live in Jackson. He turns the radio on and adjusts the volume low. An unbidden smile comes to my face when I hear the sweet sounds of Soundgarden coming out versus a country song.

"So," I say into the gloom of the interior. "We're taking a shower together, huh?"

"To clean your hand, of course," he says in a matter-of-fact tone.

"Of course," I murmur, turning in the cab to face him with the little play allowed in the seatbelt. "I'm Sloane, by the way. Sloane Meyers."

I'm proud of myself that I don't even stumble over my fake last name.

"Cain Bonham," he offers, and then says, "But I think I might just call you Right Hook."

I laugh and turn back in my seat, giving my hand a tiny shake. I can't see what it looks like due to the lack of light, but it throbs like a bitch. However, I'm not about to let that interfere with my plans tonight. When I decided I needed something to get Cain's attention outside of flirty looks or a direct come-on, which wouldn't distinguish me at all, it's like God sent that drunken leech to hit on me. I didn't even really have a plan, just knew a spectacle would get Cain's attention, and I struck hard and fast.

I figured it would get me thrown out of the bar, which I hoped would lead to some conversation with him, but never in my wildest dreams did I think he'd take me home.

And tell me he was going to take a shower with me.

I press my legs together as a different sort of throb starts to beat a bit further south than my hand. I have no clue if this half-baked plan to get in good with Cain will do anything for my story that I'm not even sure is a story, but I know one thing... tonight will be damn good regardless.

"You didn't seem surprised by my offer of a shower together," Cain says in an off-handed manner.

I could play this a hundred different ways. Most women in my position would want to solidify their status with a man such as this—do something that would stick in his memory for a long time. The best way to accomplish that at this given moment would be to take off my seat belt, crawl across the expanse of the cab, and undo his jeans. A hand job or blow job would be memorable, no doubt.

But I have a feeling it wouldn't surprise Cain Bonham, nor would it be out of the ordinary to a man such as this. The guy who did Jasmine an apparently amazing favor by fucking her in the parking lot between beers. A man who is potentially embroiled deep within a fantasy sex club has probably seen and done it all.

It's at this moment that, even as adventurous as I am in bed, I realize I might be out of my sexual element. There's probably not anything I can do to cause this man's eyebrows to raise and say, "Hey… this girl right here… she's special."

So I simply answer, "Well, there's an attraction there for sure. I'm personally glad we aren't wasting time on lame come-ons and you buying me cheap beers to get me drunk. I'd like to remember this night, personally."

Cain gives a husky laugh of appreciation and promises, "Oh, you'll remember tonight. I promise you that."

The throb between my legs gets insistently stronger, and I press them tighter together.

THE MINUTE I pull my key from the lock and step into my tiny apartment, I'm immediately filled with broiling tension. Do I just strip out of my clothes and head to the shower? Or will he pounce on me?

"Got anything to drink?" Cain says from behind me

as he shuts the door.

When I turn to face him, I find he's turning the deadbolt and closing the short set of blinds over the glass panes in the door. Locking us in and away from prying eyes.

A tiny shudder runs through me.

"Maybe some whiskey?" he asks, and I blink at him. When he notices confusion on my face, he gives a chuckle and steps toward me, tapping his index finger on my nose. "Did you think I was going to fuck you the minute we walked in?"

"The thought had crossed my mind," I mutter as I turn away and head to a cabinet above the sink. I pull down a fifth of Jack Daniels, because I'm a Tennessee girl after all.

"Need your first aid supplies too," Cain says. "Might as well get that taken care of sooner rather than later. That dude you punched looked like he could have rabies or something."

"That's all in the bathroom," I tell him by way of explanation as I set the bottle and two shot glasses on the kitchen table and turn toward my short hallway. I hear the scrape of a chair indicating Cain must be pulling it out to sit in and I imagine he's twisting the bottle open as I step into the bathroom.

After I turn on the light, I immediately look down at my hand. I must have projected my middle knuckle in the punch because it's slightly swollen. There's also a tear in the skin. It's the only open wound and didn't bleed that much; just a welled-up, large drop of blood that ran in between my middle and index finger before it started to clot.

As I reach toward the mirrored medicine cabinet above the sink, I catch my own gaze in the mirror. I study myself for a moment, noting the hint of determination in my eyes and the tiny flush to my cheeks that is indicative of my excitement.

Am I really going to do this? Am I really going to sleep with a man to try to gain a foothold on a story?

My blue eyes blink back at me without a clear-cut answer.

I mean, it's clear that I *am* going to sleep with him. I was attracted to him in that way long before I ever considered him a pathway to my end goal. But am I really going to use that intimacy to further my own agenda? Do I care if he gets hurt in the process?

I stare back at myself, and I know I don't have any answers to those questions. Shaking my head, I open the cabinet. After grabbing some peroxide and Band-Aids, I head back out to the kitchen.

I find Cain leaning back in the chair with his hands folded and lying right over his belt buckle. It's not a country-western type belt, but a plain, thick black one with an unadorned and unremarkable buckle. He does indeed wear black biker boots. On the table is a roll of paper towels he took from the holder over the sink, presumably to clean my hand. I can't imagine anything kinky we could do with that.

My eyes flick to the bottle, which remains unopened. "Thought you wanted a drink?"

"Lot of things I want." His voice is rich, low… rumbling. I feel it in my gut. "But there's a proper order to things."

"Let me guess," I say with a smirk as I pull the chair out adjacent to his, turn it to face him, and sit. "Fix my hand first?"

"Exactly," he says with a wink and takes my hand, pulling it toward him to inspect. He turns my hand before prodding at the swollen middle knuckle. "Hurt?"

"A little," I tell him with a shrug.

"Can you move it?" He holds his hand, palm up, and spread wide under me to cradle my hand.

I give him an answer by curling and stretching my fingers. "All good."

He nods and then silently cleans my hand. Peroxide, a good wiping and drying, and then a Band-Aid over the middle knuckle. I'm silent as I watch him and when the wrist on his right hand turns, I see all four of his knuckles are scraped open.

"What happened to your hand?" I grab it just as he finishes pressing the Band-Aid onto my skin. I turn his hand palm down, lightly running my index finger over his knuckles, which are already scabbed over with tiny cuts.

"I might have a right hook of my own that got used today," he says with a mischievous grin as he takes his hand away. He reaches over, grabs the bottle of Jack, and twists the cap. I watch as he pours two shots, and then he slides one my way. "Now, let's have a drink."

"What are we drinking to?" I ask curiously as I pick up the glass and hold it out.

"How about right hooks?" he says with a laugh as he taps his glass to mine.

"To right hooks," I agree and shoot the whiskey back. As expected, it burns and then settles into a nice, warm glow inside my belly. It also helps to settle my nerves a little.

"You know," Cain says as he sits his glass down and picks the bottle back up. He pours another shot for himself. I hold my glass out, and he refills it. "You're a conundrum."

Tilting my head to the side, I ask, "How so?"

Setting the bottle down, he picks his shot up, waving it in a circle toward me. "You've got this whole innocent-ly shy and sweet-looking package going on. Like you should be sitting at an afternoon tea dreaming of white picket fences and discussing some romance novel with like-minded friends. But now I'm not so sure... you turn around and beat the shit out of some guy for humping up against you."

"And that bothers you, I'm guessing." I slug back the second shot as I await his reaction, setting the glass on the table.

His brow furrows, and he scratches at his chin thoughtfully with his free hand. "I'm just not normally attracted to your type."

I narrow my eyes at him. "Your chances of getting laid are dwindling."

Cain gives a bark of a laugh before shooting down his second whiskey. He sets the glass down on the table, and I'm startled when his hands jet out to latch onto my wrists. With a sharp tug, I'm pulled from my seat and straight toward him. Sitting forward in his own chair, he releases my wrists only to bring his hands to the backs of my legs, just underneath my ass, and he's hauling me up onto his lap. My green, flowered skirt is made with mostly spandex and just a touch of cotton so it expands to capacity before sliding up my legs.

Cain flicks a glance down. I know from that angle and how high my skirt has pulled upward that he can see my panties. Of course, I knew this was my potential goal, so I dressed appropriately in a sexy, black G-string, thankful I had my Brazilian wax done just last week.

He readjusts my weight, slides his hands up to my bare ass under my skirt, and presses his fingers into the muscles. My hands come to his shoulders for balance, and I look down at him.

When his gaze rises back up to meet mine, his eyes are glittering with challenge. "I didn't say I wasn't attracted to you. Just that I'm not normally attracted to your type."

"You don't even know what my type is," I assert, leveling my stare back at him with defiance.

"Only one way to find out," he says, and my pulse skitters out of control.

Leaning forward, my fingers digging into his shoulders for balance, I place my lips near his ear. Throwing down the gauntlet, I whisper, "Bring it."

He lets out a gust of air that I can feel brush my face as I pull back to look down at him. I expect to see lust, because I certainly started feeling him get hard underneath me as I sat on his lap. And that's there, for sure, but I also see something that sets me on edge… in a sexy way. His eyes are calculating… as if he's going to test me.

"Let's see," he ruminates as his fingers stroke the skin of my butt. "Shy or bold?"

"I'm bold," I say automatically, because I know it was a direct question. And I'm prepared to prove it by pulling his jeans down, climbing aboard, and hopefully rocking his world.

God, I want to rock his world. He's so damn confident and suave about all of this. I think most guys would have pounced on a willing girl the minute we walked in, but he doesn't mind building slow, playing cat and mouse, making me work for it. It makes me assume that whatever he's making me work for is going to be well worth it.

"We'll see," he says with a smirk as he picks me up and sets me back on my feet before him. When he releases me, his hand goes to adjust the hard-on in his pants a bit to the left of his zipper. "Now, if I told you to sit back down in that chair, put your hand down your panties, and get yourself off while I watched, would you have any hesitation in doing it?"

He studies me carefully, awaiting my reaction. His eyes even flick to my cheeks to see if I'll blush.

I don't, although my pulse goes incrementally faster over his dirty talk. "No hesitation," I say as I tilt my chin up proudly, actually surprised I didn't flush from just the mere thought of it. "Sounds kind of hot, actually."

Cain's lips curve upward, and he gives me an appreciative stare. He nods his head toward the hallway and reaches for the bottle of Jack. "Good. Go into your room. Get naked and lay on your bed. I'm going to have one more drink, and while I'm doing that, I want you to play with yourself. Make yourself good and wet for me."

I'm not going to lie. I'm completely stunned for just a moment. Not that he's asking me to do anything that weird. I totally masturbated in front of a former boyfriend before, and I know he thought it was hot. I'm just surprised he wants me to do that while he sits out here having another shot of Jack.

And then it hits me. He's in control right now, and he's seeing how I'll react to it. He's also still trying to see if he can shock me—still trying to gauge what type of woman I am, because honestly... he's still just as confused as ever.

And that makes me feel powerful. It also makes my desire for this man increase tenfold to where I feel as if I might combust if he doesn't hurry up and do something to me.

But I hold my shit together, because I need to prove I am not so innocent and sheltered that I can't take what he has to dole out.

I give Cain a wink. "Better not take too long. I have some really great toys that get the job done pretty fast. Hate for you to miss out."

I am now the one carefully studying him. It's barely perceptible, but I see it... a hard swallow as he considers what I just said. His gaze drops from mine to the bottle of Jack that he picks up, and he murmurs, "I'll be along sooner rather than later then. Don't let the train leave the station without me... and that's an order."

Spinning on my booted heel, I head toward the bedroom, unbuttoning the denim top. I give him a sultry laugh and call back over my shoulder, "Sorry, babe. But God gifted us women with the ability to have multiple orgasms, and I'm not about to waste that gift."

Chapter 5

Cain

I POUR A shot, down it quickly, and then pour another.

My hand goes down to rub at my aching dick, which started actually hurting the minute she mentioned toys. If you had asked me not ten minutes ago if it were possible this sweet-looking girl had sex toys in this apartment, I would have said no way. I would have put money on her being a missionary-type of girl who considered getting fucked from behind the height of sinfulness.

But she's thrown me a few surprises tonight, and I find that it makes me even more curious about her. Makes me want to fuck her longer and harder too, and I'm glad I made the decision to come to her apartment. I'm quite sure I could have gotten both of us off nicely in the back storage room at The Wicked Horse or maybe in my truck, but now I get the distinct impression I'm going to need all night to try to peel the layers away from this girl.

Ordinarily, I wouldn't care two shits about what lays beneath the pretty exterior, but I can't help the pull she seems to have. Maybe I'm just getting tired of the same ol' pussy... women spreading their legs for the sake of spreading. Maybe I'm getting... bored?

Shaking my head, I give a laugh and down the glass of Jack.

Bored with pussy?

Yeah, never going to happen.

But I am greatly intrigued by hers.

As if to add another aching punch to my nuts, I hear a tiny moan come out of the bedroom and realize she's already gotten started. Hell, I figured it would take her several minutes to get "freshened up". Figured she'd touch up her makeup, fluff her hair, put on something sexy.

Stand in front of the mirror and give herself a pep talk that she could do this... masturbate in front of a man.

But in just under thirty seconds, she's already started and well on her way to a multiple, and I definitely like that she wants to achieve that tonight. I have no problems helping her along the way.

I quickly pull my boots and socks off, leaving them lying underneath the kitchen chair with the socks folded within. Old habits from living in the Marine barracks, I guess. As I walk down the hallway, I undo my belt buckle and start to pull it free of the loops.

When I enter the room, I freeze in place, my belt halfway off, and just stare at the vision in front of me. I didn't think it was possible, but my cock swells further... so much so it feels like it's going to burst out of my pants. I can feel the distinct pulse of blood thumping in that large vein that runs on the underside.

Sloane is lying on her bed, which is neatly made with a quilted light blue blanket. She's completely naked, her clothes strewn across the floor with that tiny, black G-string laying on the corner of her bed. Because her hair isn't overly long, really just past her jawline, it fans out in almost a halo-like affect around her head in big, barrel waves. Or rather like the rays of the sun.

I'm stunned to find her overhead light on. Figured she'd go with some mood lighting with a table lamp, but under the harsh glare of the three bulbs in a rickety old ceiling fan fixture above, I can actually see that she wears very little makeup. Porcelain skin that is clear and makes her blue eyes pop. I think they might be ringed with a little mascara, but nothing else. Her cheeks are a little rosy, but I'm thinking that might be from the fact she has a vibrator between her legs. And yes… that makeup-free face and shorter, sassier hair is what helped lend to that overall sweet and innocent vibe I was getting.

My eyes drag down her body—fantastic tits by the way—and I see her swirling a small, pink bullet between her legs. My eyes glide slowly up again, and I find her staring at me with her lids half shut and a sexy smirk on her lips. She has her free arm laying casually above her head on the pillows, one leg straight and the other bent at a slight angle. I notice pale, pink polish on her toes.

Sweet innocence with a vibrator between her legs and putting on a show for me.

Fucking amazing.

Sloane gives a breathy moan—must have hit something good, I'm thinking—and her hips give a tiny punch off the bed. This spurs me into action. Whipping my belt free of the remaining loops, I toss it on the end of the bed. I quickly pull my t-shirt off, dropping it to the floor and unsnap the button of my jeans. The entire time, Sloane watches me through those heavy-lidded eyes while she circles the bullet around and around her clit. Her moans are soft, breathy, and because her movements are slow, I can tell she didn't want a quick climax, but was content to just get wet as I instructed her to do.

Stepping to the end of the bed, I lock my legs and bend over her. Reaching a hand out, I nudge a finger in between her wet folds as she moves the vibrator just above. I sink in deep, producing a rumbling groan from her.

And fuck, so goddamn wet. I mean, *drenched*.

This is going to feel so good.

Because my cock feels like it's being strangled in my jeans, I pull away from Sloane and remove a condom from my wallet. I tear it open efficiently—lots of practice and all—and shed my jeans, stepping right out of them and onto the edge of the bed, where I kneel between her legs. I slowly roll the rubber on my dick and give my shaft a few lazy pumps before releasing it.

"Feel good?" I ask as my eyes dart to her vibrator and back up again.

She nods before her gaze drops to my cock, which is

stiff and sticking up straight in between my legs. "I expect you'll use that on me to feel better, right?"

My answer to her is simple and shows the utter confidence I have in what I can do with my dick. I snatch the vibrator out of her hand so quickly that she actually gives a startled gasp and toss it across the room. I can still hear the faint buzz of it as it lands on the carpet, but I don't give it another thought. Instead, my hands come to her hips and I flip her over on the bed, where she lands on her stomach with a small *oomph*.

I give myself just a moment to appreciate the beauty before me. A woman's backside is delectable to me; from the angle of her shoulder blades, to the dip in her lower back, to the swell of her ass. It's gorgeous and I like spending time back here. Sloane's happens to be perfection. Her ass is rounded and firm looking. I test the supposition by giving her right ass cheek a slight slap. She jerks and presses her face into the mattress, giving me a rewarding moan.

God, that's sexy, especially because I'm betting this is all new and exciting to her. She says she's bold, and no doubt, she shocked me with the masturbating, but I know there are still a million different things I could do to her that would shock her into next year. Which is exactly why I have her on her stomach. I want to test out that theory.

"I'm going to restrain you," I tell her suddenly as I reach up to grab her arms, pulling them up and backward, holding them with one hand just above her ass.

Her head comes flying off the bed, and she cranes it to look at me over her shoulder. For a moment, I suspect I see fear... probably some distrust, which is natural. She doesn't know shit about me and for all she knows, I could force some whacked shit on her once she's trussed up.

But I think that makes it all the more exciting, right?

Before she can lodge a protest, I grab my belt. With a few practiced twists, I have it looped around her wrists, pulled through the buckle tight, and the prong held securely by a specially made hole in the leather not but about six inches from the buckle. This isn't the first time I've used this belt to restrain a woman, but it is absolutely the first time I've ever asked, "You okay?"

She nods and whispers, "Yes."

"Good girl," I praise her. As I slap her on the ass one more time, she moans again, and then I tell her, "Because this might get a little rough."

I have no clue why I'm trying to scare her, but I want to see truly how much backbone she has. I figure this is the point of the evening where she might demand I let her go, but she merely lifts her hips off the bed in a silent plea for me to fuck her.

Christ, that's hot, and now I have to do just that.

My hands go to her hips and I pull them up, spreading her legs with mine in between hers. Her face remains on the bed with her left cheek pressed into the mattress. Her hair has fallen over and covered her face, and that just won't do at all. I want to see those eyes.

With a quick move, I brush the hair back from the side of her face, tucking it behind her ear and finding it extremely weird that I'm fascinated by how soft the skin on her cheek is.

Shaking my head to get my bearings, because why am I worried about the softness of her skin when I have a gorgeous ass propped up in front of me and my dick weeping to get inside?

One of the things that is really turning me on about Sloane is that she apparently waxes her pussy. It's bare and smooth without any razor burn that I tend to see from women who try to do it the easy way. I hope it doesn't make me a pervert, but that soft-looking pussy without a single hair on it just lends to her youthful innocence that I keep building up in my mind, even though she does the oddest things to tear it down.

Like right now as she pushes back against me, seeking contact. Her silent plea works too because I grab hold of my cock, twist my hips slightly, and bring myself in alignment. Wet warmth greets me as I start to rock into her. It was no lie when I said I was big, so I usually have to work my way in gently. Once I can get all the way in though, I won't hold back.

Not on this woman.

I want to see if she's bendable or breakable, or rather if she'll just take it all like a champ.

With every inch I take, Sloane's breath hitches. I might be stretching her a little too much, so I pull out a few inches and slowly slide back in, letting her own wetness soothe the sting my cock might be causing. It's slow going, but I don't want to hurt her, and I learned long ago that some of the best orgasms are the ones built patiently. While I've fucked many a woman who can take me in one fell swoop either because they like the pain or because they're not diligent with their kiegel exercises, I can just feel by the tightness of Sloane strangling my dick that she has not been overly used.

In fact, it makes me think of her as almost virginal with that creamy, pale skin, big, blue eyes, bald pussy, and sweet smile. And fuck... the mere fact that I might be tarnishing someone who might indeed be fairly innocent is what is turning me on about her so much, I think. The mere fact I can't figure it out is exciting, sure, but I realize... I want her to be ignorant of my ways, and I want to show her how good being bad is.

Pulling my hands inward along her ass, I use my thumbs to pull her cheeks apart so I can get a better view of me pushing into her. My cock is darkened with the rushing blood that's causing its hardness, and the condom is shiny from moving in and out of her pussy. I'm finding her walls are loosening, almost as if she's melting around me, and I'm able to get about three quarters of the way in when I stop my movements.

"Doing okay?" I ask her as I tilt to the side to see her face. Her lips are curved up, and she's got her bottom lip tucked in between her teeth.

With a furrowed brow and the fact I push in another inch causes her breath to catch again, she manages to gasp out, "You're really big."

"I'm almost all the way in," I say in a strangled voice, because it's getting more and more difficult to not just let loose on her. My dick is eager to pound away, and this slow in and out is for the birds.

"Will you just fuck me?" Sloane says on a wheeze as I pull out halfway, sinking back in only just as far.

To punctuate her sentiment, she rolls her hips and presses back against me. My hands tighten on her ass to still her movement and I close my eyes, telling myself she really doesn't mean that. While I have her tied up like a submissive and all ready for me to do my worst to her, I don't know that she's really built for everything I could unleash on her.

But then she undoes me with one simple, little word. Fragilely naive... asking for it. "Please."

"Christ," I mutter, pulling out almost to the tip and then punching my hips forward until my cock is lodged deeply inside of her. I feel her tender flesh give way, listen to the cry of surprise that rips from her throat, and literally cannot stop my body from pulling back out and slamming back in again.

Did I hurt her?

Do I care?

Apparently I don't, because I pull out and drive forward again, an animalistic snarl rumbling out of me as our skin cracks against each other. I should slow down.

Go faster, for sure.

Ask her if she's okay.

"Feels… good," Sloane pants.

Thank fuck.

So I go faster.

My gaze goes down and I watch as I ram in and out of her, finesse completely forgotten at this point. Pull her ass cheeks apart again, graze a finger over her tight hole, and she shivers.

That makes me smile but in no way lessens the force of my tunneling thrusts inside of her. I bring my finger to my mouth, lube it with my saliva, and bring it back down to her anus. Rubbing it around slowly while I fuck her, I ask, "Ever been fucked back here?"

Sloane shakes her head violently in between gasps and moans. I push the tip of my finger in her ass, and she cries out in pleasure.

Fuck, I groan internally. There are so many nasty things I'd like to do to her body. Cause her to scream out in pleasure… maybe with a bite of pain. I'd like to redden those cheeks with embarrassment over some of the things I would do, and then watch her flush even darker when she comes.

In fact, I want her to come right now.

Even though it knocks me off my pace just a tad, I manage to reach my other arm around her front while keeping the tip of my finger in her ass. I easily find her clit, because I could find that in the dark, and start to circle it roughly with the tips of my fingers. I lightly pump my finger in her ass, never taking it any deeper than the first knuckle. I don't want to show her all my tricks tonight.

Wait! *What?*

That would imply I want a second night with her.

Here I am… haven't even fucking busted my nut… don't even know if it will be any good, and I'm already thinking about another hookup with her?

No fucking way.

Chapter 6

Sloane

I'M NOT SURE I can handle this.

I mean… I'm a reasonably mature, adventurous, and daredevil type of woman. I'm sexually liberated, and while I may have never had a guy stick his finger in my ass, I can without a doubt say that it feels better than I ever imagined.

And I have imagined it before. I've imagined all sorts of dirty things, read about even dirtier ones, but never thought those activities were really possible. Never really believed that there were men out there who would enjoy doing that.

Seemed like fiction to me.

Romance fiction to be precise.

So even though my imagination is wild and vivid, and even though I'm not afraid of trying new and bold things, I really, truly, and utterly don't think I can handle the orgasm brewing inside of me right now. Even though my fingers are going numb from the belt around my wrists, my shoulders ache from my positioning, and I have a cock pounding inside of me that feels like it's at least the girth and length of a hard salami, I am more turned on right this very moment than I have ever been in my entire life. I'm so wet I can feel it trickling out of me with every slam of his huge dick, and I still want him to go harder and deeper into me.

The minute he puts those fingers to my clit, I know I'm done for. Then he starts talking dirty to me again, and my orgasms starts bubbling.

Yeah… you'd love having your ass fucked, Sloane.

I'd have to build you up though. Would need to try out some different plugs on you first.

Have you ever worn a butt plug? I gasp out that I have not.

You'll love it. I'll load you up and then eat your pussy. The orgasm will blow your mind, especially if I pull it out while you're coming.

And that did it for me. I moan like a wounded animal as I start to come. Wave after shuddering wave of bliss seizes my body, holds me hostage with solid pulses of pleasure, and then I scream Cain's name when it finally tears free of me. I turn to press my face into my pillows to stem the noise.

"So hot, Sloane," he growls as he fucks me harder. "So sexy when you come all around me like that… strangling my cock."

The force of my climax seems to turn Cain on even more. His hips slap against my ass in a frenzy, his hands now both back at my hips to hold me steady. He thrusts so hard that he slams my body down into the mattress, goes still, and then presses his face into the back of my neck while he starts to unload.

He lets it out with one long groan of satisfaction, grinding his pelvis against my ass as he lets my body milk him. He lies on top of me, pressing the metal of the buckle into my wrists with his weight constricting my lungs. But only for a moment, as if he knows that's not exactly comfortable, and then he's rolling off me, pulling that big and still-hard dick out, leaving me slightly sore and empty feeling.

I hear him pull the condom off—no clue what he does with it—and then his hands are working at the belt securing my wrists. He pulls it free and rubs my skin briskly. When he lets me go, I pull my arms forward and roll to my side toward him. His hand is there once again brushing the hair from my face.

Cain is lying on his side, facing me with his head resting in the palm of his hand. His eyes are lazy and his smile mellow as he stares at me. I prop my elbow up on the mattress, rest my head in my hand—mimicking his posture—and look down at the blue quilt on my bed.

Taking stock of my feelings, I'm not quite sure how to handle the afterglow of certain awkwardness. I just had the most mind-blowing sex of my entire life, but there was almost zero intimacy. It was truly about doing what felt good and decadent, yet I can't help feel that it was lacking in some respects.

"Looks like some serious thoughts going on inside that pretty head," Cain says quietly, and I raise my eyes to his.

"You didn't even kiss me," I say softly, dropping my gaze again with an embarrassed smile.

I feel his fingers under my chin, and then he's pushing upward so I look back at him. His eyes are not exactly kind, but there is a knowing sympathy there. I think it might be pity for me that I'm not recognizing this for what it was.

Just some hot and dirty sex.

"Strike that thought," I say quickly, completely embarrassed I'd even bring that up. I'm off focus here, reminding myself I have a job to do and Cain Bonham is not someone who wants to get involved with a doe-eyed innocent who wants sweet kisses while she's being made love to.

Rolling away from him, I try to change the subject. "I'm going to get a bottle of water. Do you want one?"

I don't even make a complete rotation because in a nanosecond, I'm on my back. Cain is on top of me, covering my body with his. He holds his weight off my torso by pushing his elbows into the mattress, but I can feel his shaft, now semi-hard and wet, laying against my stomach.

He intently stares down at me. "That was definitely an oversight on my part."

Lowering his face, he brushes his lips against mine before pulling up to look at me. "You have the softest lips. I've wanted to kiss them all night, but I got too caught up in the need to fuck you."

My eyes flutter closed, and my heart thumps madly

over his seductively sweet words. His mouth presses back against mine, pushes at me, and I open up. Angling his head, Cain kisses me slowly and surely, making me very much aware that he likes doing it by the rumble in his chest. My hands go to his hair, rubbing at the short bristles in the back, but then he pulls up again.

"In fact," he says slyly, "there are all kinds of places I want to kiss you."

"Like where?" I whisper, barely able to get enough air in my lungs to get the words out.

"Let me just show you," he says, his mouth going to my jaw.

It slides over to my ear, where he gently bites me.

Back to my jaw.

Glides warm lips down my neck to my collarbone, where he lightly sucks.

Cain moves his body down, pressing soft kisses over the center of my chest. He tilts his face, moves a fraction of an inch lower, and licks a nipple.

Tilts his face the other way, puts more pressure on that arm, and then bites at the other nipple. My hands go flying back up to his head as I let out a sharp cry.

Cain pushes further down my body, layering my stomach with soft touches of his mouth that cause shivers to sling up and down my spine. He takes a brief pause, lifts his head slightly, and looks up at me. "You said something about multiple orgasms earlier. We've got some work to do still."

"Oh, man," I mutter, and then his mouth is back on

me again.

For a moment after Cain pulled out of me, I felt the keen absence of something as simple as an intimate kiss. Now though, as he moves lower and lower down my body, layering dozens of kisses, licks, and nips to my skin, I find myself lost in confusion as to what this is.

When fingers push into me and he buries his face between my legs, intent on giving me those multiple orgasms, I find no clarity as to whether this is truly just physical attraction and a quest for a mutually beneficial release, or if Cain wants to indulge in something a little deeper.

Would he want more of a connection with me?

As his tongue flutters against me, causing my blood to race and a throbbing need to start building again between my legs, I have to wonder if I even really care. I'm not sure I can worry about a connection to a man who I ultimately intend to use, but I can't deny... that first kiss. The way he said he wanted to kiss me all night.

I just don't know what to think.

So instead, I decide to just give in to feeling and I let my mind drift, intent on experiencing the bliss of Cain Bonham eating me out.

THE MINUTE I wake up, I know Cain is gone. I lift my head and peer at the clock, realizing it's a little after four in the morning once the numbers clear up to my blurry vision. I roll over onto my back, groaning at my sore muscles.

My neck, shoulders, and lower back are all sore.

My wrists burn from the leather that rubbed against them.

There's a throbbing ache between my legs, and because I got an up close and personal look at the true size of his dick just before I sucked on it, I'm not surprised. I'm going to be sore there for a few days I bet.

I let my head flop down on the pillow and smile to myself because it was so worth it. For almost four hours straight, we did not stop. We may not have been actually fucking for that four hours, but we were touching and kissing and licking and groping and urging the other one to get ready for more fucking.

God, no wonder I'm so sore. If Cain's dick wasn't in me, his tongue or fingers were. He took seriously the challenge of giving me multiple orgasms and would not stop eating me out that first round until I came three times. The third one was a struggle for me because I got all up inside my own head, worried about him being uncomfortable or getting tired or bored, but he diligently dragged it out of me, smiling up at me in triumph when I stopped shaking. By that time, he was hard again and he fucked me for a second time. This time on my back with my legs up over his shoulders.

The rest of the time is a blur. His face was back between my legs, my mouth was on his dick, and his finger was in my ass again. My nipples are sore from him pinching them, and I even got brave and ran my finger along the rim of his ass. He groaned, and if I were a braver girl, I would have done more.

Maybe next time.

If there is a next time.

All I know is that after the last time we had sex, which was doggie style again, I collapsed onto my stomach and was asleep before he even pulled out of me. I have no clue if he stayed to cuddle or got dressed and left, but I was completely out of it from exhaustion.

But today is a new day, and now I have to figure out how to play this.

He's the only lead I have on this alleged sex club and Governor Hayes' tie to it, unless I want to track down Colton Stokes and try to get some more info out of him. I have to say, the notion of using Cain in that way doesn't appeal to me, but the prospect of not seeing him again doesn't either. By continuing to pursue him, I can serve the story's interest as well as my own.

Cain fascinates me. The notion that he's involved in the sex club does as well, because he whispered enough dirty things to me tonight that my mind is spinning with possibilities. Even as sore and as used as I feel right now, I'm craving to learn more.

I just know he can teach me more.

Maybe I'll just play it casual… see if he contacts me. While he didn't ask for my number or anything, we did talk enough during some short periods of rest that he knows where I work. Or maybe I'll go hang out at The

Wicked Horse and see if I can tempt him again. All I really know is that I simply can't go back to Brant with a big, fat "sorry I couldn't find anything". Either I have to prove there's a story or I have to go back and prove to him that there's nothing.

Either way, I still have a job to do.

Chapter 7

Cain

"H OW MUCH LONGER will this take?" I ask as I lean up against the concrete wall of The Silo, just to the left of the entrance door.

Luke Colson is placing the last of the screws in the new security panel he just installed. He's the best around these parts when it comes to security. With the promise of a bonus if he could get out here today, he's just about finished with the new password panel to allow members in and keep disavowed members away.

"About another fifteen minutes to get the programming done. Then I'll have to activate all the fobs you asked for," he says in between tightening the screws.

Luke doesn't question why we ordered a hundred and fifty remote security access fobs. In his job, he's learned to not ask what he shouldn't and just do his work well. That's why he'll get an extra bonus in addition to his regular fee.

"And there's no problem in rigging up the same type of panel to the new gate we're installing?" I ask as I push away from the wall.

"Nope," he says confidently. "You get the gate installed with the specifications I gave you, and I can easily adapt a locking panel to it. Same fobs will grant access."

This is a relief because while it was easy enough to tighten security on The Silo's door, we still had to worry about all of our fantasy cabins. There are thirteen cabins in all built behind The Silo. A dirt road from the parking lot of The Wicked Horse connects them but until now, anyone could drive down it if they were curious. Woolf lent a couple of his ranch hands to come out and install the gate today, and Luke will wrap up his work by installing a security panel to the lock. Then we should be all set.

"I'll be back in a few minutes," I tell Luke. He doesn't need me here hovering and besides, there's something I need inside The Silo.

Opening the door, I step into the cool hallway lit by dim sconces. From the outside, The Silo is exactly what it sounds like. A large, round building made of concrete staves and outfitted with a white-domed top and a grain elevator on the outside. From the inside, it's nothing like an actual silo and everything like what a fantasy sex club should be like.

It's approximately one-hundred and fifty feet in diameter with seven rooms constructed around the perimeter. A small, intersecting hallway from the entrance hall leads left and right, wrapping around the entirety behind the seven rooms. Concrete walls keep the rooms separated except for the interior wall that is solid glass, which is all the better for members to view the debauchery that goes on inside those rooms.

Some of the rooms are set up to accommodate certain proclivities… Gang Bang, BDSM, Swinger, Ménage, and Fetish. There's a "performance" room with just a single bed draped in black silk that anyone can use who's in the mood to be the star of their own fantasy show. Hell, once I was bored and laid on the bed, just jacking off while people watched. It's a good thing I don't get performance anxiety because that would have been embarrassing.

I make the short walk down the hallway to the center of The Silo. It's an open area with a round, black lacquered bar that sits in the center. No one is tending it now as not many members are into drinking at ten in the morning. But someone will be on duty by lunchtime. Though no food or alcohol are served between 2AM and noon the next day, The Silo is opened 24/7 for all members who want a place to escape to and fuck.

Moaning sounds filter in muted tones, and I turn my head to see someone in one of the group sex rooms. A single overhead light is on, clearly illuminating the occupants. My jaw drops slightly, not over what I'm seeing because I've seen it all and done most of what I've seen, but by who I'm seeing in there.

Angel, Rand, and Logan.

Okay, not surprised really to see Rand and Logan. They're both active members of the club and fuck around with each other on occasion. They're not gay, but they are adventurous and will try anything. From what I can tell, they've both liked most of what they've tried because those two guys will visit most of the various room and cabins in a week's time, making the rounds to the multitude of different types of sex that are available.

What does surprise me, however, is our DJ Angel. The woman has a voice so smoky rich she could probably make a man or woman orgasm with that alone, which is one of the reasons Woolf and Bridger originally hired her. She's also a prominent player in The Silo, so I'm not necessarily surprised to see her here. But not only is she a revered fantasy maker, she is one seriously hardcore dominant. So yeah... I'm stunned to see her lying on her back, legs spread wide, getting fucked by Rand, who happens to be holding onto a collar locked tight around Angel's throat.

Never in a million years did I think I'd see that woman give up control, especially since I know she enjoys pegging men up the ass and having them lick her feet.

My cock twitches as I watch them. While Rand is buried balls deep and rocking into Angel, Logan has his cock stuffed into Rand's ass. All three are groaning and grunting with unrestrained pleasure. It's hot as fuck to watch as they heave and undulate, and if I didn't have places to go and people to see, I'd unzip my jeans and rub one off to this spectacular show.

But I do have things to do so I turn my back on them and head past the bar to a small utility closet that's been built in between the BDSM and Fetish rooms. It holds "supplies" that are delivered here almost as regularly as the food, liquor, and beer are. Bridger has been able to find some seriously freaky toys and is always trying to come up with new and adventurous ways to play around with people. The other day, he told me he bought an industrial design vibrator that will pound repetitively into a woman—much like an old-fashioned jackhammer. I cannot wait to see that in play.

Pulling my key ring out of my pocket, I locate the appropriate key and open the closet. Flicking on the light, I walk down the one aisle bordered on both sides by floor-to-ceiling metal shelfing. I locate what I need, grab the two boxes I came for, and lock back up behind me. I make a note to myself to give Bridger some cash when I see him next to compensate for what I just took.

As I make my way back through The Silo, I don't cut across the center but walk the perimeter, bringing me by the room that Angel, Rand, and Logan occupy. I give a short rap on the glass with my knuckles and all three turn to look at me, narrowing their eyes to see into the gloom of the interior since none of the lights are on. But then they all smile at me in recognition and Logan calls out with an evil grin, "Come on in, man, and join us. I'll give your ass a pounding if you want."

He punctuates this by slamming hard into Rand, which causes Rand to slam into Angel. Rand hisses through his teeth in pleasure, and Angel gives a gasp of delight before her eyes roll backward in ecstasy. Goddamn, that's hot. My cock starts thickening.

However, I shake my head and wave my hand at them. "No thanks," I call through the glass. "I like my ass just the way it is."

And that's the truth. While I may have wanted Sloane to stick that slender finger all the way in last night and give my prostate a good massage, that's all that will ever see the interior of my back alley. Not that I'm averse to sex with a guy. Just not anal sex. I sure as fuck won't turn down a blow job by someone with mad skills, although I much prefer a beautiful woman with large tits.

Laughing at my thoughts, I head out of The Silo. As I pass Luke and head for my truck in the Wicked Horse's lot, I tell him, "Bridger's got a check for you when you're done."

"Sounds good," he says without even looking at me.

As I pass by the slate path that leads from The Silo to the back door of The Wicked Horse, I think briefly of stopping in to say hello to Bridger. We talked briefly by phone yesterday after my visit with Colton. I relished telling him about the encounter, and he laughed in approval.

Colton was stubborn, but only for a few minutes. He denied being the one to out us to Governor Hayes but after only one punch to his jaw, and a follow up to his gut, he finally admitted it through wheezing gasps. I imparted my message to him, and then followed it up with just one more punch, back to his mouth, which scraped my knuckles up good. But it had been so worth it, especially when he promised in a panicked voice with a blood-filled mouth to keep his trap shut.

Good boy.

I consider only briefly seeing Bridger, but then decide against it. I have more important things to do today, the first being a trip into Jackson to visit Jackson Hole Leather Emporium and deliver the gift I just took from The Silo.

The thought of just such a gift struck me not long after I came for the last time inside of Sloane. The poor girl dropped down into a dead sleep after I pulled out of her. My dick was sore, but it was a happy dick. After I disposed of the condom, I watched her sleep while I got dressed. I thought of all the dirty things I did to her and the even dirtier things I want to do to her, and then was struck with the thought of the gift.

For a love 'em and leave 'em kind of guy, the actual idea that I would see her again and deliver such a gift is an oddity, but it can't be helped. I am in fucking lust with this girl. I mean true lust, not just a generalized horniness to fuck someone. And said lust has not diminished, not even after I shot my load into her the last time. I was even then calculating when and how I could do it again. What's even odder is the realization I've clearly never been in lust before, and Rachel doesn't count. She'll never count again. But no one has held my attention past a brief night of passion. No one has intrigued me the way she has. No one, and I mean no one, has been such an enigma to me. She's sweet, yet sassy. Quite the innocent, yet intrigued by the sinful.

Proclaims to be bold, yet blushes when I tell her I want to fuck her ass. She's so many different things that she makes me feel off balance.

Most would say that's not a good thing, but I say quite the opposite. This feeling… like my world is tilting just a little and I'm venturing into unchartered territory—it feels almost dangerous… it all makes me feel alive. She puts me off balance in a good way, and I like this feeling.

But most of all, my lust for Sloane is centered on this burning desire to show her all the depraved things that can make her feel so good. She's adventurous and game, that I can tell, and I look forward to turning her existence upside down with the things she'd never be able to imagine in her most perverted dreams. I cannot wait to show her my world and maybe dirty her up a bit.

It will start with the gifts I'm bringing to her.

I cannot wait to see the look on her face.

Chapter 8

Sloane

"HERE'S YOUR RECEIPT," I tell the elegantly dressed woman on the other side of the counter. Zipping up the garment bag, I pick it up and carefully place it in her hands. It's a good thing it's completely covered too, because I may have been drooling over the gorgeous, caramel-colored suede coat lined with sheep's wool and trimmed out in red fox. At a whopping thirty-two hundred dollars, it's a luxury I could never afford on a reporter's salary.

The woman smiles big and turns away, handing her package to her husband, who follows her out the door.

"Tourists," Jasmine mutters as she comes to stand beside me, leaning over and resting her elbows on the counter. "One of the few places in the world you will see ordinary vacationers dropping that type of money on a coat they'll probably take back to West Palm Beach and stick in the back of their closet."

I laugh and turn to face her, leaning to the side and resting on my own elbows. "This is a very expensive place to visit."

Jasmine nods. "It's why I have high hopes of landing

me a sugar daddy one day. I've slept with plenty, but one will stick I'm sure."

Shaking my head, I smirk at her. "Is that all you aspire to be?"

She looks at me with all seriousness. "Well yeah... I mean, what's wrong with wanting a rich man to take care of you?"

Shrugging and feeling awkward since I'm sure I just offended her, I still can't help being honest. "Nothing, I guess. It's just... there's no safety in that."

"No safety?" she asks with a cocked eyebrow. "Did you hear the 'rich' part I mentioned?"

"But he could dump you at any minute, and then where would you be?"

"Right back here selling overpriced leather goods to tourists," she confidently says. "Just like you."

Yeah, not just like me. I have ambitions and a career path. This is just a fake job. As soon as this story is done, I'm headed back to D.C. I'll hopefully have an amazing article that will sell lots of magazines and earn me a promotion. Then all will be right in my world.

The door opens with a silvery tinkling of bells, and I look up to greet our next customer. He fills most of the doorway, projecting nothing but the shadow of a well-built man with the late morning sun bright behind him.

And then I immediately recognize the shape of his torso, the width of those shoulders... hell, I even recognize those thighs that would flex and squeeze as he tunneled in and out of my body last night.

My body temperature rises because I feel warm all over. When he steps further into the store and I can see his face clearly, I have to bite down hard on my lower lip to keep from moaning over just how fantastic he looks.

Jasmine elbows me in the ribs as she stands up, smoothing her skirt with nervous hands, and tilts her chin up at him. "Well, hello stud," she purrs as he walks up to the counter.

His gaze is pinned on me, but he does slide a quick look over at her, giving a curt nod before coming back to me. I can see the rebuff hits her hard as her shoulders slump in my peripheral vision.

"Due for a break?" he asks me in that low, rumbling voice.

Break? *What?* I blink at him in confusion because I'm absolutely stunned he's here. I mean, of course, I wanted him to come and see me because I want to continue whatever this is.

A love affair?

A selfish means to an end for me?

Shaking my head, I ask with all the eloquence of a woman completely befuddled, "Huh?"

"A break, Right Hook," he says with a lazy smile as he comes to a stop in front of the counter. "I have something for you."

It's then I notice a small, plastic grocery bag in his hand.

"You go ahead," Jasmine says quickly and even gives me a push on my shoulder. "It's dead in here, and I've got you covered. Old Man Stephenson won't come in until later this afternoon, so it's all good."

I know why Jasmine is pushing me away. While Cain's snub of her earlier may have seemed cold, I know she wasn't surprised by it. Because she told me herself he doesn't do *seconds*, and Jasmine has no clue that Cain did *firsts* with me last night. Oh, she hit me up as soon as I walked in this morning, as I was enjoying the ache between my legs as if it was a dirty secret, and she practically begged me for details.

I lied to her point blank and told her nothing happened—that Cain just escorted me out to a cab and I left. She accepted that with sympathetic eyes, and she must assume he's here sniffing around for potential opportunity.

Jasmine pushes me again, and I nervously tuck some of my hair behind my ear as I sort of stumble out from behind the checkout counter.

"Got a break room?" Cain asks.

I nod and turn toward the back door that says *Private*. The owner, Leonard Stephenson, has a small kitchen with a table that seats four. We're allowed half an hour for a lunch or dinner break, depending on our shift, but otherwise, he expects us to be out front to help customers. I'm not worried because as Jasmine says, he doesn't ever come into the store until late afternoon and we are the only ones on duty. I know she won't bother us.

Cain follows me through the door and the minute

it's closed, he places his hand on my elbow. The kitchen is dead ahead but he steers me to the left, right to the unisex bathroom all the employees share. With one hand still on my elbow, he pulls the door open and pushes me gently inside. His hand flicks the light, and the door is shut and locked behind us.

"What are you doing?" I ask as I turn to him, but he curls one hand around my neck and presses a kiss on my mouth.

A hard, deep kiss with tongue and a moan of greeting in his throat.

And oh, hell… my knees almost buckle from the sensation and the fact that he brought me here, for privacy, because he wanted a kiss. My hands snake up, running over the hard lines of his chest, over his shoulders, and around his neck.

But I barely get my fingers laced before he's pulling away and giving me a devilish grin. "Didn't want to have another kiss oversight."

I almost swoon—*almost*—but he doesn't give me the opportunity before he's throwing me for another loop.

"Turn around," he orders as he reaches into the plastic bag he brought with him, pulling out two small boxes that fit in one hand. "Put your hands on the edge of the sink and bend over."

"What?" I practically yell, my eyes dropping down to the boxes he's holding. "No way."

"Yes," he says, talking over me.

I cross my arms over my chest and glare at him. "Not

until you tell me what's in those boxes and why you want me to do that."

Cain isn't pissed over my denial but rather snakes a hand out, curling back around my neck again and pulling me in for another rough kiss. He laughs into my mouth and lets me go. "Sassy. I like that. I should redden your ass for it, but it's going to be tender enough—"

"What's in the boxes?" I interrupt, trying to get a look at the plain white package with minimal words written on them. I've already forgotten his highhanded attitude, more than a little turned on by the threat to redden my ass. Completely curious and even a little afraid by why my ass will be tender, but yeah... mostly turned on.

Laying one box on the edge of the sink, he takes the other and opens it up, shaking out the contents into his hand.

A butt plug.

I recognize it at once, not from any personal experience but from research I did before coming out to Wyoming. I had no clue what happened in a sex club, but I was smart enough to guess that toys might be part of the agenda. I searched a lot of popular sites, sometimes strangely fascinated by what I saw—at other times, perplexed. Once, really, really disgusted when urine was involved.

But I definitely recognize a butt plug.

"I want to get your ass ready for my cock," Cain says in a low voice, and my eyes snap up to him as my body jerks from the sexy tone.

"Like right now?" I ask, my voice semi-hysterical.

"The plug right now. My cock… that's not going to happen right away. I'll have to move you up to bigger plugs." He sounded so casual and calm as he explained this to me. I, on the other hand, felt my world spinning over the implications.

First, and foremost, he wants to stick that massive dick in my ass. I could barely take it last night in the place it's supposed to normally be and wouldn't have if not for a lot of careful prodding by him. The thought of him doing that both titillates and scares the shit out of me.

Second, and this is equally as important, it sounds to me as if Cain is saying he wants to be with me again. I mean, if he plans on graduating me up in butt plugs, that requires more than one night together, right?

"Now put your hands on the sink and bend over," he says again. His hazel eyes are a shade darker than what I remembered from the bright light of my bedroom. More brown than green at this moment, and I wonder if that has anything to do with the nature of our conversation. My eyes dart down and see he's got a hard-on pressing against his jeans, so probably.

"Sloane." He says my name softly, as a means to get my attention.

My gaze slides up. Before I can talk myself out of it, I turn toward the sink, drop my chest, and stick my butt out.

"Nice," he growls as he steps up behind me. I look up into the mirror over the sink, seeing him looking down at my ass with undisguised lust.

"Hold this," he says as he presses the plug into my hand. It's heavy, made of what appears to be smooth, stainless steel, and it isn't very big... no wider than my index finger. It has a narrow, rounded tip that flares a bit wider before curving inward again. I read enough about them to know this is to keep it from falling out once it gets past my ring of muscle, and the wide, circular bottom will keep it from getting sucked in.

Damn... I'm nervous but so turned on right now. I feel like crying.

Cain draws my skirt up over my legs to my hips. It's a pastel blue floaty thing I paired with a white, off-the-shoulder blouse and sandals. I'm wearing simple white lace panties underneath, something I think he appreciates as I hear him hum low in his throat as they're revealed.

I don't know what I'm expecting... maybe for him to just get the deed done with a quick pat on my head, but I'm stunned when he snakes a finger in between my legs from behind. Right into the edge of my panties, brushing back and forth against me.

"Just checking," he says in triumph. "Wanted to see if the thought of this turned you on."

"And the verdict?" I gasp as he slides his finger in all the way.

"You're flooded," he murmurs before pulling out of me and pushing the tip of his finger against my clit.

"And I'm going to get you off really quick to help relax you."

I drop my head, staring at the sink as my hand curls reflexively around the plug. Cain's fingers are talented. They're calloused and rub in tights circles around me, faster and faster. I'm so wet that he glides effortlessly... his stimulation and the fact he's doing this while I'm bent over the sink at my place of employment makes this all the more exciting. It takes me no time at all before I'm bursting apart with a short sob of relief, my hips rotating with no control against his fingers.

"Fucking beautiful," he says as he gives a last tap against my clit and pulls his hand from in between my legs.

Sucking in air, lifting my head. I can feel Cain now pulling my underwear down as he says, "Spread your legs a bit."

I'm so languid feeling right now that I do as he asks, until my panties sitting at mid-thigh stretch and bite into my skin.

Cain reaches over me to grab the other box, and I'm relieved when he opens it up and I see a new tube of lubricant.

I gaze up, finding him looking at me in the mirror. He winks at me. "It's going to feel good. I promise."

And I believe him because everything he's done to me so far has felt better than anything I've ever felt in my life. No lie.

Cain's face drops back down so he can concentrate

on his work. Because I can't see what's going on, I close my eyes and take a deep breath. I concentrate on sounds and feeling.

First, Cain's large hand caresses my bare ass. I hear the click of what I'm thinking is the lubricant being opened, then his slick fingers are pressing in between my ass cheeks and rubbing up against me, all around. I feel a cool trickle hit my ass, and he's massaging more lubricant onto me.

"Hand me the plug," he says, his voice hoarse.

Holding my hand up by my shoulder, I feel him take the plug. I keep my eyes closed.

"Deep breath, Sloane," he tells me with one large hand fanned out over my lower back.

I do as he says.

The tiny tip of the plug touches my anus, and I will myself to hold still. I let my breath out slowly just as he starts to push it in. It doesn't hurt, but I expect that's because it's no bigger than his finger. It feels… good actually.

Damn good.

Who knew?

I'm stretched a little as it gets pushed in to the hilt, feeling my muscles contract around it and settle as soon as it's all the way in. Cain gives a little tap to the circular end, causing it to jolt within me, and I gasp.

"Nice, right?" he says thickly.

I open my eyes slowly and nod. "Yeah, actually."

Cain's hands go to my underwear, and he pulls them

up my legs. I straighten up, feeling the plug move slightly as it adjusts. My skirt drops, and Cain actually smoothes it down before bringing his hands to my shoulders and turning me around.

"I want you to wear that all day," he says as he peers down at me. "Do not remove it."

"But—" I start to argue, because there's no way I can do that. I won't be able to concentrate.

"What time do you get off work?"

"Huh?"

"Work, Sloane," he patiently says. "What time do you get off?"

"Four," I say, confused at the rapid change of subject, especially since I am still prepared to argue against that plug staying in me all day.

"I'll be at your apartment waiting for you," he says as he leans down and quickly kisses me. "I don't start work until seven, so we have a few hours to play. I'm going to lick your pussy hard and pull that plug out as you start to come. Trust me… you'll thank me for it later."

I swear I almost orgasm right then and there. My jaw drops open in disbelief, but Cain is giving me another quick kiss and then he's walking out of the bathroom.

Did that seriously just happen?

Chapter 9

Cain

I SLAM INTO Sloane one last time, the muscles in my back tensing exquisitely, my balls pulled up tight, and I explode viciously inside of her.

F-u-u-u-c-k, that feels good.

So goddamn good.

I've had a hard-on practically all day since I left her in that bathroom with a plug in her ass. I practically jumped on her when her car pulled in front of her apartment as I was already waiting there for her. I wasn't sure what to expect, but I was immensely relieved when she sashayed up to me and hissed, "Get this damn thing out of me. I better come hard like you promised or there will be hell to pay for what I went through today."

That right there... that got my cock to go to full attention. We raced up the stairs, flew down the hallway, and then tore each other's clothes off. I did as promised... licked her pussy furiously, whipping her up into a frenzy. It took her less than a minute to orgasm. When she said, "I'm coming," I pulled on the plug, felt the resistance, felt it give, and when it popped free, she actually shrieked in ecstasy. Her hips also punched off the bed so hard, she caught me in the chin with her pubic bone, snapping my neck backward.

"Damn, Right Hook," I said with a laugh as her ass fell back to the mattress.

She shuddered while looking at me with sex-blurred eyes. "Sorry," she muttered, and then another quake rolled through her.

"I'm not," I told her earnestly as I opened up a condom from the jumbo box I brought with me. I rolled it on and because she was exquisitely loose after that orgasm, I was able to sink right into her tightness without a wince of pain.

It was fucking perfect.

The orgasm that continues to rumble through me is fucking perfect. I huff a few breaths as it settles, and then suck in some more air to further calm my heartbeat.

Glancing at my watch as I roll off her, I figure out I can fuck her one more time... maybe twice if I can talk her into sucking on my overused dick after round two. I pull the condom off, tie a knot in the end, and drop it over the edge of the bed to the floor. I'll pick it up later on my way out, with the other condoms that will be joining it.

Flopping to my back, I lay next to Sloane while we get our breathing under control and think about what just happened between us. Some supreme sex, that's for sure.

The most supreme, in fact. I'm not sure I've seen a woman come that hard, and the fact I made her do it actually swells me up with some silly pride. I mean, I like getting women off. It's a challenge to me as all women are built different. But I don't care about the nature of their orgasms. One's just as good as the next, and besides... that's what sex is, right? Tit for tat. You get me off—I get you off.

That's sure as shit not how I felt about Sloane when I was with her last night. I was driven to pull as many orgasms out of her as I could, even as she was begging me to leave her alone. I want to do that again, and in fact...

"How do you know so much about things like butt plugs and anal sex?" Sloane asks me. I feel the mattress dip. As I turn my head her way, I see she's rolled to her side, laying her head on one of the pillows and curling her arm under her. She looks well fucked and completely relaxed.

I shrug and turn on my side to face her, resting my head on a pillow and reaching out with my hand to take her free one. I lace my fingers with her. "I'm just adventurous," I tell her.

I'm damn well not going to tell her I got my initiation into this world by working at a sex club over in Driggs, or that I currently work at one now. Even as curious as this sweet little girl is, she'd freak the fuck out.

Maybe.

Hell, I don't know because I don't know much about what she really thinks of all of this. "What did you think of it?" I ask as we stare at each other. She knows I'm talking about the plug.

"I liked it," she says with a smile. She drops her eyes, and then looks back up at me with pink cheeks. "That was the most intense orgasm I've ever had."

Nodding at her in understanding, I squeeze her hand. "It was beautiful to watch. Can't wait to see you take my cock."

A small gasp of shock comes out of Sloane. I love when my dirty words can cause that. She shakes her head and says, "I don't know, Cain. I don't think I can take you back there."

"You can with the right amount of prep," I tell her with confidence.

"You have lots of experience with this?" she asks sarcastically and maybe with a little jealousy.

It makes me laugh, and I feel compelled to roll forward to give her a quick kiss. "I have some experience with anal sex. I mean… been with women who enjoy it, but they're used to it. You're my first virgin ass."

"That implies you want to continue seeing me," she says hesitantly. "I mean… you said it will take time."

"True enough," is all I tell her, because while I know I want to see her again… fuck her again… I'm not sure what I want past that.

"And if you are continuing to see me, would you perhaps be continuing to see other women at the same time?" she asks, sounding uncertain. Hesitant.

I blink in surprise because the immediate answer that almost just popped free was, *Fuck yes I'm going to see other women,* but something stops me. Maybe it's her wide eyes staring at me earnestly, or the fact she just trusted me enough to let me plug her ass during the workday, but I'm shaking my head in the negative. "I'll keep my dick solely on call for you, how's that?"

She grimaces and asks for clarification. "That means no fucking girls in the parking lot of The Wicked Horse?"

I blink in surprise at her. "How'd you know that?"

"Jasmine," she says simply.

"Jasmine?" *Who the fuck is Jasmine?*

"Jasmine," she says with a pointed look. "My co-worker. You fucked her not long ago in the parking lot."

Shit... I knew that girl looked familiar, and I wasn't sure why. Now I know. Don't exactly remember the details, but it makes sense.

I give Sloane's hand a squeeze. "I promise, no other girls while you and I are fucking. You promise to give me that ass... let me do whatever it takes to get you there, and you'll be the only one."

She grimaces over my crude words, but fuck... what can I say? They're all true.

"Why is anal sex so important to you?" she asks with a curious tilt to her head.

"It's not," I assure her. "But your ass is."

"My ass?" she says with confusion.

"You're sweet and innocent, curious and adventurous. You have a virgin ass, and I'd love to pop that cherry. It's a fantasy of mine. At least, it's become a fantasy since last night."

Awww… isn't that sweet? She blushes and looks down again, I think warmed by my admission that it's only her ass I'm fantasizing about right now.

Chuckling, I reach out and pull her into my arms. Pressing her in close, I feel fucking compelled to kiss her forehead. I cuddle her for a few moments, relishing in the feeling. I mean, sure… I've done that before, but really just to make the girl feel good after. Maybe soften the sting of a quick departure or something.

But with Sloane… something actually feels kind of right about this.

Loathe to release her right away, and besides, I need a few more minutes to recharge before we can fuck again, I provoke her embarrassment a little further. "What's your fantasy?"

She jumps in my arms slightly and pulls her face back to look at me. "Fantasy?"

"Yeah… your fantasy. What type of dirty fantasy gets you worked up?"

"I don't have one," she says.

A little too quickly.

"Oh no you don't," I tell her as I push her onto her back and roll on top. I nudge her legs apart with my own, press my hips down, and feel my dick start to get some life back into it. Damn, that was fast, but I keep on point. "You are not avoiding that question. Every man and woman has a fantasy. Something they think about when they masturbate. Something that makes them come fast and hard when they're playing with themselves, or are otherwise engaged in a boring fuck. You've got to have something, Sloane."

She cuts her eyes down and to the right, sucking her lower lip in between her teeth. Then back to me with those big, round, baby blues and says, "Well… there is one thing… but…"

Her words trail off, and her face gets red. I lean down, graze my lips over hers. When I pull back, I smile at her in encouragement. "You can tell me. I promise the most that will happen is it will make me horny and I'll fuck you."

"Well," she says slowly. "I mean… I'm not really sure that this stuff ever really happens in real life, but… my fantasy is to be gang-banged."

There is nothing that Sloane could have said to me that would have surprised me more. And even though the thought of that scenario happening is provocatively hot, I have to get some clarification. "A gang bang?"

"Yes." Another blush.

"Sloane, do you even know what that means?" I ask her carefully… gently.

"Yeah… multiple guys, one girl… lots of sex," she says, her chin tilted stubbornly at me. "And you're judging me… you said you wouldn't do that."

"No," I assure her with a shake of my head and an encouraging smile. "Not judging. It's just… typically, you know… in porn and the like, a gang bang is kind of rough. It can be violent and unless you're into pain and humiliation, it's not something I think you'd get off on."

Sloane's eyes flare wide with understanding, and she vigorously shakes her head. "Oh, God… then no, that's not my fantasy. I just meant multiple guys… you know, all focused on my pleasure. Definitely not into pain and degradation."

My lungs deflate in an instant, so relieved to know that all of my instincts about Sloane weren't wrong. She truly is innocent to this stuff, which really fucking turns me on.

I tilt my head, lean over, and kiss her neck. "So… what you're saying is your dirty fantasy is to get serviced by multiple men."

"Yes," she moans as I push down a bit, dragging my teeth down her skin.

"Would another woman be part of that fantasy?" I ask, feeling my cock start to swell as I think about another woman licking between Sloan's legs.

She giggles and says, "No. Just men."

Damn.

"How many guys?" I ask her, intent to have her describe for me all the details, knowing it's going to ramp up her desire right now. I know it's certainly ramping up mine, as I'm quickly hardening.

"Three," she says breathlessly, her hands coming to my head as I move to her breasts. "No, wait… four. I think I want four total."

"All hung like me?"

"God no," she gasps as I lick around her nipple. "I'd die with that much big cock at once."

"Would you take three guys at once?" I ask her, looking up to see her reaction.

She stares at me, and I almost come right there against her mattress when she admits in a whisper, "I don't know if I could, but that is part of my fantasy. I'd totally try."

Fuck.

Fuck, fuck, fuck.

Why did I even get started down this path? Why did I ask her something that would lead to this moment... a single, clear moment when I realize I have the power to give that fantasy to her? It would be so fucking easy to set up.

It would be so fucking hot to watch her having every dirty desire fulfilled. It's one of the things I love best about being a fantasy maker for the club... indulging members in things they don't think they could ever have. Giving them the ultimate pleasure.

Now I simply have to fuck Sloane because it seems her fantasy may have just become one of mine at this very moment. I push up from her, grab another condom, and rip it open.

I was going to eat her out again, but I'm too damn horny now thinking about this. I need inside of her.

And then I need to decide if I should give her what she wants.

Chapter 10

Sloane

SEX.

Big dicks.

Butt plugs.

Gang bangs.

God, what has my world been reduced to?

I woke up this morning feeling out of sorts about Cain and the myriad of emotions I've been feeling the last few days. I'm attracted to a man who is completely out of my comfort zone, who I'm using to gain subversive information from to further my career, and I'm willingly immersing myself into a world of kinky sex to meet my goals. When I made the decision to pursue a journalism degree in college, I was well aware of the boundaries that reporters constantly push in search of the truth. They put themselves in war zones, go deep undercover, and risk their very freedom by protecting their news sources. I knew all of that then, and I know it now, but I'm still struggling.

My stomach is churning wondering how far I will go with all of this, particularly when I'm not even getting a whiff of a true story here. I just don't see how to make the connection from a sex club—which is totally legal, by the way—to a dirty politician.

And trust me… I want to find that Governor Hayes' is dirty. I want to prove it and take him down, because he'll be the first true notch in my bedpost of justice that I take down solely as a result of my own hard work.

I suppose that's truly the thing that keeps me going here as I war with myself over my own moral dilemmas. How far will I go with Cain? Will our hearts start getting involved, especially as the bounds of intimacy are stretched? Without a doubt, since I let him stick a plug up my ass as if he owned me, I definitely feel something of a bond with him. When he rolled out of my bed yesterday afternoon, leaving me a quivering mass of satisfaction on the mattress, he leaned over and gave me a soft kiss. His eyes were warm, sated, and triumphant. He merely said, "You are amazing," and I felt my heart thump in response to that, the one part of my body that still had some strength of its own.

But now even that's weakening.

My phone starts a vibrating buzz on my kitchen table beside my empty coffee cup. It's face up so I can clearly see Brant's number and I grimace even as I reach to answer it. "Hi, Brant."

"We need an update, Preston," he says brusquely, addressing me by my last name as if I'm a recruit in his military platoon. "You've been there three weeks."

Sighing softly, I reach out and circle my finger around the edge of my coffee cup. "The first week was spent developing my cover and making contacts," I remind him.

"Then you've had two weeks to dig something up," he says in exasperation. "We can't fund your vacation there forever."

"I'm not sure there's a story here," I tell him resolutely, ignoring the vacation comment. "I'm just not picking up on anything yet."

"Come on, Preston," he says in a hard voice. "It's a sex club and a politician. Of course there's something there. You just have to spin it right."

I bristle against those words because we're not the fucking *National Enquirer*. We don't need to fabricate or inflate this shit; there's enough corruption in our government officials without chasing sordid stories like this. Still, I'm careful when I say, "I've gotten in with the head of security at the club. I've planted the seed, and I think I'm close to getting an invite. Once I get my foot in the door, I'll be able to assess the situation better."

"That's good," he practically purrs into the phone, and I wince. I can almost imagine him rubbing himself by the lewd tone. "You do whatever it takes to get the goods, you hear me?"

"I'll do whatever I can that doesn't put me in danger," I tell Brant firmly. "If you're not willing to let me work this with regards to my own safety, then you need someone else here."

"Of course your safety comes first," Brant says quickly and in a soothing voice. "But I don't have to remind you... sometimes it's the tiniest detail you come across that can break a story wide open. Just keep plugging away. This story will make your career."

Ironic that he used the word "plugging".

"I understand," I tell him.

"Plan on calling me at the end of the week with another update. We really need this, so I'm going to push you hard. That clear?"

"Clear," I tell him with a leaden weight settling in my stomach.

"And word of advice," Brant says as an afterthought. "You better be thinking of another angle than your current source."

I had already thought about that because I was feeling all kinds of rotten now that I'm getting to know Cain. The thought of using him in this respect isn't setting well with me. Colton Stokes is on my list for sure. I'm going to hit him up today. And I'm also trying to figure out an angle with Callie Hayes. I've done some research on Governor Hayes' platform and because his campaign is officially launching soon, I think I know the perfect thing that could possibly get me in the door with her.

PART OF MY research when I moved to Jackson was to learn all I could about my source, Colton Stokes. Thirty-one years old, never married, currently not dating anyone. Drives a brand-new Chevy Suburban. Operations manager of his father's cattle company. Net worth not a hell of a lot since Daddy owns the company, but he does have access to a modest trust fund.

I also happen to know he works out at the gym every Monday, Wednesday, and Friday mornings, and I wait patiently sipping on coffee for him to come out. The morning is heating up nicely and there's not a cloud in the blue sky. I'm not working today, and I'm not sure what to do with myself after I take care of this. Maybe I'll drive around, check out the scenery. Ideally, I'd be up for spending some time with Cain, but he told me he's got some work to do before his shift starts at The Wicked Horse tonight.

I've suppressed the urge to do a deeper background check on Cain beyond the employment stuff. I know I should so I can avert any surprises, but I feel guilty enough trying to use him to get my foot into the club. He didn't tell me details, only that he worked two other part-time jobs when work was available as he had some debt to pay. However, he did ask if I was coming by The Wicked Horse tonight. I played it vague and told him it was a possibility. His reply was, "Well, I won't be able to spend any time with you while I'm on duty. I just don't want you to be upset by that."

I thought it was cute he needed to explain that to me, but I was more than cool with it. I saw firsthand in my early observations of him how serious he is about his work. In fact, I think I won't bother going because he's honestly the only reason why I'd want to, and I don't want to just stare at him all night with my tongue hanging out.

The door to the gym swings open, catching the glare of the sun. Colton Stokes walks out, putting on a pair of sunglasses. He immediately notices me leaning my ass against the front bumper of his Suburban with my arms crossed, staring at him. As he walks closer, he gives me an unsure smile and says, "Can I help you with something?"

I push my own sunglasses off the bridge of my nose and up to my head to rest there, standing up straight. Holding my hand out, I say, "Sloane Preston."

He takes my hand, not a hint of recognition in his face, and shakes it. It's a bit of a risk to reveal myself to him, real name and all. I suppose there's a small chance he could rat me out to Bridger Payne or Woolf Jennings, but I think not. The fact he wanted to be *anonymous* in his tip tells me he wants to stay far under the radar.

"*Revealed* magazine," I say, and his eyebrows shoot up as he drops my hand. "We talked on the phone a few weeks ago. I'm here investigating the story you alerted us to about Governor Hayes."

Colton looks wildly left and right, then steps in closer to me and hisses, "Not about Governor Hayes. I told you about Woolf Jennings and his sex club."

"And then you told me about his daughter dating Woolf Jennings," I remind him. "We're a political magazine, Mr. Stokes. What did you think would happen if you waved that bait in front of us?"

Colton takes his sunglasses off and scrubs an agitated hand through his brown hair. My eyes are immediately drawn to dark bruising to the left temple, curling just under his eye. And as I peer closer, I see bruising on his jawline.

"What happened to you?" I ask, my eyes narrowing on his injuries.

Leaning back in toward me, he mutters, "Let's just say a message got delivered to me from the owners of The Wicked Horse. Woolf and Bridger were not happy with me."

"They know you called me?" I ask, a moment of fear starting to claw at me.

"No," he says loudly before lowering his tone. "No, they have no clue I called a reporter. If they did, they'd probably kill me. They're mad I told Governor Hayes about the club."

"And they beat you up?" I ask incredulously.

With a bark of a laugh, he says, "They wouldn't dirty their hands. Sent one of their goons to deliver the message."

And it hits me all at once... the cuts on Cain's hand the other night.

He beat Colton Stokes up for telling Governor Hayes about the sex club and I'm assuming about his daughter's role in it.

And another idea strikes me practically stupid. "Wait a minute... if you told Governor Hayes about the club, and Woolf and Bridger are mad about it, that means

Hayes didn't know about it at all, right?"

Colton carelessly shrugs. "I don't know. He acted surprised. Pissed as hell."

"Fuck," I curse loudly as my gaze wanders aimlessly around the parking lot. I'm seeing this story go down the drain. If Governor Hayes' didn't know about the club, he has no culpability. There's no dirt on him.

The only potential thing that could possibly stick would be if the money Jennings gave Hayes was from the club, but again... what's the point in running that if the governor didn't know it?

All my plans to shake Colton Stokes down for more information sort of evaporate, but I still ask to make sure, "Is there any connection that you know of between the governor and the club?"

"Just that his daughter goes there and is sexually in-volved with one of the owners, Woolf Jennings. She was involved in an orgy there. And now the governor knows it too. So, I guess in a way... he's condoning that lifestyle."

"I did a preliminary search on The Wicked Horse. The deed to the place is registered solely in Bridger Payne's name and has been since the place was construct-ed. Are you sure Woolf Jennings is an owner?"

"Positive," Colton says as he puts his sunglasses back on. "And it sits on Jennings' land."

That's true. I confirmed that already and just because Bridger Payne's name is on the deed to the actual building, it does not mean he's the sole owner of the business. Hell, there could be several owners for all I know, but that's not spelled out on any typical paperwork that I would have public access to—like deeds. Regardless, I am just not sure what to do about this… and that means a call to Brant for an update.

Just fucking perfect.

"Now if you'll excuse me, Miss Preston, I need to get going." He pushes by me and reaches for his truck door, but then levels a stare at me. "And I'd appreciate you not mentioning me to anyone."

"I protect my sources," I tell him straight up. I might not like him, but I will protect his identity. I sort of feel obligated now; I'd hate to see what Cain would do to him if he found out. And this also confirms for me as well… Cain clearly is involved with the sex club aspect of the business, but I'd suspected as much.

Stepping back from his vehicle, I pull my phone from my purse and watch as Colton gets in and drives away. When he's out of sight, I walk toward my own car, dialing Brant's cell.

He answers on the second ring. "Speak to me, Preston."

"I just did a follow-up interview with our source here. He says the governor had no clue about the sex club, so I don't think there's a connection there."

"Fuck," Brant mutters.

While I hated everything about using Cain to get the story, I'm all of a sudden feeling saddened that once the story is killed, I'll be leaving out of here probably as early as tomorrow. That means no more Cain and while I've only known him a few days, I'm already mourning the loss of the tenuous connection we made. It's there and it's something real… of that I'm sure. But sadly, it will probably die right along with the story once I move back across the country.

"We'll have to come at this from a different angle," Brant says brusquely. "Exploit the daughter in the sex club angle."

"What?" I ask, astonished over his suggestion.

"The daughter being in the sex club and the fact she'll be his campaign manager is enough. We'll run the story on the moral high road. Play up the depravity angle."

"But there's nothing wrong with her being a member of that club," I blurt out.

"Not to you or me," he says with a chuckle. "But to the millions of conservatives out there, they won't want an elected official with that grime attached to him."

"So we're going to kill a man's career because of something his daughter did that he had no knowledge of… and that isn't even illegal?"

"We're not killing anyone's career, Preston," he admonishes me. "We're merely reporting the truth. Besides… you don't know for sure the governor's not involved, right?"

"No, but—"

"And you're being paid to get the scoop on what's really going on there," he says, rolling right over me. "So roll your sleeves up, get in there, and figure out what you have to work with. At the least, you have an opinion piece on the morality aspect, and if you're really lucky, you dig up something concrete about Hayes."

"Brant… I'm just not feeling—"

"Do it," he orders into the phone with an icy voice. "Or look for another job. It's quite simple."

He hangs up on me. I sit in the parking lot of Colton Stokes' gym for half an hour after, trying to determine what I could do with my life if I quit my job. I had no answers other than the fact I could continue to dig and see what popped up. Try to shine some more clarity on what is important to me within this career.

As of now, I'm feeling a bit disillusioned.

Chapter 11

Cain

⁂

I LEAN UP against the wall to the left of the entrance doors inside The Wicked Horse and carefully survey my domain. My guys are all at their posts, alert and watching the crowd. The bartenders are handling the customers with ease and there have been no major disturbances unless you count Billy Stooks barfing in the men's bathroom because he always goes into tip-over when he switches from beer to liquor. We packed him up in a cab and sent him home.

I've done three walk-throughs of The Silo tonight, not because security is really needed there, but because I can't stop thinking about Sloane and her fantasy.

Shit... if that girl had a real gang bang, she'd freak the fuck out. The minute she took a slap to the face, a vicious twist to her nipples, or a hand squeezing her throat closed to keep her from screaming in protest, she'd probably pass out from the terror of it. Christ... just the image of that happening to her twists my guts up. Even though that exact scene has turned me on before with countless other women, I know I sure as shit couldn't let her ever do something like that. Like I told her… that scenario is built for women who like the pain and fear.

By the third time I'd walked through The Silo, I realized I did so eyeballing the various members who had come out to play tonight. Evaluating them. Wondering who would be willing to give her the fantasy that she really wants without crossing lines. Yeah… the thought of it… Sloane getting well fucked by four men as we all stand around and watch her blush deepen with every pounding, well hell… I'm getting hard thinking about it. It's definitely one of my fantasies now.

But there's a problem.

As much as I want to… as much as I know it would be the hottest thing ever to put her in a fantasy cabin and have her screaming out all night in pleasure… as much as I want to dirty up all of her innocence and sweet ways, I'm still deep down questioning the sanity of it. Questioning whether it's fair to change her world this way, even if she comes out on the other end completely satisfied and thrilled to her core. She won't be the same.

I'm afraid I won't either.

With my mind in a turmoil, I decide to seek the advice of one of the wisest people I know when it comes to the games of sex and kink.

Pushing off the wall, I head back to Bridger's office. I know he's in there because he left The Silo a little bit ago after putting on an eyebrow-raising show with one of the original members. I have no clue what Bridger's back story is. I know he moved to the area when Woolf returned home from college a little over ten years ago. He's worked out at the Double J as a ranch hand, and he and Woolf are best friends. I was not surprised Woolf and Bridger opened up a sex club, but I was surprised as fuck when I first found out that Woolf liked this lifestyle. I was working at Scandalous in Driggs, and the fucker walked in one night with Bridger while I was getting my cock sucked on center stage. We ended up sharing some beers and the same girl who had been sucking my dick. As they say, the rest is history.

While I don't know much about Bridger, I would say there's some seriously whacked shit in his past. I've seen some hardcore BDSM stuff before, but nothing compares to the pain he can hand out. He does it sparingly, and there are only a handful of members in this club who can handle what he doles out. No, correction... they actually *need* what he doles out. Their sexual satisfaction is dependent on it.

Watching Bridger is like watching an art show. He's methodical and deliberate. He can land the end of a whip on a nipple from clear across the room. He can practically carve a pattern in someone's back that's symmetrical and precise. I've seen him whip men and women to where they are screaming in pain, refusing to use their safe word, and when he lets them come, it's the most explosive, freeing moment you can imagine. Bridger rarely fucks on these occasions. If I had to hazard a guess, I'd say it's because most of this stuff doesn't really turn him on. While it's morbidly fascinating to watch, I know it sure as hell doesn't turn me on... watching those specific instances that are true BDSM acts. Where pain and sometimes blood are required for a person to get off.

A lot of the people who play at the club like to pretend they're into that shit, but it's just a toned-down version. We carry a huge stock of soft, suede floggers designed with wide, flat lashes that barely put a blush on the skin. They feel pretty good actually, producing just enough of a tiny sting to enhance the experience.

But when Bridger wields a flogger, you can be assured it's one that will hurt. He often uses a leather one with braided lashes that are knotted on the end, but if he wants to dole out maximum pain, he'll use a horsehair one he keeps locked in his office. While it looks soft and fluffy, it actually produces an exquisitely intense sting. I once made the mistake of poking fun at it, and he cracked me on the back of the hand, causing me to yelp. He then laughed his ass off. Thereafter, I held major respect for the person on the receiving end of that device.

Heading straight through the building, I cut across the dance floor, and turn down the hall that leads to his office. I give three short knocks, assuming he's in there, but I can't hear anything because the music is so loud. However, in just a few seconds, the door is open and he's motioning me in.

He looks tired, but I expect those performances take it out of him. When he's flogging, the man is truly working up a sweat with the repetitive swings.

"What's up?" he says as he walks back to his desk, straightening up what looks to be spreadsheets strewn across the wood surface.

"Need to ask you for some advice," I tell him straight up as I take a seat on the couch, propping an ankle on my knee.

"I'm listening."

"I've got this girl," I tell him.

"You got a girl?" he asks in amazement.

"Well, not like a girlfriend or anything. We're fuck-ing and—"

"As in more than once?"

"Yes, more than once," I say in irritation, and Bridg-er chuckles. "Anyway... she has this fantasy of getting fucked by multiple guys."

"Dirty girl," Bridger says in amusement. "You know how to pick 'em."

"Actually no," I tell him soberly. "She's sweet. Kind of naive about this stuff, but she's adventurous. I figured what the hell... I've got the means to give her what she wants."

"You want to soil her," Bridger says, and the senti-ment is so accurate that I rear backward on the couch a bit.

"Why would you say that?" I ask in astonishment, a bit wigged out he pinpointed my very innermost dilem-ma.

"It's a classic fantasy," Bridger says with a shrug of his shoulders. "Trust me... the prince didn't want to just kiss Snow White to wake her up. He wanted to fuck the innocence out of her."

I snort and shake my head. "You've ruined that movie and my childhood for me."

"The point is, in our line of work, purity is like a gateway drug. You find someone who is ignorant of this world but has a tiny curiosity, and the possibilities are endless. You do a little nasty to her, watch her shriek louder than anyone you've ever been with, and you're hooked. You want more."

Holy shit, this guy is freaky accurate. I'm thinking the minute I sank that plug in Sloane's ass was the moment I might have become addicted to her. When I pulled it out as she was coming and watched her thrash in the throes of the most magnificent orgasm ever, I became irrevocably lost to the notion of doing more to her.

"So I should give her the fantasy?" I ask him for clarification.

"I like a good gang bang," Bridger says with a laugh. "Easy enough to arrange."

"Yeah, can't do that exactly," I say as I scratch my head with a sheepish smile.

"Why's that?"

"She… well, I don't think she could really handle something like that. It would have to be toned down."

"That can be done. Just need to pick the right people," he observes.

"I was thinking Rand and Logan for sure."

Bridger nods in agreement. "If some guy-on-guy action turns her on, I'm sure they'd be glad to oblige."

"I'm sure," I drily say. "They'd fuck a watermelon if that turned her on."

"Want me to join you?" Bridger asks, and I blink in surprise at him. Bridger rarely participates in anything outside of the few BDSM members he services. Past that, he does his fucking in private… usually right here in this office.

"I don't want to put you out, man," I say hastily. "But I'd probably set it up early next week."

"No trouble," he assures me. "Sounds fun."

Yeah, fun and Bridger don't exactly go hand in hand, but I'm not going to pass up this opportunity. While he's a master with the lash, he's also the most intuitive person I've ever met when it comes to reading people's sexual desires. I want this to be good for Sloane. While she's going to get off with what we'll do to her, I know Bridger can maximize it.

"Will you direct?" I ask him, because in these situations, it's easy for it to get out of control. I know Bridger will be able to read Sloane like a book and deliver to her what she needs.

"Sure," he says with a smile. "But once you put me in control, I won't give it up."

His tone is firm but there's an ominous ring to it. It gives me a slight shiver.

"You got it, boss," I say as I stand from the couch with a two-handed slap to my thighs. "Now I better get back to work."

"Take the rest of the night off," Bridger says as he looks back down to his spreadsheets. "Go see your girl."

"She's not really my girl," I feel compelled to clarify.

Bridger snickers without taking his eyes off his work in front of me. "Go see your girl," he commands. "Consider it an extra bonus for the excellent work you did with Mr. Stokes."

"But it's a Saturday night."

"Go see your fucking girl," Bridger snarls.

I open my mouth to argue with him further about the nature of my relationship with Sloane, but then I think about her all curled up in her bed, maybe even in a conservative nightgown that deserves to be ripped from her body, and I can't help myself. I ignore Bridger's "my girl" comment and give him a nod of thanks.

He doesn't see it though because he's intently focused on the work in front of him, and I'm already forgotten.

Chapter 12

Sloane

SOMETHING HEAVY ON me starts to rouse me from sleep.

The hand over my mouth and the one between my legs causes a stab of electric fear to slam into me, and I'm fully awake. I'm disoriented for only a minute as I take in the fact my bedside lamp is now on, a man is on top of me and his fingers inching under my panties. Just as I start to try to buck him off with a surge of fear-induced adrenaline, I realize it's Cain on top of me, grinning down.

"It's me," he whispers.

"Nnnhh shhttt," I yell into his hand, and he removes it. I clarify in a more moderate voice. "No shit."

He laughs, leans down, and gives me a deep kiss just as his fingers brush through me. "Surprise."

"How did you get in?" I ask, trying to sound mad but gasping in pleasure as one finger slides home.

"Your lock was ridiculously easy to open with my driver's license," he says, holding that finger still inside of me for the moment. "I was going to knock, but then I just couldn't resist the surprise."

"You're lucky I don't sleep with a gun," I tell him.

"I checked under your pillow first," he says, and then curls his finger upward. I groan and tilt my hips, and he laughs again... this time in triumph.

"What are you doing here?" I ask in a strangled voice, my mind starting to disconnect and my body starting to take over as evidenced by my hips rotating against his finger.

"I'm here to get you off," he says as he rolls to my side and props himself up casually on his elbow while still keeping his other hand lodged between my legs. He looks calm, utterly relaxed, and slightly mischievous.

"You're supposed to be working," I say sternly, then my eyes roll in the back of my head as he pulls his finger out and starts to rub it on my clit.

"Shut up, Sloane." His voice is amused, but his eyes are intent. "Let me get you off and then we can talk."

Okay, if I must.

I close my eyes and let him do whatever he wants to me, because my desire to have him get me off takes precedence over my curiosity to know why he's not at work.

SLOANE, WAKE UP.

Come on, Sloane... it's time to get up.

I hear the voice, but I'm so warm, sated, and sleepy. I ignore it. Strong arms are wrapped around me, and I feel the sweet call of slumber pulling me back under.

Hands moving on me, sliding up my ribs, over to my breast... nice, and I'm not sure if this is real or a dream, but I'm digging it.

A sharp pinch on my nipple, followed by a hard twist, and I give out a surprised yip of pain and shoot up out of my dream state, right off the mattress.

I'm confused as Cain is pushing me back down and latching his mouth to said tweaked nipple, rolling his tongue over it in gentle, soothing strokes.

And holy hell that feels good with the tingle of pain still sizzling beneath it.

Cain raises his head and looks up at me with a grin. "Told you to get up."

"That hurt," I whine softly as I bring my hand up to prod at my sore nipple.

"I know," he says with a triumphant gleam in his eye. "But you liked it... admit it."

"No," I say in a petulant voice, but it doesn't have much strength behind it because damn, that was amazing.

"Yes," he argues with me.

"No," I bicker back.

His hand latches onto my wrist and in an abrupt change that leaves me spinning, he's pulling me out of the bed. "Come on and get a shower. I'm taking you out to the Double J today."

"What?" I ask in confusion. I stumble slightly as he pulls me out of my bedroom and down the hall.

"My friend Woolf's ranch," he explains. "I have to do some work out there today, and I'm bringing you with me. I'll have some time to take you horseback riding."

"Wait... no, I can't," I say as I pull against his hold. It makes no difference; he pulls me right into the bathroom. "I have to be at work at ten."

"Call in sick," he says as he reaches into the shower and turns the water on.

"But I'm not sick," I say resolutely.

We're both naked so standing in my little bathroom makes me acutely aware of his magnetic sexuality. I force myself to hold eye contact with him and not drop down to that massive dick that spent plenty of time between my legs last night. After I got over the shock of him breaking into my apartment, I immediately submitted to his wicked ways. He did, indeed, get me off with just his fingers. I was so wrecked after that, we didn't bother with any conversation as he promised. Instead, he played my body to his satisfaction, which included a slightly larger butt plug he insisted I try because as he said, "It will feel amazing as I'm fucking you from behind."

I flush warm just thinking about it because it felt like nothing I've ever experienced before, every thrust into my body rattling the plug within me, causing it to bump and jostle against nerves back there I never knew existed prior to meeting Cain Bonham.

"Hmmmmm," Cain hums low in his throat as he steps into me... a knowing look on his face. "Whatcha thinkin' about? Your face sort of got red there."

"Nothing," I say as I give a slight cough to clear my throat. "Now, about work—"

He steps in closer, and I feel his erection brush against my stomach.

I will not look down.

I will not look down.

I will not look down.

Cain grabs my hand, startling me, and hauls my body toward him. Right to his cock where he curls my fingers around it and makes me squeeze him hard. He groans from the sensation and then with his grip on my hand, makes me stroke him up and down. His eyes flutter closed, he removes his hand from mine, and he says, "Yeah… just like that, Sloane."

My eyes drop immediately and I look down at my hand, looking so small as it's wrapped around his hard girth. I squeeze harder and increase the pace of my strokes, fascinated as fluid leaks from the tip, hits my hand, and lubes his skin for me. I stare in absolute fascination, feeling tingles break out all over my body as I jack this sexy man off. I want to watch him come, have it hit my stomach with warm bursts and hopefully deep groans from him.

"Take off work today," Cain says in a hoarse voice as his hand comes back to mine. He grips me hard and stops my movement, holding me absolutely still. His dick jumps in my hand, but he ignores it.

My head snaps up to his and while a sizzle of lust still remains deep in his eyes, I also see something else there.

Almost a need that can't be assuaged with my hand on his cock.

I've got an immensely strong work ethic. While this may just be a cover job, I don't like to leave people hanging. I've never in my life called in sick when I wasn't.

But when I see Cain looking at me like this... pleading for something—I'm not sure he even knows what, nor do I—it causes something inside me to shift. I've not been able to exactly figure out what Cain and I have going on here, because up until this moment, it's really just been sex. But now it's turning into something different and I have to make a decision how to roll with it.

If I say yes, I could lose my job. Ultimately, not a problem, as the magazine is paying my expenses. I'd get the added benefit of possibly gaining a further foothold within Cain Bonham's world. This, I need, if I'm going to do the job that's being demanded of me by Brant. On its face, it seems like the best move for my undercover operation.

But that's the part that's causing me doubt. I don't want to spend the day with Cain just so I can figure out how better to use him. I want to get to know him, find out his story, and connect to him on more than just a sexual existence. I'm thinking he wants that to. Otherwise, why would he invite me?

"Why are you doing this?" I whisper suddenly. If I'm to figure out what to do, I need to know his motivation.

"Doing what?" he asks with surprise.

"Asking me to spend the day with you," I say with a small degree of skepticism. "I thought what we had was just sexual."

"Who says I'm not going to fuck you at the Double J?" he asks with a mischievous smile.

"Because this is just sex, right?" I ask him for clarification, not giving into his amusement.

The smile slides off Cain's face and his eyes sober. Batting my hand away from his dick, he steps in closer to me, leans his face down to compensate for the difference in our height, and murmurs, "Not just sex, Sloane. Fucking amazing sex. Mind-blowing sex. Trust me when I say I'm coming back for more of it."

My heart instantly pangs with hurt that he doesn't feel a connection like I thought, but then it becomes immediately relieved when I realize I can just concentrate on my job and use Cain to my advantage.

But then he causes another sharp stab of emotion when he touches his mouth to mine briefly before saying, "But that's not what today is. I figured you'd like to see some of Wyoming and there's no prettier place than the Double J. I only have to do a few things for Woolf, and then I can take you out horseback riding."

Shit.

Damn, shit, damn, shit.

I might have doubted myself before now, but the minute he says those words and I realize there's more to Cain Bonham than just unbelievable orgasms, I know

I've got some major feelings twisted into this. Otherwise, the excitement of spending some time with this complex man wouldn't be warring so hard with the guilt I'm feeling for the way in which I'll ultimately take advantage of him.

Chapter 13

Cain

"**Y**OU'RE AWFUL QUIET," I say as our horses plod alongside each other.

Sloane turns that beautiful face… one I always think of as sweetly innocent… and gives me a smile so bright it almost hurts to look at it. Those two dimples fascinate me because they do the weirdest thing and make me want to smile back at her just as big.

"It's just so beautiful," she says as her face turns back toward the Teton mountain range. "I mean… our mountains in Tennessee are lovely, but these are incomparable."

True enough. On this bright summer day, the riot of colors on the range is stunning. Deep green grass and trees, slate blue rock formations, and snowy white peaks. I'll never get tired of it.

Sloane hung out at the barn while I did some minor repairs on one of the stall doors. It wasn't an urgently needed fix, but Woolf always throws work my way when he can and I'm appreciative of that. It took no more than an hour of my time and then I got two horses saddled. Because Sloane was an inexperienced rider, I put her on the fattest, laziest horse in Woolf's stock and assured her she wouldn't move faster than a snail. She was nervous at first but once she realized this was just a relaxing ride over some well-worn trails, she gave over to the thrill of the scenery and I think forgot she was on a horse, despite the fact she was still clutching the horn as if her life depended on it.

"So… you're like a cowboy or something?" Sloane asks out of the blue, her eyes still set on the mountain range ahead of us.

"The Double J employs a lot of people. I worked through high school here and part time in between other jobs."

"And you were in the Marines, huh?"

"The tattoo's kind of obvious, right?" I chuckle.

"It does kind of stare me right in the face when you're on top of me," she says primly, and my chuckle turns into an outright laugh.

She'd be right about that. In a moment of pure stupidity when I was eighteen and had just graduated boot camp, me and my buddies went out and got tattoos to display our pride in being Marines. I opted for a devil dog on my right pec. A tough-looking bulldog with a severe underbite and a Marine Corps collar around its thick neck. It glared out from my chest with the letters U.S.M.C. tattooed underneath in red and gold.

"I was in for six years and admittedly, that tattoo was a mistake," I tell her.

"What did you do in the Marines?"

"Infantry," I tell her simply. "It's why I ended up back here in Wyoming after I got out. Not a lot of transferrable skills in that MOS."

"MOS?"

"Sorry," I tell her as I tug on the reins slightly to move my horse closer to hers. "Military Occupational Specialty. I was 0351… an assaultman. I basically operated an anti-tank weapon."

"Were you in Afghanistan?" she asks, her gaze now coming to mine with somber curiosity.

"Twice."

"Is that how you got your scar?" she asks, and I blink at her in surprise. No woman I've been with has ever asked me that question. Granted… it's been a long time since I've been on a date with one, and granted… most times I'm just giving a hard fucking to someone over at The Silo and there's no opportunity for questions, but the simple way in which she asks catches me off guard. It's not with a morbid curiosity, but rather a desire to know me better. I can see in her eyes the truth of that because she doesn't drop her gaze from mine.

Shaking my head, I tell her, "Afraid it's not that glamorous of a story. I was working at a bar over in Idaho. A jealous husband came in looking for his wife. Tried to drag her out by the hair. I took exception to it, and he took exception to me taking exception to it. He got me with a broken beer bottle."

"Holy crap," she says with her jaw hanging low. "Was he arrested?"

"Nope," I tell her with a smirk. "But I kicked his ass after that. I was satisfied with the outcome."

"You're such a badass," she says with a giggle and fuck... but I love that sound. So young, carefree... makes me want to turn that giggle into a moan of lust-filled passion. That's probably not going to happen out here, so I'll settle for a blush.

"You know what I should have done?" I say as I reach out to grab the reins of her horse, right near the bridle so I can bring it to a halt with me.

She turns slightly in her saddle to look at me, both hands still clutching hard on the horn. "What's that?"

"I should have loaded your ass up with the plug before I put you on that horse. Do you know how good that would have felt with you rocking against that saddle?"

Sloane's face goes beet red, which causes me to grin at her, and she shakes her head no. "Absolutely not. I wouldn't have let you do that."

"You would have," I confidently say.

"No, I wouldn't," she argues.

"You'd let me fuck you right now if I pulled you off that horse and threw you down in that patch of wild-flowers," I tell her as I nod toward the ground, hoping to make that blush go brighter.

"Not going to happen," she says firmly. "We're out in the open. Anyone could see us."

"We're miles away from anyone," I counter.

"The moose might see us, or a bear could sneak up

on us," she sniffs.

Winking at her, I say, "You have a point. I don't think I could battle a moose or bear for you."

Releasing my hold on her horse, I kick my heels in, give a cluck, and urge my horse to walk again. Because Sloan's horse is also dumb in addition to being fat and lazy, it follows along without a second thought.

"I have Tuesday night off," I tell her offhandedly, hoping this sounds casual. "Interested in hanging with me?"

"Like a date?" she asks with wide eyes.

Hmmmm. Not sure setting up multiple men to fuck her as a surprise is a date, but sure, why not? "Yeah... something like that."

"Sounds great." Her smile pops with those dimples again.

Fuck, they kill me.

"You work an awful lot," she says in contemplation. "Is that par for the course?"

"Pretty much," I say simply as I scan the area, looking for a place we can stop for a bit. She says she won't let me fuck her out here, but I'm betting I can get her to change her mind. And it's her own fault really... flashing those dimples at me.

I pull my horse to a halt and dismount. Dropping the reins to the ground, knowing the horse isn't going anywhere, I walk to Sloane's horse and hold my hand up to help her off.

"Why are we stopping?" She looks down at me with

uncertainty, her hands still gripping the horn hard with reins trapped in between. Fucking adorable.

"Just giving the horses a bit of a break," I lie smoothly to her.

She accepts what I tell her and releases her grip on the saddle. Ignoring my hand, she swings her leg over but as she starts to lower herself to the ground, I put my hands on her waist and ease her down.

"Thanks," she says and pushes her hair behind her ears. I've noticed this is a nervous move she makes, and I like that she's on edge with me.

Turning from her, I take the reins of both horses and lead them over to some rabbitbrush growing near the trail. I toss the reins into the branches, knowing the horses won't move. Pulling a rolled saddle blanket from the back of my mount, I shake it out.

The trail we had been riding was bordered on one side by a thick grove of juniper, birch, and pine and to the other side by a wide, flat meadow. About a thousand yards further and we'd hit the Snake River. I'd chosen this trail because it rides perpendicular to the mountain range so I'd wow Sloane with the beauty, but mostly because there aren't any cattle on this part of the ranch. No cattle means no cowboys.

That means privacy.

Grabbing two bottles of water out of my saddlebag, I tell her, "Follow me."

I have two choices. Plop the blanket in the meadow grass or move into the woods and hope for a decent spot free of too much of nature's debris. The woods would be ideal, offering more privacy and hopefully loosening Sloane's inhibitions, but I choose the meadow because I like a challenge. Besides, fucking in a field under a bright blue sky? Nothing better.

I find a nice spot perhaps no more than twenty feet from the trail and lay the blanket down. The grass is fairly sparse and clumps of sagebrush around us sweeten the already pristine air. I sit, stretch my legs out, and nod toward the spot beside me.

"Take a load off, Right Hook."

She gives a soft laugh and plops down to my right, crossing her legs and reaching out for a piece of sage. Picking it off, she holds it to her nose, giving it a long sniff. "Mmmm… that smells good."

"I never get tired of that smell," I say as I tilt my head back to let the sun warm my face a bit. I didn't have my cowboy hat since it was too far out of the way to swing by my house, so I made due with a ball cap I had in my glovebox. Luckily, the sun isn't too brutal today, although I won't keep Sloane out here too long because her skin is definitely on the delicately pale side.

"So why do you work so hard?" Her voice cuts through my moment of commune with the sun, and I turn to look at her beside me. "You work full time and fill your off hours with extra work. Sounds like a man on a mission to me."

"I'm taking time off now, aren't I?" I say with a wink and lean toward her. I bring a hand to her thigh and angle my head in for a kiss.

Her head pulls back and her hands come to my chest. "Seriously… why do you work so hard?"

Sighing, I give her leg a squeeze, pull away from her, and lay back on the blanket. I plant my feet on the ground and rest my hands on my stomach. It takes no more than a moment for Sloane to mimic my actions and then she's lying on her back beside me, both of us now staring up into the blue Wyoming sky dotted with white clouds.

"I was married," I tell her simply, but there's nothing simple about this story and it's not one I've told many people. "Five years ago. My wife had some addictions… several actually. Cocaine mostly because Rachel loved to party. But she was also addicted to shopping. She ran up about fifty-thousand dollars of credit card debt that I'm stuck paying."

Sloane's head pops up, and she turns on her side to face me. I just angle my head to the right so I can see her.

Her brows are furrowed as she asks, "But isn't that debt split when you divorce? Why do you have to pay it all?"

"Because we didn't divorce," I tell her. Her eyes flare wide with shock, so I quickly let her off the hook. "She's dead. Been about three years now, and the cards were in our names jointly."

Sloane places a hand on my chest, and her face melts into a symphony of sorrow. "I'm so sorry."

"I'm not," I say coldly as I sit up and Sloane's hand

falls away. She nibbles on her lower lip with worry and confusion. "I'm glad she's dead. She didn't deserve this life."

Rearing back, Sloane tilts her head in astonishment as if she couldn't believe I'd say something so cruel about another human being. She opens her mouth to say something, then shuts it just as quickly and right there... in her eyes, I see it. She starts to disconnect from me.

And that just won't do. I told her the truth but not all of it, and I'm not about to lose something else to the destruction that encompassed all that was Rachel Bonham.

Snaking my hand out, I grab hers and hold onto it before she can pull away further. "She killed our child," I say gruffly. I know it's a bit dramatic, but I need Sloane to understand that despite the drugs, cheating, and running up astronomical bills I couldn't afford, there's only one true reason I'm glad she's dead.

"What?" Sloane says and she goes to her knees, inches her way closer to me with concern etched over her face.

Taking a deep breath, I blow it out harshly and tell her what very few people know about me. "She was twelve weeks pregnant. I had no clue, but she went and had an abortion behind my back. I found out from a fucking credit card bill."

A deep gasp of dismay comes from Sloane's lips, and she whispers, "That bitch. That evil bitch."

"She was so drugged out, I'm not sure she really

cared what she was doing. She died about three weeks after from an overdose."

"I'm glad," Sloane says, but I know she doesn't really mean it. She doesn't know Rachel or me, but even as heinous as my situation was and as much as she empathizes, I can tell Sloane has a soft heart and wouldn't wish Rachel's horror of a life on anyone.

I wish I could be as forgiving, but remembering that pain and misery is good for me. It helps to keep me at arm's length from others so I don't fall for that shit again.

Some would look at me right now, sitting in a sunny meadow with a pretty girl and would just shake their head with humor at the situation, but they'd be wrong in thinking I'm falling for Sloane. No, I like having sex with her. She's cool and all, and fun to hang with, but this is one thing and one thing only.

It's about dirty sex with an angel-pure type of girl. Once I get her dirtied up, I'm sure I'll cut her loose.

Chapter 14

Sloane

"WHERE ARE WE going?" I had asked Cain when he showed up at my apartment to pick me up for our date tonight. I wasn't sure how to dress because I hadn't heard from him since our time at the Double J two days ago. Well, except for a short text that said, *I'll pick you up at 8pm.*

His response?

He merely held up a black, silk scarf and said, "It's a surprise."

In that singular moment, a thrilling quake of adrenaline laced with fear and excitement raced through my body as I suspected Cain was taking me to the sex club.

I willingly let him tie the scarf around my eyes, shutting me in absolute darkness. He kissed my neck and whispered, "I hope you like it."

And that was the last thing he said to me.

He helped me out to his truck and buckled me in.

He never said another word, despite my questions and nervous chattering. He was purposely ignoring me, which was doing nothing more than focusing that fear and excitement into an almost painful cramp of tension low in my belly and between my legs.

I have no clue how long it took us to get to our destination. With the silence and tension and darkness, my mind was racing with possibilities, so I stopped paying attention to my physical surroundings.

"We're here." His voice rumbles low and breaks the silence like the crack of a whip. I jump slightly and my hand rises to the scarf.

"Don't take it off," he commands me. "Not yet."

My hand drops, and I hear him get out of the truck. In moments, my door is opening and I feel cool air against my legs as I'm able to get the seatbelt off. The forecast called for the temperature to drop into the mid-50s. Because I wasn't sure if we were going casual or dressy, I chose an outfit that was in between. A mint-green circle skirt, pleated at the waist and flared out, hanging mid-thigh. I paired it with a form-fitting black turtleneck, black tights, and black ankle boots with a high heel. A cheetah-print scarf around my neck, silver hoop earrings, and a swipe of mascara were all the other accessories I'd chosen. I looked mostly sweet, which I've figured enough to know turns Cain on, but the high heel on the booties adds just enough sex appeal that Cain won't forget the other side of me that he's drawn out.

Cain's hands go to my waist and he lifts me from the truck. When my feet hit the ground, I sense hard-packed dirt as Cain puts one hand at my lower back and takes my other hand to lead me to the great unknown. My heart flutters madly within my chest, going faster and faster as he walks me toward something I'm sure is going to change my world.

Up three steps that make hollow thumps and creak as we step on them. Wooden, I'm guessing.

Four more steps, a pause, and I hear Cain turn the knob to a door.

Is this the sex club?

We step in, the air feels slightly warmer, and I hear the door close behind me. I'm slightly disoriented as I expected to hear more. I mean, if this is a sex club, I expected voices, maybe some music and moaning. I expected lots of moaning.

Instead, my ears strain against the silence, and that, accompanied with the darkness I'm still immersed in, causes my pulse to soar practically out of control.

Cain steps in close to me; I can tell it's him by his smell and the change in the air around me. A hand to the back of my head and the scarf is being pulled away.

I blink several times, the light around me harsh on my sensitive eyes, and I realize I'm in what looks like a large living room. A couch to my right with a framed painting mounted on the wall. Confused, my eyes slide to Cain's, but then a rustling sound behind him catches my attention. I lean slightly, look past Cain's shoulder, and see a man leaning casually up against the adjacent wall that borders a dark hallway. He stands with his arms crossed across his massive chest, dark brown hair worn in messy, long layers with whiskey-colored eyes.

He's stunning, but what catches me off guard the

most is the strand of thin, white rope in his hands.

A slight cough behind me causes me to spin.

Two men stand there, both staring at me with not unfriendly faces, but not with open smiles either. One has a slightly amused look though. They're tall, well built, and extremely good looking. One has blond hair that's shaved on the sides but really long on top, so long it falls to one side and hangs down to almost his jaw. He has a full, thick beard and an eyebrow ring. The other has short, dark hair, eyes just as dark, and a goatee that surrounds a set of generously full lips. He reaches down and rubs his crotch while he stares at me, and wow... just...

"Sloane," Cain says softly. I whip back to him, feeling like my heart is about to burst forth from my chest. His hands come to my face where they hold me gently, so I focus on him. "This is for you... your fantasy."

"But—" I start to question.

So many questions.

Where are we?

Who are these men?

What are they going to do to me?

Will I die from pleasure?

Or will this be a terrible, terrible mistake I'm making?

"No buts," he cuts me off quickly. "I only want to know if you're in or out. I promise you won't be hurt. I promise it will be phenomenal, and you will come over and over again. But if you're in, then we're starting and the only way we're stopping is if you use a safe word, okay?"

"A safe word?" I mumble, feeling like my thoughts are drowning in mud.

"You say the word and we stop immediately," he explains. "Normally, a safe word is to stop the application of pain if it gets to be too much, but I promise you that's not what we're doing here. Remember I told you that you're not really cut out for a gang bang? We're modifying things a bit. Giving you a lighter version, okay? But if it gets too overwhelming… too intense… you say the word and we stop. You can't pick the word 'stop' though, because we'll ignore it. I expect you might say that a time or two as things get intense, so choose your word carefully."

My head swivels, trying to see the three men… trying to see if there are any more.

"But who are these guys? Where are we?" I ask, mostly in an effort to try to ground myself, but also because I'm confused. Are we in someone's house? This isn't a sex club.

"The only thing you need to know is that this is private property, you're safe, and these are guys I work with and trust."

I peek at the large guy standing behind Cain with the rope. He's a bit scary looking in his intensity. "Are you going to introduce me—?"

"Sloane," Cain says firmly and my eyes slam back to him. "This isn't a social. You're going to get fucked by strangers—and me, of course—but you don't need to

140

know them. They're going to do with you what they want, and that's part of the fantasy, right?"

"But you're going to be involved too, right?"

His lips curve up, and he smiles at me in understanding. "Wouldn't miss it for the world."

"And… um… I don't think I'm ready for…" My words trail off, complete embarrassment overtaking me that these men are listening to this.

"No cocks in your ass tonight," Cain affirms with a chuckle. "I've already told them it's mine, but that doesn't mean other things won't be in there."

A massive shudder hits me from his words. While I can see that amuses Cain, it also turns his eyes dark… the green disappearing and the brown overflowing, which I've come to recognize as hot desire.

So now it's decision time. I can be a big girl, tell myself this is all to further my career because it will help me get better intel. I reason to myself that if I go through with this, show Cain how much I love it—even if I have to fake it—then he'll invite me into the club. I keep him interested with my adventurous innocence, worm my way in, and find exactly what I need to write my article.

Or… I can be honest with myself and admit that I might possibly be doing this for other reasons. Maybe perhaps because I feel something with Cain that I've never felt before. Something has awakened inside of me, and it seems to be begging for more.

And if I go ahead and admit that to myself, what does this mean for Cain and me? Once this is over and done with, will he look at me the same? If it's different, will it be increased desire or disgust?

This concerns me.

"Cain," I whisper as I lean in toward him, my hands coming to rest on his chest while he still frames my face with his own. "What about us?"

"What about us?" he asks in a low voice, his eyes searching mine for clarification.

"Well… how do you feel about other men… with me? I mean, there's no way in hell I'd let you do this with four girls. It doesn't seem to make sense to me."

Understanding fills his eyes, lightening them up a bit. He gives me a sympathetic smile and a soft kiss. "Sloane… this fantasy of yours… it turns me the fuck on. Thinking about and watching you get pleasured… I've been obsessed with the idea since you told me. Trust me… this is as much for me as it is for you. I think you've figured my tastes run on the kinky side, right?"

I nod, because yeah… I figured that out.

I have no clue if this will really turn Cain on or end our relationship. I have to trust him when he says he's cool with this, and the reason I have to trust him is because I have to also trust his promise that I won't be hurt. I am putting my life and part of my soul in his hands right now, because I will be changed by this experience. Of that, there is no doubt.

Taking a deep breath, I give him permission to let the games begin. "Then my word safe word is *Tennessee*."

Cain slams his mouth on me for a deep and possessive kiss with hands now gripping my jawline tightly and his entire body pressed to mine. I go dizzy, try to latch onto his arms, but he's pulling away and releasing me.

He takes a step back and to the right, and the man with the rope in his hand comes into full view. He is truly magnificent both in form and face. He's bigger than Cain and the other two guys, with muscles bulging under a tight, navy blue t-shirt and soft, faded jeans. His eyes are lasered onto me as he casually saunters forward, one hand holding the rope, the other letting his fingers idly stroke the silken-looking fibers.

"Get her naked," the man says in a rough voice full of so much command, I almost start to pull at my clothes to obey. But then hands are all over me... Cain to my front and the two men behind me, and I'm stripped quickly. The minute my underwear clear my legs, I have a sudden moment of panic caused by my nakedness in front of three strangers and Cain... a man I've only known a few days.

"Cain," the large man says as he drops the rope to the ground without taking his eyes off me. "Make her come real quick... let's loosen her up a bit."

I'm surprised when Cain doesn't question the man or hesitate, but instead drops to his knees in front of me, his hands coming up to stroke the outside of my legs. He looks up at me, his dark lashes framing his eyes, which are now luminescent with more green than brown. "I'm going to fuck you with my tongue, Sloane."

My legs almost buckle under me just from the weight

of pure sex in his tone, but I'm saved when the blond and dark-haired men behind me press in closer. I'm stunned when the blond curves his hands around me from behind, drags them down to my mound, and peels me apart right in front of Cain's eyes.

Heat crawls across my face, down my neck and to my chest as I'm drowning in absolute embarrassment. This causes Cain to chuckle, his hands to slide higher to grip my ass, and I can feel his rumbling laugh when he presses his mouth to me. He goes in for the kill, and I'm not surprised. He's done it before, and the man is deadly with his tongue.

The pleasure is exquisite, hitting me squarely between my legs, yet my entire body seems to be immersed in sensation. The blond man's hands are holding me for Cain's pleasure, the dark-haired man's go to my breasts, and the large man surprises me by pulling his t-shirt up and over his head, revealing a massive but sculpted chest tattooed with flying blackbirds up his ribs.

I take all of that in quickly, then my eyes flutter closed because Cain is working his mouth hard between my legs and the decadent sinfulness of these last few moments is overwhelming to my senses. I feel an orgasm curl into a knot deep within me. Cain lashes at me hard and I break apart, letting out a long moan of relief as I climax.

Cain pulls his face away from me, giving me a languid smile. I return it and have to restrain myself from reaching out to him in a show of gratitude and tenderness. For a brief moment, no one else is in the room with us. It's just him and me, sharing a moment that belongs to us alone. In this brief moment where everything else is excluded from my existence, I have almost an epiphany of sorts. That this… what we're getting ready to do… is going to change not only me, but also Cain as well. I can't tell you how or why I know this, but I can just sense that both of us are standing on a precipice, getting ready to take the jump, and we're either going to soar or plummet, but whichever way it is, it's going to be life-changing.

"Goddamn, that was hot," the blond guy says, with his hands still between my legs. He tilts them inward, dragging his fingers through me, and I'm embarrassed again over how wet I am.

Cain's brow furrows almost in confusion as our moment is shattered. The large man with the blackbird tattoos squats down, catching my attention. I watch as he picks the rope up from the ground, slides it through his hands, and stands back up straight again. Cain also stands up but takes a deferential step back as the big guy starts to circle me. I feel the blond and dark-haired guys' hands fall from me as they step back.

The giant of a man circles around me, and I warily twist my head to watch his progress. My heart is pounding, partially fearful of this guy who looks like he could command legions of warriors and partly with exhilaration at what he could possibly do to me. My nipples harden in response to my thoughts. As he comes around to my front again, his gaze flicks down to them with a satisfied smirk on his face.

As if he knows what I was thinking and was expecting my body's reaction.

"Rand... tie her up and have at her," the man says suddenly, tossing the rope to the blond.

At least I know his name now, and I'm not sure if that makes it better or worse.

"My pleasure," I hear him say, and then my arms are being tied behind my back with the rope. It's soft feeling against my skin, except when he pulls it tight, then it a produces a sharp bite. I hold back a whimper because I know innately that these guys have been told to go easy on me, and I don't want to look like a wimp. I can handle this.

My eyes flick to Cain, and he's watching with the focus of a hawk. I start to shoot him a smile but then a hand is on my head, fisting my hair into a stinging grip. The dark-haired guy comes to stand in front of me with a lecherous smile.

The big man steps forward and brings a hand to my jaw, pressing in slightly at the hinges, causing my mouth to open. He bends, moves his face close to mine, and whispers, "I want you to suck Logan's dick. And make it good, okay?"

My eyes flick to Logan and his smile actually warms. He gives me a conspiratorial wink. With Rand at my backside, seeming to wrap endless loops around my wrists, and the man I now know to be Logan holding my hair, I'm stunned when the big guy... whose name I don't know... gives me a sweet kiss on my cheek before letting my face go. He stuns me further when his hands go to Logan's jeans and he deftly pops the button, dragging the zipper down. I'm beyond shocked, and God help me turned on beyond measure, when he pushes Logan's jeans down just a bit and pulls his dick out, which is swollen with need.

It's such an intimate act, completely kinky, and I can't help myself. I look to the big guy and blurt, "What's your name?"

His eyes move from Logan's dick, which he casually starts stroking in his big hand, causing Logan to groan, and slide over to me slowly. His eyes squint in amusement, and he chuckles, "Bridger, darlin'. Nice to meet you."

I smile at him, weirdly relieved to know his name. It makes him slightly less intimidating.

Until he says, "Now get on your knees. You got four men who need servicing."

Chapter 15

Cain

SOMETHING ABOUT BRIDGER'S tone of voice catches me off guard. I'm achingly hard already just from stripping Sloane bare and watching her blush in front of three strangers while I ate her out. Watching Rand tie her hands up and Logan hold her hair got me even harder.

But the way Bridger just spoke—or maybe it was the actual words used—get me on edge a bit. I don't want Sloane scared and while she's been daring so far, this is a huge fucking deal that she's doing this. People don't wake up one morning and think to themselves, *Hey, I think I'll get fucked by four guys today.*

It just doesn't work that way, and she's dealing with enough of a shock that I sprung this on her.

I did that with purpose, wanting to have her make a quick decision on whether to do this. I knew if I told her about it ahead of time, she would have probably talked herself to death on the pros and cons. No clue what her ultimate decision would have been, but tonight, she went with a gut instinct and that told her to go for it. This confirms my suspicion there's a whole lot of gumption deep in that girl, and I want to bring it out tonight.

I just don't want her scared at the same time.

Bridger turns, dips his hand into a bowl that rests on a small table, and pulls out a handful of condoms. He tosses each one of us a foiled packet. Logan uses his grip on Sloane's hair to push her to her knees. I note with relief that she goes willingly and with a spark of excitement in her eyes. He releases her briefly so he can get the rubber on.

She waits patiently as Rand, Logan, and I open our pants and pull our cocks out. Her eyes flick back and forth between us, wide and blinking. God help me... she licks her lips once.

Logan gets suited up first, and he wastes no time. His hand shoots out, gripping a fistful of Sloane's hair again at the back of her head. With his other hand on his cock, he pushes it toward her face. "Open up, baby."

She does without hesitation, and I hold back a groan as I watch his dick disappear into her mouth. I know how good that mouth is. She's got a fucking phenomenal mouth now that I think about it and as her cheeks hollow inward to suck on Logan, I can't help but stroke my own aching dick.

Rand drops to his knees behind Sloane, sticks both hands to the insides of her thighs, and urges her to spread her legs a bit. She does so awkwardly, not having much leverage with her hands tied behind her back and Logan's dick in her mouth. Rand rewards her by sliding two fingers inside of her, a move that causes her hips to buck, a lustful groan coming out of her mouth as Logan's cock slips free. Bridger laughs darkly.

I take a few steps closer, my eyes flicking up to Bridger's. He gives me a look that says, *We're just getting started*, and that causes a thrill to race up my spine. I want this to be so good for Sloane, and I get what Bridger's doing now. He's starting out with a mind fuck, making her think this is all about the men in this room. Telling Sloane she's servicing us. He did it to throw her off kilter, take away any security I may have given her by telling her that we're going a bit easy. She doesn't know what to expect now, and that is purposeful on Bridger's part. He did it to flame her fears a bit, knowing it will magnify the sensual pleasure.

Logan lets out a long groan as Sloane takes him extra deep. "Fuck, that's good."

She responds and bobs on him faster.

"Let her bend over, Logan," Rand says roughly as his fingers pump in and out of Sloane as she rotates her hips, seeking more. She needs fucked and right now.

Logan pulls out of Sloane's mouth, drops to his knees, and then leans back so his ass rests on his heels. With both hands to Sloane's head, he pulls her back down on him so she's now taking him from a hovering position above his cock. This causes her back to go more perpendicular to the floor and her ass to tilt upward.

"Perfect," Rand says gruffly as his fingers slide free. In one punch of his hips, he shoves his cock into her from behind.

Sloane gives a startled groan and her eyes flutters shut in pleasure. Everyone stills… Rand lodged deep in her pussy, Sloane with just the tip of Logan's cock in her mouth, and Bridger and me watching to see what happens.

It's Sloane who gets the action going again. Pulling forward a bit from Rand, she rotates her hips and pushes back, a silent plea for him to fuck her. She then starts bobbing up and down on Logan again, who brings his hands back to her head to help guide her. Rand starts pumping his hips in but goes at a leisurely pace, not wanting to knock her off the blow job game.

Rand and Logan look at each other, a beautiful, naked woman stretched and bound in between them, one fucking her from behind, the other fucking her mouth. I find myself insanely jealous of them at this moment.

"Give it to her deeper," Bridger says in a low voice. Every one of us except perhaps for Sloane knows that Bridger is talking to Logan. He's been studying Sloane's skills, and he thinks she has more in her.

With his hands to Sloane's head, Logan lifts his hips up on a downward swing from her. It causes his dick to go deep, and she gags. He quickly pulls her head up and she gulps a lungful of air before he pushes her back down again. "That's it, sweet girl," Logan murmurs to her as she gags again when he hits her throat. "You like choking on my cock, don't you?"

Logan pulls her up free again and I see Sloane's eyes water, not sure from the lack of oxygen or if she's scared, but either way, I don't give a fuck the cause, because it's going to stop.

"Ease the fuck up, Logan," I growl as I take a step toward him.

Rand pushes into her deep and goes still, interested to see what happens. Logan holds Sloane's face hovering over his dick and rather than answer to me, he turns to Bridger for direction. To my relief, he gives a short nod of affirmation.

Logan turns to Sloane, gives her a soft smile, and then pulls up on her head a bit as he leans into her. He kisses her mouth gently and says, "Sorry, sweet girl. My bad."

Sloane's eyes are filled with immediate relief, which immediately relieves me. I'll never forgive myself if she walks away from this as a bad experience.

"Let's try something else," Bridger says as he kneels down beside Sloane. Rand doesn't stop fucking her though, but he goes slowly so as to not knock her off balance. Bridger quickly undoes the knot against her wrists and unlaces the intricate pattern that's binding her. He pulls the rope away swiftly and says, "Stand her up."

Rand pulls free, his dick wet and bobbing while Logan helps Sloane to her feet.

Bridger also stands straight, his dick also still hard and ready for some action at some point. "Hold your arms out, darlin'," he says to Sloane.

She complies. Bridger immediately takes the rope

and starts to retie her wrists from the front, leaving about a two-foot length free at the end. Logan doesn't miss an opportunity to further his apology to Sloane for choking her because he puts a hand between her legs and starts rubbing at her clit. She moans, drops her head back, and pushes her hips into him. She looks at me and I give her a smile, my hand absently tugging on my own cock to try to give it some relief.

In less than a minute, Bridger is pulling on the rope and Logan steps back and away from her. Bridger leads her to the middle of the living room we're in, which is one of the newer fantasy cabins that happened to not be in use tonight, and says, "Hold your arms up."

Sloane does, no hesitation, as she doesn't understand what's getting ready to happen. Bridger takes the free end of the rope and reaches his own hands above his head, tilting his head back. Sloane does the same. Her eyes widen as she watches him tie the end to a large hook bolted into the ceiling. He pulls on it, removing all slack and even causing her to go on her tiptoes a bit. I know it will be biting into her skin but I also know she can take it.

Bridger stands back and says, "Rand... Logan... have at her. Fuck her good and then Cain and I will finish her off."

Chapter 16

Sloane

R AND COMES TO stand in front of me. He looks up at
the rope tied to the hook above, and then back to
me with a mischievous glint in his eyes. "Now, now,
now… all kinds of things we can do with you like this,"
he says in a playfully ominous tone. I dig my toes down
into the carpet, bracing myself for whatever's coming.

I will have to say, I've never been flooded with such
an array of emotions all at the same time. Excitement,
fear, pleasure, pain, worry, gratitude, horniness, trepida-
tion. All of it just completely throwing my entire system
out of whack.

For a moment, when Logan was trying to deep
throat me, I almost panicked. Not because I was truly
afraid of him, and honestly, I sort of liked the rough
handling a bit, but I seriously didn't think I'd be able to
breathe if he kept it up. More confusing to me than all
the stuff I'd been feeling prior to that, was hearing the
deadly tone in Cain's voice when he told Logan to stop.
While I know reasonably in my mind that this is just a
sexual experience that is devoid of feelings and intimacy,
the way Cain stepped forward in protection of me struck

me straight through the chest. Then I had another moment of exquisite doubt that this was all wrong. That this could ruin anything between Cain and me for the future, but just as quickly, I had to remind myself... what future? I'm using him to do an undercover story.

So I pushed that worry aside and decided to ride this experience out.

"How about a kiss first before I fuck you?" Rand asks me. He has the prettiest green eyes set off by long, blond lashes. I can see tattoos peeking out from the collar of his shirt, and the punk-styled haircut and nose ring lend a very cool edginess to him.

"Sure thing," I tell him with a saucy smile, figuring to keep up with the way this has turned sort of playful.

I wait for him to press his mouth to mine, and I even see a flash of silver indicating his tongue is pierced when he smiles back at me, but he shocks the shit out of me by dropping to his knees and sticking said pierced tongue right between my legs. I'm so surprised that I actually cry out from the sinful invasion as he stabs his tongue into me, pulls it out, and licks straight up my center. He then merely stands back up and grins at me. Giving his lower lip a lick, he says, "Fucking delicious."

Then Rand bends his knees, grabs me under my ass, and lifts me up. My legs go wide, and he unceremoniously shoves his dick inside of me. He's not as wide as Cain is, but he's just as long because he immediately knocks into something deep within me, which I suspect is a direct assault on my G-spot. I moan and sag against the ropes, causing them to bite into my skin more but I just don't care.

"Oh, sweet Sloane," Rand groans as he moves inside of me. "You're fucking perfect."

I'm vaguely aware of Logan walking around me, and then his arm circles around my waist from the rear. Pressing his cock, which is still wet with my saliva up against my ass, his hand goes in between my legs, where he softly pinches and rubs my clit. Rand starts to fuck me hard, ramming into me at a furious pace... hitting that spot deep inside me each time. Sweat breaks out on his forehead and within moments, both of us are grunting almost in tandem with every thrust. Logan's fingers on me cause a second orgasm to start forming, and then he does the unimaginable.

He brings his other hand down to grasp the bottom of Rand's dick, counter stroking him while he heaves in and out of me.

"Yeah," Rand groans as his eyes close in pleasure. "Fuck yeah."

Oh, jeez... that's hot. Watching a man jerk another man off while he's fucking me.

Orgasm has launched.

I cry out... a strange, gurgling sound, but it's overshadowed when Rand slams into me, throws his head back, and starts shaking. "Oh, man, that's good."

I can feel his dick thumping inside of me while he unloads into the condom and Logan's fingers still pluck at my clit. I gasp in lungfuls of oxygen, my heart ready to explode, and I mentally say to myself, *One down… three to go*.

Logan releases his hold on Rand's dick and pulls back on my hips, causing Rand to slip free of me although he still holds my legs. The minute the head of his cock is gone—before I can even take in another breath and get my bearings—Logan is shoving into me from behind. I cry out from the sudden invasion. My eyes flick over to Cain, just over Rand's shoulder, who seems to be holding his own dick in a strangle hold, his eyes glazed and his jaw locked tight. His eyes are pinned to my pelvis area, watching as I'm jolted from behind with every thrust that Logan is giving me.

"Easy," Logan murmurs in my ear as he fucks me. "I've got you."

He heaves up and into me, his breathing harsh in my ear and at odds with his tender words. I close my eyes, give into the sensations of the second guy who's fucking me tonight, knowing that it's not even done and it's the most intense thing that's ever happened to me in my life.

"Get out of the way," I hear Cain say and when I open my eyes, he's shoving Rand away. Cain takes my legs and lowers them to the floor. I can feel Logan adjusting his stance behind me but he never misses a stroke, except now the angle has him moving even more shallowly within me.

Cain leans in, gives me a swift kiss. When he pulls away, he murmurs, "Want to taste you again."

Oh, God.

He wouldn't?

Not while Logan was…

Cain drops to his knees and hikes one of my legs over his shoulders, while Logan continues to pound me from behind. He has to shift slightly again, and he must be bending his legs because now he's able to drive up into me again with bruising force.

Then Cain's mouth is back on my pussy. I immediately start to convulse again as I realize he has to be licking at Logan while he fucks me. There's just not enough room down there otherwise. I moan, trying to hold off my orgasm, but then I make the mistake of looking down at Cain's head bobbing in between my legs, and I lose it. Knowing he's down there, eating me out, probably licking Logan's cock… it's just too much. I come apart from the inside out and scream from the force of the pleasure.

"Who's going to be next?" Logan grunts as he moves even faster within me. Cain stands up, wiping his mouth off with his hand.

"My turn," Bridger says gruffly, and my eyes fly to him. He's the one I've been worried about. He's the one who scares me the most, and yet I feel like he's the one who's going to push me in just the right way.

"Get ready, dude," Logan pants. "I'm about to come."

Logan's cock pumping in and out of me like a jack-hammer feels so good, and I watch with wide eyes as I now take in Bridger stepping up to me. His jeans are open, pushed to just below his hips, and he is massive. Around the same size as Cain and shining from the tip of his cock is a barbell pierced through the head. He strokes himself roughly with one hand while ripping a foil packet open with his teeth.

"F-u-u-c-k," Logan curses as he slams into me, his fingers digging down hard into my hips and my feet momentarily coming up off the floor. He leans his face forward, clamps his teeth onto my shoulder, and bites into me as he starts to come. The tingles left over from the last orgasm Cain handed me seem to spark again, and I'm vaguely aware of Bridger rolling the condom on over that massive erection as I sag against the ropes even more, all feeling in my hands gone.

Logan steps away, the loss of him inside me almost leaving me barren feeling, and then Bridger's strong arms are releasing me from the hook. My knees buckle, and he's surprisingly gentle as he lowers me to the carpet. I look at Cain, who has a half smile on his face, his hand idly stroking at his cock again.

Bridger turns me, places me on my knees, and pushes me forward. My tied wrists come out in an attempt to support my upper body, but Bridger pushes on me harder so I go down to my elbows. This leaves my ass high in the air and he pushes a jean-clad leg in between mine, swiping it back and forth to spread them further apart.

"Lube," is all he says, and it sounds like a surgeon asking for a scalpel during surgery. The skin on my neck prickles and a jolt of fear travels from head to toe.

I try to turn my head to see what's going on, but I can't get a good look down on my elbows. I feel hands on my ass, pulling my cheeks apart, and a cold drizzle of lube hitting me dead center.

"Don't," I say as I try to rise up, but Bridger places one large hand on my back to hold me in place and smacks the other against my ass just hard enough to get me to shut up.

"I know you don't want a cock in your ass, darlin', so quit worrying," he says gruffly. It doesn't ease my anxiety because I know something's going back there.

"Relax," I hear Cain murmur and I take a deep breath, choosing to trust he won't let this large man hurt me.

Bridger's fingers go in between my ass, rubbing up against my opening, and then dropping lower, pulling the lube along. He rubs all over my pussy, pushing fingers inside of me and massaging my insides. I groan, drop my head down, and stare at the carpet briefly before closing my eyes and just concentrating on the feeling.

His hand is gone, but then I feel the head of his cock rubbing there. Even through the latex of the condom, I can feel the nuances of the piercing against my flesh and I can't help shuddering. He pushes in, just the head, and I take a deep breath to get ready for his invasion. Instead, his hand slaps at my ass again, this time hard and making the sound of a cracking whip.

"Shit," I cry out, my head rearing upward, and then

he slams inside of me, rocking my whole body forward.

And Christ, that feels good, despite the sting on my ass and my tender flesh he just stretched wide.

Bridger starts a steady pace, his breathing loud and choppy. I glance up, seeing Rand and Logan sitting on the couch watching us. They've disposed of the condoms, and their cocks are soft as they lay against their stomachs. Rand shoots me a wink, and then just to shock the hell out of me I bet, Logan reaches his hand out and curls his fingers around Rand's dick, lightly rubbing his thumb over the soft head. Rand lets out a contented sigh and his head falls back against the couch, eyes closed in bliss. He starts swelling right before my eyes and under Logan's strokes.

It's too much. I drop my head back down again and concentrate on the feel of Bridger... the third guy to fuck me tonight.

And just when I didn't think I could get overloaded any further, Bridger starts to talk dirty to me.

With fingers pressing into the globes of my butt cheeks, Bridger asks, "You like this, Sloane? Like getting fucked by multiple guys?"

I grunt my assent.

"Is your pussy sore yet?" he taunts as he tunnels in and out. "Because it ain't a good fucking unless it hurts."

I can't even answer; the words are so filthy and provocative that I wouldn't trust my voice. But I don't think he wants an answer because he says, "Next time... you're going to take three of us at once and you're going to love it."

God, I think he's right. I think I would, but then again… I'm full-on delirious at this point.

"I heard you want Cain's cock in your ass," Bridger says thoughtfully, never pausing in his thrusts. "I think I'll help move that along."

That's all the warning I get before he's pushing a finger inside of me. And not the gentle easing in that Cain did the other night, but straight in deep and to the third knuckle, causing me to cry out in astonished pleasure. With the same motions of his thrusts, he pulls that finger out and rams it back in. It feels good, I don't want him to stop, so I actually say, "Don't stop" when he pulls his finger free, only to scream out when he pushes two back in.

The invasion burns, causing tears to prick my eyes, but immediately morphs into a fullness that ramps up the pleasure of his cock inside of me. In and out his fingers go, his dick matching pace. I feel dizzy from the overload of pleasure, now grunting like some kind of animal.

Then Cain is in front of me, kneeling down… resting his ass on his heels. His hand comes under my chin and he lifts my face up, holding tight as my entire body is being rocked back and forth by Bridger. His eyes are filled with a mixture of worry and lust. His cock is swollen and dark through the latex of the condom.

"You okay?" he asks. I immediately nod, and then gasp as my ass starts burning again. I think Bridger just stuck a third finger inside of me. I can't tell for sure though because I'm about ready to pass out from the avalanche of sensations.

"I bet she'd take your cock back here right now," I hear Bridger say, but Cain shakes his head in the negative.

"Suit yourself," Bridger says as he removes his fingers, and then both hands are at my hips. He really plows into me from behind, slamming into me so hard our skin cracks against each other. He hits me so deep it almost hurts, and my mouth falls open in a silent scream of pleasure.

"Gonna come," Bridger says roughly, and I'm surprised when he pulls out. I can hear the sound of the condom snapping and then warm liquid hits my back. I turn my head, pulling away from Cain's fingers still under my chin, and see Bridger with his head tilted back and eyes squeezed shut. His hand works his cock, jacking himself through an orgasm as he unloads his semen onto me.

This stuns me, but I don't question it. It's sort of dirty hot, and I don't mind.

Three down, the best yet to come.

Cain takes me by the shoulders and helps me up into a kneeling position. I feel Bridger's semen sliding down my back onto my butt. As if reading my mind, Cain whips his t-shirt off and reaches around me, wiping the mess up and then tossing it aside.

He then puts his hands to my face again and gives

me the sweetest kiss he's ever bestowed on me. There's not an ounce of lust in it, although I know by the massive erection he's sporting that he's turned on like nothing else, and this relieves me.

"You are like the sexiest woman I've ever been with," he murmurs, and then kisses me again. "And I can't wait to fuck you right now with these guys watching."

I don't have a chance to respond, not that I'd know what to say to that, but I do know that a new flood of wetness seeps out of me at the thought of Cain giving me the best I'll have tonight to make this an unforgettable experience. One of Cain's hands comes to my tied wrists where he latches onto them, and the other goes to a shoulder where he gently eases me onto my back.

"Little help here, guys," Cain says. Rand and Logan push off the couch, both of their dicks now standing at half mast from their open flies.

Cain pushes up off the floor. To my surprise, he starts taking off the rest of his clothing. While Rand, Logan, and Bridger remained completely clothed, which was sort of hot and made me feel dirty and vulnerable in a way, I'm touched that Cain wants to be completely naked with me.

As he disrobes, Rand and Logan kneel down on the carpet beside me.

"She's ready for a hard fucking now," Logan says in a low voice.

From the other side of me, Rand says, "Cain's going to own that pussy of yours, Sloane."

A shudder ripples through me, knowing that they are talking filthy for my benefit. Rand even takes a hand, puts it between my legs, and slides a finger into me while Cain pushes his jeans and underwear off.

"She's soaked for you, man," Rand says, then pulls his finger out and lets it circle my clit in soft strokes.

"She's fucking beautiful," Logan murmurs.

I groan, rotate my hips… silently demanding more.

Cain looks down at me for a minute… eyes intense and his scar vivid and angry looking, making him appear dangerous and even more sinfully unattainable. His eyes then flick behind me to Bridger. I tilt my head back and get an upside-down view of Bridger sitting in an arm-chair, his dick tucked away and one leg crossed casually over the other. He's resting his chin in the palm of his hand, elbow on the chair, smiling at me in amusement.

A soft thud catches my attention, and I look down my body to see Cain has fallen to his knees in between my legs. Without a word of encouragement or instruction, Rand and Logan's hands go to my thighs.

They each grab one of my legs.

Raise them up.

Spread them wide.

I know in this moment that I am not the first girl these two men have played with. They're too synchronized, and a stab of jealousy goes through me as I also realize that Cain probably was with them as well.

Cain crawls over me, my hips raised up off the floor, my pussy wide open for him to take. He grabs his dick, lines up, and then presses down into me with both of his hands supporting himself near my ribs.

"Christ, that feels good," he mutters as he closes his eyes briefly. When they open back up, I almost combust from what I see in his eyes.

Lust.

Care.

Determination.

He's going to make me come again.

Cain starts slamming into me hard, jarring my spine against the carpet. It hurts but what's going on between my legs feels so good, I can't complain. A bead of sweat rolls off Cain's temple and lands on my chest.

I take all of this in at once.

Three guys surrounding me. All of them holding me down. One watching from a casual perch as if all of this is normal. All of them having fucked me. I've come three times already. When Logan slips a hand across my stomach and down between my legs, I start orgasming again the minute he touches my clit.

"Yes, Sloane," Cain grunts as he hammers into me faster and faster. "I can feel you trembling all around my cock when you come."

My hips punch up, trying to pull Cain into me deeper. I tear my legs free from Rand and Logan, wrapping them around Cain's lower back and pressing my heels in hard to grab as much of a physical connection with him as I can. My bound hands reach up, go over his head, and I pull him down to me. I see a smile on his face just before his mouth connects with mine. Shoving my tongue in, I kiss him hard, and that's when I feel his entire body seize up. The muscles in his neck contract under my palms, and he groans hotly into my mouth as he grinds down against me while he comes.

He seems to come forever, his hips rotating, his pelvis pressed flat to mine with Logan's hand caught in between us. It sets another ripple off through me and for a moment, I think I might lose consciousness.

Chapter 17

Cain

THE MINUTE I pull out onto the highway and put a few miles between us and the fantasy cabin we were just in, I reach over and pull Sloane's blindfold off. She was confused as to why she would need to wear it on the way out, so I had to scramble with a blatant lie and tell her it was Bridger's house, and that he didn't like anyone knowing where he lived.

My gut burns over that lie, and it burns even more when she asks, "How do you know men who will do stuff like that?"

My mind races, trying to come up with another lie, but she piles on more questions. "I mean... you've clearly done that with them before. Have you done that with lots of other girls?"

Her voice is curious, but I hear an underlying tone of vulnerability that a flat-out lie won't ease.

"Sloane... I've known those guys forever. We enjoy some kinky shit, so yes, we've all done stuff like that before. But not like we did tonight."

"And I still don't understand... doesn't it bother you to watch other men with me?"

Finally, I can tell a truth. "It hasn't before," I say quietly as we drive down the darkened highway. "But tonight… I had some problems."

"Like what?"

"Jealousy," I say simply. "Envy. Doubt."

"Doubt about what?"

I take a deep breath and let it out slowly. "About whether it was the right thing to bring you there tonight. Whether I even had the right to ask you to do something like that."

She doesn't respond but chooses to look out the passenger window at absolutely nothing since the highway is desolate and black as midnight.

After three more miles, I slow down and put my blinker on, even though there's not a car in sight. I start to turn left into my driveway when she asks, "Where are we?"

"My house," I tell her as my truck bumps down the dirt lane. "It's late, and I didn't want to drive all the way back into Jackson tonight. I'll take you home in the morning."

And yeah… that's definitely different. I've never brought a woman to my home before. I lived in town with Rachel, but I decided I liked solitude after the shit storm she put me through, so I rented a little cabin that is closer to my work at The Wicked Horse.

We pull up to the side of the house, my headlights illuminating my Harley that I'll soon need to cover for the winter season. Sloane gets out of the truck wordlessly, following me onto my small porch as I work the key into the lock. I push the door open, flip the light switch on just inside, and motion for her to precede me in.

She does so, glancing left and right to take in my small abode. It's not much, but then I don't need much. Besides that, I can't afford anything more. It's a small, two-bedroom cabin with pine floors, a large front room that combines as the kitchen/living room, and a short hall with two bedrooms separated by a shared bathroom. The guy who owns it usually rents it out to tourists but was more than happy to accept a year-round lease from me for the stability.

"It's nice," Sloane says as she sits her purse down on an end table.

I flip on another light for the kitchen area and head toward the fridge. "You want something to drink?"

"I'm good," she says and walks over to a small book-case I have beside a desk on one wall of the living room. The place is so small that I don't even have a couch. Just a ratty old recliner, my desk, a side table, and the book-case. She peruses the photographs on one shelf.

"Family?" she asks.

I walk over to her, stand beside her, and point to one frame. "That's my mom and stepdad, Walt."

"How long have they been married?"

"Most of my life. My dad took off when I was little; traveling a rodeo circuit. Walt's like my real dad, I guess you could say."

"And who is this?" she asks, pointing to a pretty brunette with her arm wrapped around a big, burly guy and two dark-haired kids standing in front of them.

"That's my sister, Claudia, her husband J.C. and my niece and nephew… Carrie and Tucker."

She looks at some other photos. They're of the same people because they're the only ones important enough to me to hold a place here. I'm in a few of them, usually with a big, toothy grin. What can I say? I dig my family.

I tuck my hands in my pockets, unsure of what to do. Normally when I'm with Sloane, I have a hard time keeping my hands off her. Conversation hasn't been our main priority, and I'm not even sure how to just hang out with a woman.

"Want to watch some TV?" I lamely say.

Her gaze goes over to my recliner, the only place to sit other than my desk chair, and then over to my small TV that sits on the edge of my desk because there's nowhere else to put it. She looks back to me with a smirk on her face and a cocked eyebrow.

"I meant in my room," I tell her with a grin. "Let's go get a shower and crawl into bed. I'm sure there's something we can watch."

"Okay," she says quietly, eyes lowering to the floor, and I realize she might feel just as awkward as I do right now.

Pulling my hands out of my pockets, I take her by the shoulders, pulling her into me. I wrap myself around her and give her a kiss on top of her head. "Tonight was amazing, Sloane. Possibly the most amazing sexual experience of my life."

"So you liked it?" she asks hesitantly.

"Liked it?" I ask with mock affront she'd even ask such a question. "Watching you come over and over? Watching you get pleasured until I thought you might pass out? Hell... fucking you so hard I thought I might pass out?"

I drop my voice, squeeze her harder. "Watching you do something daring and brave and oh so very dirty?"

"So you liked it," she concludes, her voice semi-muffled since her face is pressed into my chest.

"I fucking loved it," I assure her.

And I did. God, I fucking loved it, even if I had a hard time swallowing down some jealous tendencies. Before, when I've done something like that with the guys, I've never really thought too much about the woman. I wanted her to enjoy it, and I worked hard to make sure that occurred, but honestly... those experiences were about me first and foremost, and then after that, I wanted my buds to have a great time.

But tonight... it was all about Sloane and I hope she understands that.

"Come on," I say as I release her, taking just one of her hands in mine to lead her to the bathroom. "Let's get in the shower, and then I'll tuck you into bed. I know you're exhausted."

She follows behind me, her hand firmly clasped in mine. "I don't need you to be sweet to me, Cain. I'm a big girl."

"I know that," I tell her, and then add on, "I apparently just can't fucking help myself where you're concerned."

She gives a husky laugh as I flip the light on to the small bathroom. It's got a tub, shower, and small vanity beside the toilet. It will be a tight fit for both of us, but I am looking forward to soaping her body down good.

I turn on the water, adjust the temperature, and turn back to Sloane. Her hands immediately go to my belt buckle, where she loosens it and pulls the leather free. She quickly undoes the top button, unzips my fly, and then reaches her hand in to grab ahold of my soft cock. It immediately comes to life, and I groan when she squeezes me. "What are you doing, Sloane?"

"Going to give you a blow job," she says simply.

I swell even harder, but I shake my head in denial. "You're exhausted. Let's get you to bed."

"I am exhausted," she agrees. "But not so exhausted as I can't do this for you."

"For me?" I clarify.

"Because of what you did for me tonight."

"It's not necessary—" I start to say, but then she's stroking my cock and the words just die in my throat. There's no way I can turn down this offer.

SLOANE IS DEAD to the world, her head on my chest and an arm thrown across my waist. It didn't take her long to fall asleep after our shower. Hell, after that amazingly fantastic blow job just before the shower, I should be ready to fall asleep too but my mind is racing.

Racing with all things Sloane Meyers.

Like why in the hell I brought her to my house? Or why I'm content to lay in this bed with her? Or for fuck's sake, why did I tell her we'd get up early so I could take her to breakfast?

Breakfast!

I don't take women to breakfast. I sneak out of their beds and hope they don't wake up.

And since I'm thinking about all the ways in which my head is fucked over this woman, I can't believe I bucked up against Bridger tonight. He was directing our scenario, and he told Logan to give it to her deep. That meant Logan should give it to her deep until she couldn't take it anymore, and that meant I should sit there and stroke my dick and watch. But I directly contravened his order by telling Logan to ease up. Watching her gag and tears come to her eyes, I was ready to fucking throw a punch if he didn't do as I said.

I mean... what in the ever-loving hell is wrong with me?

Deciding that perhaps holding her soft body against mine and smelling my shampoo in her hair isn't helping matters, I gently slide out from under her. I can't help myself when I pull the covers up over her shoulders, but I absolutely restrain myself from brushing her hair from her face. I'm not that much of a pussy over this girl.

Yet.

I walk naked out into the living room, cross into the small kitchen, and grab a beer from my fridge. After twisting the cap and disposing of it, I take a hefty pull.

Then another.

Maybe I should get drunk, then I'll stop obsessing about her and how fucking hard I came in her tonight. It's like watching Rand, Logan, and Bridger fucking her caused some sort of caveman to come out in me. I had to fuck her harder and better. Had to make her come longer. Had to bury to the hilt and unload the biggest nut ever inside of her.

And there was a moment I wished I wasn't wearing a condom. I wished I was squirting into her bare pussy, coating it and marking her from the inside as mine.

What the ever-loving fuck?

Sighing, I head into the living room. I sit on the cold, plastic desk chair and run my finger over the pad of my laptop to wake it up from sleep mode. I don't use it for much… surfing for some porn at times, but mostly to check email.

I pull it up, glancing through the subject lines, deleting spam as I go along.

Then I see the subject line "Friday Night?" and the sender is Amy Mason.

I double click on the email and read it.

Cain,

I signed the fantasy agreement with Bridger today, and he said he'd email you a copy. I'm really looking forward to seeing what you've got for me. I suggest Friday after this one. Will that work for you?

Amy

Christ.

I had forgotten all about Amy and the fact that I'd told Bridger I'd do a rape fantasy in her house for her. While most of my concerns had been alleviated by Amy signing an agreement laying out the scenario, the decision to take this job was done before I ever met Sloane.

Before I promised her monogamy while we were together.

Shit.

I scrub my hand over my hair, itching at the short bristles on the back as they prickle with tension. Can I fuck Amy as part of my job with The Wicked Horse and still keep my word to Sloane? My gut tells me no… that no sane woman would consider that a reasonable exception to the "no-cheating" rule.

What's more important is the fact that I absolutely don't want to fuck Amy Mason. Sure… great pussy and all that, and fuck yeah… those types of scenarios are seriously hot. But for the life of me, the thought of it is almost distasteful to me for some reason.

Still… I have a job to do, and Sloane Meyers has been in my life less than a week. I might just be merely infatuated with her, and I can't let something fleeting fuck with my world as I know it. I'm not giving up this gig and the money that will come as a result for anything.

I quickly type back a reply, even though my stomach cramps with each word that streams onto the screen.

Amy,

Friday after this one is good. But just to give me some added protection, respond back to me with the details of what you want. I know you signed the agreement, but I'd feel better if I had the email from you, especially since Charles isn't going to be involved in this one.

I don't even sign my name, but I hit *send* before I can talk myself out of it. I'm going to honor my commitment to her and Bridger because I said I would. It's a job to me, that's all.

I know that won't ever fly with Sloane, so as much as it's causing my chest to squeeze, I'm going to have to call it off with her before then.

The only question is when?

That leaves me with a week and a half to get her out of my system. Perhaps if I just fuck her soundly every night before then, the fantasy of this girl and what she does to me will wear thin. Then I can cut her loose and have a clean conscience when I fuck Amy Mason.

At least I think that's how this will work.

Chapter 18

Sloane

IN THE BRIGHT light of day, as we pulled out of Cain's driveway onto Highway 191, I immediately had my bearings. The blindfold last night had left me disoriented and because we were in what appeared to be a house, I had no clue where we were. But as I recognize Sleeping Indian Mountain on the eastern horizon and knowing we're heading toward Jackson, it hits me that we must have been near The Wicked Horse last night. While we were definitely not in the building that Colton referred to as The Silo, we must have been on the property. And who knows… maybe it was Bridger's house, but maybe it was something else.

Despite the fact that last night was the most intense, sensual, and erotic thing I ever could have imagined happening to me, I still don't know jack shit about the sex club. I had hoped by carefully prodding Cain about his relationship with Rand, Logan, and Bridger, something would be revealed that could clue me in on where to turn. But he was tight lipped and honestly, I can't blame him. He's been hired to protect a secret, and it's clear he also has tight bonds of friendship with those guys. I'm nothing to him and completely untrustworthy.

Which is why I realized last night before I drifted off to sleep that I would have to work the Callie Hayes angle instead. And yet, once again… I'm going to try to use Cain to get my foot in the door to try to build a story I don't believe exists. I'm scrambling to save my job and career, and I'm doing it at the expense of a man who in just a few short days I've come to care about a great deal.

And yes, I do care about him.

There's no way I could share that experience with him and not feel a bond.

There's no way I could have slept in his embrace last night, or felt his lips on mine for a good morning kiss, and not feel something for him.

And the problem is I actually feel too much for him. So much so that perhaps I need to consider a new job and just leave all this sordidness behind. Maybe I could just work at the leather store for the rest of my life and let Cain fuck me each night, hoping that something deeper would continue to develop.

Shaking my head and trying to get back on track, I start a calculated conversation that I hope will lead to some fruition. "So what do you have planned today after breakfast?"

Cain doesn't take his eyes off the road but says, "Not much actually. I was hoping Walt would have some work for me. He owns a construction company, but he rarely has any part-time openings in the summer months. Want to do something?"

I take a deep breath and spit out my lie. "I can't actually. I have to be at work at noon, but I'm hoping to run by Governor Hayes' local office here and see if I could talk to someone."

Cain actually jerks in his seat and looks at me briefly before turning back. "Governor Hayes?"

I give a girlish laugh, tuck my hair behind my ear, and continue to build my story. "Yeah... I've been reading up on the local politics and saw he was throwing the weight of his office behind a bill that's been introduced to put tougher controls on doctors prescribing pain medications."

His head now swivels completely my way, his eyebrows raised in surprise. "And you hope to do what by going to his office?"

After another girlish laugh, I give him a sheepish look. "Oh, well, I want to volunteer in some way for his campaign. I've always had a big interest in politics, especially at the local level. Worked as a page in the Tennessee senate, volunteered for some election campaigns, stuff like that."

Cain silently digests that and before he can start poking holes in my story, I decide to lay a truth on him to help ease my conscience a bit. "And I've got a vested interest in that issue."

His head swivels to mine again, giving me a questioning look before turning back to the road. "What's your interest in that?"

I take in a breath, close my eyes momentarily, and

ask my mom forgiveness for me using her this way. "My mom has struggled with addiction to pain medications. She overdosed once… intentionally."

"What?" Cain exclaims, his head now snapping my way with disbelief in his eyes.

I hold his look. "Six years ago. She had so many drugs in the house. Prescribed by various doctors, not checking in with each other—pharmacies not communicating. It was just too easy for her to have the power to try to kill herself."

"I'm sorry," he says softly, taking one hand off the wheel and reaching out to grab mine. He raises it to his mouth, presses a kiss to my wrist, and releases it. "I can't even imagine."

"But you can," I point out to him solemnly. "Rachel died of an overdose."

He nods in understanding but makes a better point. "Not the same. Those were illegal drugs, and she was just being stupid. It sounds like your mom may have been very lost."

Tears suddenly well up in my eyes because Cain just described my mother perfectly.

Absolutely lost.

One tear slips out and runs down my cheek in a warm river. I hastily wipe my hand over it, but Cain notices. His hand comes back to grab mine, and this time, he doesn't let it go. He holds me securely, conveying a sadness he shares with me and giving me permission to continue to grieve if I want.

I have the sudden and overwhelming urge to throw myself at him. Make him pull the truck over, crawl onto his lap, and snuggle into him. Demand he wrap his arms around me and tell me that he would forgive any stupidity on my part for the terrible lies I've been telling him, and more importantly, for using ugly truths to get a stupid fucking story.

The sound of Cain's cell phone ringing cuts the silence, and he releases my hand so he can grab it off the seat beside him. He takes a quick look at the screen, and a smile lights his face.

"Hey Mom," he says when he connects.

He turns his head to me, gives me a smile, and turns back to the road. He listens to his mother on the other line, and finally says, "Yeah... I'm almost to Jackson now. I'll swing by really quick and take a look, but I can't stay long. I've got someone with me and we're heading to breakfast."

He listens some more before shaking his head with amusement. "Yes, it's a woman and yes you can meet her."

Cain gives a hearty laugh and says, "Bye, Mom."

I can still hear her talking on the other end when he disconnects.

After he tosses the phone back on the seat again, my heart flops over like a puppy getting belly rubs when he takes my hand again, giving it a squeeze. "Hope you don't mind stopping by my mom's shop for a minute. The hot water heater isn't working, and I'm betting the pilot light just needs relit."

"Wow," I say with a chuckle. "Meeting your mom. This is just moving way too fast for me."

Cain laughs, squeezes my hand, and then makes an ache form between my legs when he says, "I don't think so. Not after you made all my dirty dreams come true last night."

My face flushes red, and I know he's teasing me. He's not taking me to meet his mom. I just happen to be along for the ride.

"Listen," Cain says, his voice now serious again. "I know Governor Hayes' daughter. We went to school together, and she's involved with my friend Woolf that owns The Double J. I could arrange an introduction if you want. Callie's going to be managing his campaign, and I'm sure she'd love you to volunteer."

And just like that, Cain gives me exactly what I was hoping to get when I brought up my interest in Governor Hayes.

An introduction to his daughter.

And I feel so terrible about it that I just want to throw up.

"WORD OF WARNING," Cain says just before he pulls open the glass storefront door of Molly's Dream Nails. "My mom can be a bit intense, so try not take what she says too seriously, okay?"

"Oh-kay," I say slowly, not quite sure what to expect.

Cain opens the door, motioning me in. I step into what looks to be a very fashionable and trendy nail salon with six tiny desks made of black and hot pink lacquer, and two cushy reclining chairs of cream leather with large foot basins at the bottom for pedicures. Three of the desks are occupied with technicians doing nails of what looks to be local women by the way they're dressed, but I don't recognize Cain's mom as one of them.

Cain strides by the technicians, who are all young and look at him with appraising looks, as does one of the customers who has to be approaching sixty years old. He tips his head, pops those dimples, and says, "Ladies."

They all giggle and smile, fluttering their eyelashes. I want to roll my eyes, but I hurry along behind Cain as he heads toward a closed door.

Just before he opens it, I nudge his elbow and give him an amused smirk, "Do you always leave a wake of giggling women fanning themselves wherever you go?"

Cain blinks at me in surprise and points to his face, "With this ugly mug? I don't think so."

"Ugly?" I ask in confusion. "You have one of the most beautiful faces I've ever seen. Hell, I want to fan myself half the time I'm around you."

He blinks at me again, looking stunned and disbelieving. He even cocks his eyebrow and levels a skeptical smirk at me.

"What?" I say in exasperation. "You surely know how hot you are? You don't need me to say it to you, and your ego is plenty big enough without me needing to stroke it—"

Cain's mouth on mine effectively shuts me up. His tongue in my mouth and his hand on my ass causes me to moan. I think I hear a few of the women give dreamy sighs behind us. The kiss is all too brief, but he only wanted to make a point. He levels a metaphorical exclamation point on it when he pulls his mouth from my lips, tilts it toward my ear, and whispers, "If we didn't have an audience, I'd go for much more than a kiss right now."

"Maybe there's a bathroom," I suggest breathily, because I'm so down with going for more. To hell with breakfast and meeting his mom and the women gawking at us.

Cain chuckles, but he whispers low. "Let's stop talking about this right now. I don't need to be sporting a boner in front of my mom, and she's just on the other side of this door."

When he pulls his face back from me, his eyes are filled with laughter and amusement. It makes him even more stunning to me, and my tongue gets all tied. So I just mumble, "Okay," and Cain nods, opening the door.

He walks in first. I can't see anything but his broad back for a minute, then he bends over and says, "Mom... get off the floor."

Extending his hand out, he squats a little and then stands back up. I move to the side to see him helping his mom up.

"What were you doing?" Cain says in a loving but exasperated voice.

"Seeing if I could tell if the pilot light is out," she says as she brushes dust off her jeans.

"But you don't even know where—" Cain starts to point out, but then he's ignored as she turns to me.

Cain's mom is small… maybe an inch shorter than me. She has his same dark hair and hazel eyes that she wears very short with wispy fringes around her face. If I had to guess her age, I'd say early fifties only because I know Cain is thirty, but she'd pass for way younger.

"Oh, my word," his mom says as she steps forward, arms outstretched and to the side. Her eyes rake me up and down, and I'm wearing the same outfit that I wore to my very first and probably only gang bang. Luckily, it wasn't too rumpled and was at least stylish and chic. Her arms come to my shoulders and she beams at me. "You are just gorgeous."

I blush prettily and watch as Cain's mom turns to him, still holding me firm in her grasp.

"Isn't she gorgeous, Cain?" his mom asks him with the same sparkling smile of pure joy that her son has brought a woman to see her.

Cain shakes his head in amusement and slides his eyes to me. His gaze pins me in place and my stomach flip-flops when he says, "Totally gorgeous."

His mom's smile burns brighter, and she actually sighs. I hold my own sigh in, but it's hard because damn… that was swoon worthy.

Turning to me, she gives a push and guides me back toward the door we just came through. She loops an arm through mine and starts to usher me that way. "I'm Molly Bonham, Cain's mother, but you probably already figured that out."

"I'm Sloane Meyers," I tell her as we go through the door, leaving Cain behind. I've known Cain's mom for all of thirty seconds, and I've already lied to her the minute I told her my fake last name.

Molly leads me over to her technician table, and the other women all look at me with avid interest. Molly indicates a chair on the opposite side, and I sit. She takes her own chair and then reaches her hands out, snapping her fingers in an indication she wants my hands.

I hold them out to her uncertainly. She grasps them and studies, turning them left and right. "You have beautiful hands. You come back and I'll give you a manicure, but for now, I'll just give you a massage while we talk."

Molly pumps some lotion in her hand from a bottle on her desk and starts rubbing it into one hand, her fingers digging down into the muscles of my palm, and damn... that feels good.

"So, how long have you and Cain been dating?" Molly asks with a cheery smile. "And don't leave out any details. This is practically unheard of. Well, not since—"

"Rachel?" I blurt out.

Molly blinks at me in surprise, and then shakes her head with disgusted look on her face. "Lord, no. He never brought Rachel to meet me when they were dating. I was thinking of his high school sweetheart... oh, what was her name? At any rate, he was crazy about her, but she was a heartbreaker. Broke all the boys' hearts if I remember, but that was high school crush-type stuff. Well, and then, of course, he was gone in the Marines and hardly had time to come home and visit, and since Rachel, well... he's not had much interest..."

Molly goes on and on about Cain, and my head spins trying to keep up with her. This little dynamo of a woman who is vigorously massaging my hands and laying out her son's entire dating history to me is absolutely charming. I listen... absorbing everything I can about this mysterious man.

A man who takes his job seriously.

Fucks women in parking lots.

Has kinky group sex with his friends.

Puts butt plugs up my ass at my workplace.

Hell... Molly is so damn normal and "mom-like" that it starts to give me new perspective on Cain. It's almost as if I can envision him as a normal guy.

"...and then he just works so hard between his job at The Wicked Horse, then working part time at the Double J, and for my Walt. I worry about him, and he needs a girl to keep him straight. He has to know there's more to life than working to pay off all that debt Rachel left him."

"She sounded like a bad piece of work," I comment softly.

"She was the worst," Molly says in a low voice as she leans in on me. "She cheated on Cain... ran around with all sorts of bad folks, high on drugs. Ran up all those credit cards. Honestly, while I hate for anyone to die, I couldn't help but be relieved she was out of his life. And now here you are... the first girl he's seemed interested in since her."

I find it interesting Molly didn't mention the abortion Rachel had. It could be she just didn't think it was couth to mention it to me as a stranger, but I'm betting she doesn't know. Knowing what I do about Cain, I'd put money on the fact he didn't share with his mother because he didn't want to cause her pain.

"So how did you two meet?" Molly asks as she pumps more lotion and starts to massage my other hand.

"Um... actually at The Wicked Horse," I tell her with a mischievous grin. "I ended up kicking a guy in the balls who tried to touch me on the dance floor and Cain had to escort me out."

"And you've been dating ever since," Molly says with a romantic sigh.

Yeah, well... not dating.

We're fucking, Molly. Just fucking.

In fact, your son brought me to a strange house last night and fucked me with three of his buddies.

It's hard for me to even reconcile that notion... that it just happened last night, and here I am having a conversation with Cain's mom. It's just surreal to me.

The door to the back room opens, and I turn my

head to see Cain coming out. He gives me a quick smile, rolling his eyes when he sees his mom rubbing my hands.

"Okay, Mom… let Sloane go now. We've got to go," Cain says as he walks up to us. "Pilot light was out. I relit it for you."

Molly pats the hand she was massaging and looks at me. "It was lovely to meet you, Sloane, and I hope to see you again."

I give her hand a squeeze as I stand from the chair. "It was really nice to meet you too, Molly. Hope to see you again soon."

"Well, let's make it this Sunday," Molly says with a devious smile leveled at her son. "Cain usually comes to eat Sunday lunch with us. His sister and her family will be there too. You come with Cain, okay?"

My head swivels to Cain, who I imagine might be gritting his teeth over his mom's offer, but instead, he just leans over and kisses her cheek. "We'll be there around one."

I'm stunned he wants me to go to a family dinner with him. We just had wild monkey group sex last night, and now he's taking me to the family homestead?

But I recover quickly and turn to Molly. "Can I bring anything?"

"Just yourself, dear," she says and then winks at Cain. "I like this girl, Cain. She's a keeper."

This time, Cain doesn't humor his mom but instead gets a tight lock to his jaw. He just nods and says, "We'll see you Sunday, Mom."

I follow Cain out of the shop, no doubt what I just saw on his face. He may have been sweet and doting in there just now in front of his mom, but Cain Bonham has no plans to keep me around for very long.

That was very, very clear on his face.

Chapter 19

Cain

CAIN BONHAM OUT on a date.

A double date at that.

Bet no one saw that coming.

I have to say, it's not as awful as I thought it would be. I'm trying to remember the last date I went on, and I guess it was when Rachel and I first hooked up. We didn't start out with a date but with some wild sex in the back of my truck, and I think we eventually ended up going to dinner after. But with her, it was only sex and more sex, and I got sex and love confused back then.

Not so now.

I'm clear and levelheaded on what the stakes are, and I also know Sloane Meyers doesn't belong in my life long term. In fact, this time next week, I'll be fucking Amy Mason and Sloane will be a memory.

My gut twists at the thought, but I ignore it. Instead, I look at Sloane and Callie talking.

The women hit it off, and I mean hit it off. They haven't stopped fucking talking since we got to the restaurant, and Woolf and I have been stuck having to entertain each other.

At least we always have sports to talk about.

Sloane wasn't making light of her interest in politics. I was amazed at her knowledge and involvement at the state level back in Tennessee, and she worked on two campaigns, one of which was a US senator. Frankly, that shit was boring to me, but early on in the conversation, my interest was caught when Sloane told Callie more about her mother.

"So why do you want to help with my father's campaign?" Callie had asked her as they sipped on glasses of wine and we all picked at the overpriced shrimp cocktails.

"He's supporting House Bill 137," Sloane said.

Callie nodded in recognition. "Requiring doctors to check a database before prescribing highly addictive drugs."

"Among other things," Sloane said. "But yes… that's the most important part of the bill."

"Cain said you're new to the area. Why the desire to get involved in local politics?"

Sloane told Callie about her experience, going into some mind-numbing detail that caused Woolf and me to have a spirited discussion about baseball, but then my attention was dragged back when Sloane said, "It's personal to me. And since I'm making this my home for the immediate future, I'd love to get back involved in the political scene."

"Why is it personal to you?" Callie softly asked.

Sloane's voice was strong as she told a bit more detail

than she gave me a few days ago. "My mom had some lower back surgery. Got prescribed some pretty addictive stuff. She couldn't give them up. That was compounded by the fact that she was severely depressed. She took too much… overdosed. I found her not long after she took them and was able to get help in time."

"Oh, God," Callie said with her hand coming to cover her mouth in astonishment. She then just as quickly puts her other hand over Sloane's and squeezes it. "I'm so sorry. Is she okay now?"

"That was a few years ago," Sloane said, running her finger around the edge of her wineglass and staring at the red liquid to avoid Callie's questioning gaze. "She's off the pain pills, but she still has issues."

Luckily at that time, the waiter came up to take our order, so Sloane got a reprieve from further questions. The minute he left, I gently steered the conversation back to Sloane's request to volunteer, and the girls were off and running again.

Woolf and I talked about football.

Eventually, the talk turned away from politics and we all had a good time hanging out. That had never been a chore between Woolf, Callie, and me, seeing as how we all knew each other for years. But it really didn't surprise me that Sloane fit in so well. She's laid-back like us but sharp as a tack, with an amazing sense of humor. We all four lingered after dessert for over an hour, just talking and laughing, and it was almost 10:30 PM by the time we left.

By the end of the evening, Callie and Sloane had made plans to get together the very next day to do some shopping and "talk politics". It seems as if Sloane is not only getting back into a hobby she enjoyed but has also made a new friend as well, and I'm glad. I suspected they would like each other, and honestly... that eases my conscience that she'll perhaps have a friend she can lean on when I have to cut her loose next week. Callie's going to give me so much shit about it, but at least she'll understand as she knows all about the sex club. And she'll also give Sloane some comfort as well.

Ordinarily on a Saturday night around this time, either I'd be working at The Wicked Horse or I'd be fucking someone in The Silo or fantasy cabins. But tonight, after we say goodbye to Woolf and Callie in the restaurant parking lot, I ask Sloane what she wants to do.

She shrugs. "I don't know. Go back to my place?"

The last two nights, I worked, but it didn't keep me away from her. I drove all the way back to Jackson and let myself into her apartment, pleased to find her already naked and waiting for me. But tonight, I kind of want her in my bed.

"Or my place," I throw out, inviting her to my home for a second time. This is stupid because it smacks of a strengthening relationship, which is fucked up since I have no intentions of keeping this going in the long term.

"Okay," she says with a smile.

I take her hand as we walk over to my truck, head

already spinning with what I want to do to her when we get there.

SLOANE STRADDLING ME, riding my cock.

My hands on her hips, helping her to bounce up and down.

Fantastic tits jiggling.

One of her hands between her legs, rubbing her clit.

Sloane fracturing apart and crying out as she orgasms.

That's all I need. I slam her down on me as I plant my feet firmly in the mattress and punch my hips upward. My cock goes so deep, she gives a startled yip even as she shakes and shudders. I unload viciously, gritting my teeth and riding out a pleasure so intense, it almost doesn't seem real to me.

Sloane immediately collapses on top of me, her body as slick with sweat as mine. My arms come up and around her, my hand to her back where I feel it rising and falling as she gasps for breath.

"Am I crazy?" she says between pants. "Or was that really, really good?"

"You came three times," I say, equally out of breath. "I think I just blew the head off my dick. So yeah... that was really, really good."

Sloane giggles and nuzzles her face into my neck.

And I fucking love that sound and that feeling, and

fuck… I'm going to miss that for sure.

The sounds of *Bullet with Butterfly Wings* starts playing and Sloane jerks, sitting straight up on top of me, looking at her purse sitting on the floor. She scrambles off me, my cock sliding free and now feeling utterly cold and abandoned. Dragging the sheet off the bed with her, she hastily wraps it around her body before grabbing her purse and diving in for her phone.

It comes up to her ear. She gives a slight cough to clear her throat and answers, "Mom? Are you okay?"

Leaning up on my elbows, I watch as worry crosses Sloane's face and she listens intently on the other line. Her eyes rise to meet mine, and she gives an apologetic look while holding up one finger to me. I return an encouraging nod and she walks out of my room, taking the privacy she just wordlessly requested of me.

With a sigh, I roll out of the bed, pulling the condom off as I go, dumping it unceremoniously in a garbage can on the other side of my nightstand. While I'm totally cool with walking around butt-ass naked, Sloane covering herself with the sheet to talk to her mom told me one thing.

That this conversation was potentially upsetting or painful, and she needed some type of protective cloak, even if it was just shielding her nakedness from me. So in deference to her, I pull my jeans on without the underwear and sit back down on my bed.

My house is so small that I can hear Sloane even though she's talking quietly. I don't think she's trying to hide what she's saying though, because while her words are soft, they are clear.

I'm sorry you're having a bad night. Did you try to call Kent?

Long pause as she listens.

I know you don't like the way they make you feel, but you need to stay with it.

A shorter pause.

Yes, Mom... it's important.

And then in a lower voice. *I'll try to come home soon. Maybe in a week or so I should be able to.*

A really long pause, and then, finally... *It will be okay, Mom. You know to call Dr. O'Loughlin if it gets bad, right?*

Short pause.

All right. I have to go, but I love you. I'll call you to-morrow to check on you.

I wait a few more minutes, assuming Sloane will walk back into my bedroom, but she doesn't come. Pushing myself off the bed, I pad down the short hall into the living room. She's sitting in my recliner, feet curled up under, tightly wrapped in the sheet. Holding her phone in front of her, she stares at the screen and gives a curse under her breath, then her thumbs are flying across it as she messages someone. Her face is livid with anger. The subtle whoosh sound of an outgoing text chimes even as Sloane continues to glare at her phone.

"You okay?" I ask her and she jerks, immediately shutting off her phone. I expect to see worry and exhaustion perhaps from the side of the conversation I just heard, but instead, she shoots me a slightly guilty look.

I glance down at the phone and then back to her, wondering who she just texted and why it would cause her to look angry and then guilty, especially right after ending a call with her mother.

Sloane's worried features smooth out, and she gives me a quick smile. "Yeah. Fine. That was just my mom. She's a little blue and wanted to talk to me."

"Is anything wrong?" I push at her as I walk into the living room, coming to stand before the recliner.

She looks up at me, thumb idly stroking the edge of her phone. Taking in a breath, she lets it out. "My mom just got out of the hospital about a month ago. A psychiatric hospital. She had a bit of a meltdown and voluntarily checked herself in."

I kneel down in front of Sloane, bringing my eyes level to hers. Placing my hands on her thighs, I squeeze. "I'm sorry. I didn't know."

"Well, it's not something you just tell total strangers," Sloane says with a humorless laugh.

"We're not strangers," I tell her.

"We've known each other a week."

"But look at the things we've done in that week," I counter argue with a smile and a pointed look. "And here you are, laying all your dark secrets on my doorstep."

Another flash of guilt in her eyes, and I realize she's not sharing *all* her secrets with me.

"Is your mom okay right now?" I ask so she doesn't

shutdown.

"Yeah," she says softly, pushing her legs out from underneath of her. I move my hands so she can uncurl herself and place her feet on the floor to either side of where I kneel. "She'll be okay. Sometimes she just likes to hear my voice... I think it grounds her."

"Sounds like you're planning a visit back to see her soon," I say offhandedly as my hands go back to her thighs that are enshrouded in layers of sheet.

Sloane blinks at me in surprise, so I clarify, "I overheard your end of the conversation."

"Oh," she says distractedly and I can see the wheels in her head turning, trying to remember exactly what she said. She's definitely hiding something from me.

"Who were you texting?" I can't fucking help asking. I just found out that Sloane's got some serious shit to worry about with her mother clear across the country, something's upset her tonight, and she sent what looked like an angry text out just a bit ago. It's driving me nuts not knowing what this is all about, particularly because now I want to help her in whatever it is.

"My brother," she says quickly.

Too quickly and I know it's a lie.

"Your brother?"

"Yeah... Kent. Older than me by four years. He lives in the same town as Mom. I want him to check on her."

Well, shit... that sounds plausible, but still. I don't think that's right. The tone of voice she uses just now in talking about her brother is soft... loving. There's genuine affection there.

She's not pissed at him. At least not tonight, but I decide to let it go for now.

I've certainly got no business poking around all of Sloane's dark secrets. Not when I have my own. Especially when I intend to cut her loose in a few days, making any of this interest moot.

So instead, I do something I know both of us love and choose to hold onto that connection instead. I push the sheet up her legs, running my fingers over her bare skin as it's revealed. When her pussy is open to me, the sheet bunched around her waist, I put my hands under the backs of her thighs and haul her legs up over my shoulders.

Pressing my mouth to her, I give her a rough lick. She cries out as her hands go to my head to hold me tight.

Yeah… I'm going to miss this too.

So fucking much.

Chapter 20

Sloane

CALLIE HAYES IS one of the most amazing people I've ever had the privilege to know and hang out with, and that little fact right there has compounded the guilt on my shoulders. She's beautiful, smart, and funny. Overly compassionate and equally passionate about issues that matter. The oppressive weight of my culpability feels like a cinder block on my chest, only made worse by the fact I have now targeted this lovely lady. My mission is clear. I'm to find some sordid dirt on this unsuspecting woman merely because she happens to be the daughter of a politician and my magazine wants to profit off the situation.

"Want a margarita?" Callie asks as we're shown to a table at the back of The Merry Piglets for lunch. We spent the morning just browsing some of the stores on the town square, not with the idea in mind to shop, but really more of a casual meeting where we could get to know each other better.

The thought of food or alcohol actually makes me want to puke because my stomach is so knotted up, so I just shake my head with a smile and say, "Too early for me."

Callie snorts and says, "It's never too early for a margarita," and then snags one of the waitresses walking by, latching onto the tie to her apron. "Kimmy... two classic margaritas."

"Sure thing, Callie," the young woman says with a wink and heads over to the bar.

"You're popular here," I comment with raised eyebrows and a smirk.

"I used to work here in high school," she says with a laugh. "Our family has known the owners forever... the Sanchezes... and my dad's done political rallies standing right up there on the bar."

"Now that's cool," I say with admiration, because I could never imagine my dad doing something like that. Too much starch in his underwear back when he was representing the great state of Tennessee in the U.S. Senate. Of course, now he's a bit different.

"So what kind of hours could you commit to me on the campaign?" Callie says as she unrolls the utensils from the paper napkin. She places the cutlery on the table and tosses the napkin on her lap.

"I work roughly thirty-five hours a week, give or take. I have early mornings open all week, and every other weekend off. I'm usually off by four PM, so use me however you want."

Callie's eyes gleam mischievously. "Girl... you don't know what you just offered. It's easy enough to find people who are all gung-ho and fired up to help, but not so easy to find someone with your knowledge and experience. If I had the money to do it, I'd hire you for the campaign instead of asking you for some volunteer hours. But I won't be able to take on employees for a few months yet until the campaign officially kicks off."

I try hard not to wince as that just added a whole new level of guilt onto my shoulders. And fuck, I hate doing this.

Hate it, hate it, hate it.

I hate Brant for making me do this. I hate my career and politics and my fucking father who started me down this path to begin with.

I just hate it all, and I have the overwhelming urge to run straight out of The Merry Piglets, drive my rental car back to the airport, and book the first flight out no matter where it's going. Leave everything behind, start over somewhere new.

Except, the actual thought of not seeing Cain tonight is almost just as unbearable. Or not going to dinner at his mom's house tomorrow.

He has enough of a hold on me at this point in our very young relationship that I have constantly battled myself over what to do. The sane part of myself... the part that still has integrity... wants to tell *Revealed* magazine to kiss my ass and walk.

The other part of me though... the one that will do anything to protect her mother, even if it means submitting to blackmail... well, it's the part that's winning the war within my conscience at this point.

Yes… it's come down now to blackmail.

After I hung up the phone with my mom last night, I decided to check my texts. Acid backed up in my throat when I saw one from Brant that said, *You're not working fast enough. I want an update first thing in morning, and I need something solid.*

Asshole!

He told me he'd give me two weeks last time we talked. It's only been a week, and I was hoping that within the next few days, I'd be able to come up with a miraculous solution that would make all this go away and let me stay in Cain Bonham's bed—possibly his heart—for, oh, about forever.

I sent Brant a furiously quick reply back that merely said, *You told me I had two weeks.*

Then Cain came into the living room, and I shut my phone off.

Next morning, there was a message from Brant and he wasn't fucking around. It simply said, *Call me by 9AM or you're fired.*

For a brief moment, I thought about not calling and taking the termination. It would be so easy and my conscience would be alleviated. I could figure out what to do with my life after that. But the thought niggled at me that if I called him, and told him there just wasn't anything to be found, he'd let the matter go and put me on another story.

So I called him as soon as Cain dropped me off at my house after we got a quick breakfast. It was 8:55am and I was pushing my luck, but I couldn't make the call with

Cain around. As soon as he pulled out from the parking lot to my apartment, I hit Brant's number on speed dial.

The conversation deteriorated rapidly, any hope of me being able to salvage my pride and perhaps Cain and Callie in the process was obliterated.

"Brant," he answered, even though his Caller ID would have identified me.

Asshole.

"It's Sloane," I said in a tired voice.

"Cutting it close," he remarked.

I didn't respond and let the silence lay heavy.

"I need some sign of progress right now. Apparently, investors are questioning the longevity of the magazine since sales have dipped last two quarters. We need something juicy to renew interest."

"I don't have anything," I told him, trying not to sound too whiny. "I'm getting nowhere on the sex club, and I just met Callie Hayes. I'm hoping to start doing some volunteer work with the governor's campaign soon, but that could take a few more weeks to find anything."

It was my hope he'd understand the futility of it all and let it go. No such luck.

"Then get in tight with the daughter. Get her to talk to you—get her to disclose her involvement. I'm sure it's something a few bottles of wine will easily flush out."

I sighed because I knew he was right. Callie and I hit it off amazingly well at dinner. You know how you can just tell when you have a connection with someone? Well, I felt it with Callie, and I know she felt it with me.

She has the potential—if I wasn't here perpetuating a fraud upon her—to become best friend material.

My heart squeezed so hard over the thought and I blurted out words that would eventually seal my fate. "I can't do it, Brant. These people are nice. They've done nothing wrong. We can't tie anything to the governor. This isn't right."

"You're not paid to bring your morality into this, Preston," he barked at me over the phone. "And right now, you are entrenched and have made two good contacts with key players. You are going to stick with this and you are going to get the story, do you hear me?"

"Or what?" I sneered at him, wishing he was standing in front of me at this very moment so I could kick him in the balls. I was so angry over his lack of integrity that was being aimed at destroying two people I had come to care about, that I didn't care if he fired me. I was bracing for it actually.

"If you don't do as I say," Brant said in a very low voice, deadly calm and ice cold, "I'm going to run the next juiciest story I can find."

I had no clue what he was talking about, but his tone was so threatening that I swallowed hard.

"Want to know what the story is about, Preston?" he taunted, and then gave a deep, husky laugh as if this turned him on. "It's about a senator who couldn't keep his dick in his pants, fucked a hot, young thing while on a trip to Brazil, and fell in love. Carried on an illicit affair using taxpayer dollars to fund his travel to do so, that apparently everyone in Washington knew about except for his poor, unsuspecting wife, daughter, and son. And then, when he was outted and the story revealed to the world, the poor wife, who by the way, was addicted to prescription painkillers, tried to kill herself. Isn't that just the yummiest of political scandal?"

My fingers clutched onto my phone so hard, I thought it might crack. My teeth gnashed so forcefully, pain shot through my lower jaw. My voice was barely controlled fury when I whispered into the phone, "That happened a long time ago. That's old news."

"But it's new news that your mom just had another breakdown and landed back in the psych unit. We're coming up on the five-year anniversary of your dad's marriage to his hot, young Brazilian wife. It would be an interesting piece to do a profile on a disgraced senator who now prefers to live on a beach in Rio with his new wife and twin girls, while his ex-wife jumps in and out of psych hospitals."

My blood pressure spiked so high, I got momentarily dizzy. My hand went out to the counter where I steadied myself, and the first thought that ran through my mind was one of murder. I considered hopping a plane, flying to Washington, and stalking Brant home from the office where I'd unload an entire magazine of bullets into his black heart.

My plan fizzled quickly though when he said in a calm, businesslike voice, "You've got a week to get her to disclose something to you or I'm going to be splashing poor Delilah Preston's pretty but fucked-up head all over the front of the magazine. You hear me?"

"I hear you," I rasped out, tears filling my eyes and then flowing down my cheeks. I hung up the phone without saying another word, and then I tried to figure out how I was going to get Callie Hayes comfortable enough with me in just a week to admit to me that she attended an orgy at a sex club with her boyfriend, who is a secret owner.

The waitress comes back and sets two frosty glasses filled with pale green, margarita heaven rimmed with salt. Callie looks up to the waitress with a smile to thank her, and I lean forward and place my lips around the straw, sucking hard on the alcoholic beverage for fortitude.

"Whoa," Callie says with a laugh. "Thought it was too early to drink?"

"Apparently not," I say with a slight cough after I release the straw. The drink is potent and my eyes water.

"Hey," Callie says, her brow furrowing with a concerned look. "Are you okay?"

I start to shake my head in the negative, because I couldn't begin to tell her all the ways in which I'm actually very sad right now, but then I'm struck with horrible, calculating, and dirty inspiration.

I let my lips slide into a frown and raise my eyes to her, filled with conundrum and worry. "I don't know," I say vaguely, cutting my eyes around to make sure no one is nearby who can hear. "It's just... I'm not sure..."

Callie takes my cue and leans across the table, whispering herself, "Tell me what's wrong, Sloane. Sometimes it helps to talk about things."

So I put the bait out there.

I cut my eyes around again, and then focus them back on Callie. In a low voice, I say, "God... I'm not sure I should even say anything... but, well... it's about my relationship with Cain..."

"He's crazy about you," she says with a confident nod of her head and a satisfied smile on her face.

"And I'm crazy about him too," I assure her with a soft smile, but then drop my eyes to the table. "But..." My voice filters away to indecision of whether to share, and Callie pulls on the bait harder.

"But what?" she asks softly, and my duplicitous eyes rise up to hers.

Totally clear and earnest eyes of fern green stare at me in solidarity and support. She's saying, *I've got your back.*

Whereas I'm trying to stab her in hers.

I almost bolt out of the restaurant as that thought crosses my mind, but the image of my mom lying in a hospital bed, drugged to capacity so she doesn't harm herself, flashes vividly, and I press forward, setting the trap.

"Well... Cain is in to some really kinky stuff," I say, my face flushing red with embarrassment, and that's not an act. I've never been very good at sharing stuff like this, and what Cain and I did almost can't be described.

Callie doesn't say anything, but there's no judgment there. On the contrary, there's a bit of a knowing gleam, and that makes it a bit easier to lay it all out there.

"He... had asked me what my fantasy was, and I thought we were just... you know... talking out our ass or something. And I told him it was to have sex with multiple guys."

Callie's eyebrows rise slightly, but she nods in understanding. "Women have fantasies just like men. Nothing wrong with that."

"Well, he provided me with the opportunity to fulfill mine," I tell her bluntly. "And I took it."

"Oh," Callie says as her eyes go round with surprise and then understanding. "Oh, *wow*. That must have been intense."

"You have no idea," I say, an absolute truth amidst all the lies I've told recently. "It was life altering in some ways."

"You sound conflicted," Callie observes. That's exactly how I tried to sound, so that's good.

My eyes drop to my margarita glass, and I fiddle with the straw. "It's just... it felt so good and right, and Cain's made me feel all kinds of confident about it, but I can't help but continue to worry that it was wrong. Being with other men when Cain and I promised to be monogamous with each other. I mean... no way would I let him do that, so talk about double standard. I should have said no, right? I should have never indulged in that. And what if that ultimately ends up disgusting him?

Makes me like a cheap whore or something in his eyes?"

I end by drawing in a long breath, because that was a mouthful, and I realize that much of what I just said is actually true. Every one of those doubts and conflicted thoughts have plagued me since that wild and amazing night.

Callie takes a quick look around, then back to me with sympathetic eyes. Her arm comes out and she covers my hand with her own, giving me a squeeze. "You didn't do anything wrong, Sloane. If Cain said he was good with it, then I'm sure he was. And if something like that happens and everyone is consenting and understanding of the ramifications… if you go into it with your eyes wide open… then there is nothing wrong with engaging in something that's out of the norm like that."

"Easy for you to say," I say with a snort and give a laugh of nervousness that is totally manufactured by this point. "You're so sweet and normal. I'm the one sitting here feeling like I should be branded the town whore."

Callie narrows her eyes at me and slaps me lightly on my hand before grabbing and squeezing again. "Now you listen here, Sloane. You are not a whore. You are a consenting adult, as was everyone else who participated that night. If it felt good and everyone had a clear conscience about it, then what's the problem?"

She's still not giving me what I need. She's giving me enough innuendo about her personal experience, which I suspect is true now as I wasn't going to accept Colton Stokes' word alone. But she's not giving me the details I need to give to Brant so he'll leave my mother alone.

So I prompt just a bit further, "You sound like you know something about this type of thing."

Callie's cheeks go red, but she holds my eyes and tilts her chin up almost in defiance. "I do. Know something about it. I did a three-way with Woolf and his best friend. And it was the most erotic experience of my life, and God help me... I'd do it again if the opportunity presents. I was totally wigged out about it though, like you. But Woolf helped me to understand that what I did with the other guy was nothing but a sexual act, and one that he enjoyed watching very much. It changed nothing about our feelings for each other, except perhaps cemented our bond and trust."

Holy shit!

Callie's been with Bridger? That has to be who she means when she says Woolf's best friend. I mean, according to Stokes, they own The Wicked Horse together.

And suddenly, I actually have a new and different type of respect for Callie. That she was brave enough to try something out of her comfort zone, particularly with someone as intimidating as Bridger. If this stupid fucking story wasn't so necessary to protect my family, I'd relish sitting down with this woman and sharing all kinds of secrets with her. It would be nice to have another female who understands the conflicts that come when fantasy meets reality.

"Now," Callie says dramatically as she picks her

menu back up. "Let's figure out what we're going to eat. I'm starved."

And just like that, our conversation is over and I'm still left with nothing but an admission that she had a three-way. Far less than what I need to appease Brant.

Chapter 21

Cain

OUTSIDE OF RACHEL, and only because we were together for a few years, I've never fucked one woman as many times as I have Sloane. While we've known each other a little less than two weeks, the amount of times we've gone at it together has astounded even my inner horn-dog nature. And each time gets better.

Each orgasm stronger.

The connection deeper.

It means I'm fucking screwed.

And now… having her on the back of my bike as I take advantage of a warm early August day… I can't imagine anything feeling more right in my life.

The Harley rumbles gruffly as I slow down to turn into Mom and Walt's driveway. They live just outside of Jackson on the opposite side of the Elk Refuge, about twenty minutes from my house. But it was the perfect day for a ride, and I wanted Sloane pressed up against me. I wanted to take every advantage of feeling her because time was running out for us.

Five more days is all I had, and I wasn't going to

waste a second of it. If I couldn't be balls deep inside of her, I at least wanted her touching me. If she couldn't be touching me, I at least wanted to see her. Which is why I asked her to hang at The Wicked Horse last night while I worked. I actually breached my own rule about not mixing business with pleasure.

And it was a pleasure to be able to look at her whenever I wanted while I also let my gaze roam around the club, checking for trouble. I didn't pull any time over at The Silo, of course. Asked one of my other crew to handle sweeps through there, and I didn't miss it for a second. Normally, I got a thrill walking through while on duty, listening to the passion permeate the air, watching bodies undulating against each other, knowing that I couldn't partake just then, but when I got off duty, I would more than make up for the lust I let build inside of me. Delayed gratification has its benefits and all, but I couldn't have cared less last night. I was completely happy letting my lust build just by watching Sloane dance, and while my intention was to wait until we got to my house to have her, I couldn't control myself when we got out to my truck. Sloane didn't even put up a fight, letting me lower my tailgate, bend her over, and hike her skirt up so I could fuck her in the shadows.

As if she could sense my trip down memory lane, Sloane presses in tighter to me, giving a squeeze to my waist with her arms. I pull the bike up beside J.C.'s truck, engage the kickstand, and kill the engine.

"That was so much fun," Sloane says as she jauntily

stands and swings her leg up and over the back of the bike to dismount. She does so with her hands pressed into my shoulders for leverage, and I hate the thickness of my leather jacket dulling the feeling.

Sloane and I take our helmets off, place them on the seat, and head up to the house. Her hand slips into mine, and I like that feeling too. I never much cared for PDA. Never held hands with Rachel, but again... this just feels right.

We trot up the steps and I open the front door, pulling Sloane inside, through the living room and straight back to the kitchen where we always hang out. The aroma of roasted chicken fills the air, and my stomach grumbles. My mom is a hell of a cook, and I try to make most Sunday dinners she holds after they all go to church. Mom, Walt, Claudia, J.C., Carrie, and Tucker all attend Sunday services at the Methodist church. I don't, usually because I work late and I'm too tired to get up that early, but mainly because I've just never felt the connection.

However, for a brief moment as I walk in and see everyone in their Sunday finest, I have a fleeting wonder of what it would be like if Sloane and I had gone together. We'd sit with my family, taking up one long pew. Probably hold hands the entire time as we listened to the minister and sang songs. I can't believe I'm even fucking thinking about something like this and I push the thought away because that smacks of something deeper and more infinite than I could have ever hoped to have with someone, and it can't be Sloane.

Not at this point in my life.

"Cain... Sloane," my mom says in a happy voice as she sees us. "Come in... we're about ready to eat."

My sister is already at the table with Carrie on one side, Tucker on the other. She moves her hands in quick fashion, communicating to Tucker to put his napkin on his lap. Carrie watches, gets the message, and does the same.

J.C. is carving the roast chicken at the counter, and Walt is pulling a beer out of the fridge. They all turn around and levy warm smiles as we walk in.

I make quick introductions. "Everyone... this is Sloane. Sloane, you know my mom, but that's J.C. on chicken duty, my stepdad, Walt, and that's Claudia sitting in between the rugrats, Carrie and Tucker."

Sloane sweeps her gaze across everyone, nodding with a smile. Then she walks over to the table, and sits down opposite of Claudia. Beaming at Carrie, she says, "Hey cutie... I love that dress you're wearing."

Carrie gives her a toothless grin, but she lowers her eyes in shyness.

Sloane turns to Tucker, and I jump in to explain. "Tucker's dea—"

But I'm stunned silent when Sloane's hands start moving quickly, using sign language to say, *Hi Tucker... I'm Sloane. It's nice to meet you.*

Tucker gives the quick sign back for, *Hello.*

"You know sign language?" I ask, and her head turns

slowly to me.

She answers me but signs directly toward Tucker to explain her knowledge. *My brother Kent is deaf so I know sign language, although I'm a little rusty.*

Turning to me, she says, "He got a cochlear implant when he was about twelve, so we didn't really use it that much afterward unless it was around his other friends."

"Well, you're still perfect at it," Claudia says, and then reaches her hand across the table. "It's really nice to meet you."

I stare at Sloane in amazement. It's not that knowing sign language is a big deal because plenty of people do, but it's the fact I keep finding things in this woman to endear me to her more. They showcase that despite the fact I thought she was my opposite because of her sweetly innocent ways, we actually have other things to bond us besides sex.

The mere fact that she can carry on a conversation with my nephew just makes me more enamored of her.

Our family dinner is exactly as it always is, and maybe even better. We spend a few hours at the table, the food quickly eaten but the conversation, laughter, and jokes taking far longer to dissipate. It's made even better with the addition of Sloane. Tucker took to her quickly, as usually he's the one who sadly gets left out of conversation with new people he meets because they simply can't communicate with him.

It was late afternoon by the time we were ready to leave. I had to be at work in about three hours, and I wanted some alone time with Sloane before then. I had asked her to come hang at The Wicked Horse tonight while I worked, but she begged off, stating she wanted a good night of sleep before work the next day. I did get her to promise to stay at my house, and we even packed up a bag with a few essentials for her. If I have my way, she'll be in my bed every night this week.

Until I let her go.

"WHAT ARE WE doing?" Sloane asks as I bring the bike to a stop and cut the engine. I put the kickstand down but don't bother to dismount.

"Watching the sunset," I tell her. "This is a great place to watch it from as it sinks below the Tetons."

"Ooooh." She gives a girlish squeal as she hops off, tugging at her helmet straps. "I knew you were a romantic."

When both her feet are on the ground, I reach out and snag her by the waist. I pull her toward me so fast that she drops the helmet onto the dirt road I had taken that winds behind two large buttes with a protected, private view of the Tetons. It's a public road, used by fisherman to reach a nearby stream, but no one is parked out here now.

Perfect.

"Get up here," I say gruffly, urging her on my lap, facing me in a straddle. I dig my boots into the ground for leverage additional to the kickstand.

Sloane doesn't argue or waste time. She scrambles up and wraps her jean-clad legs around my waist. Her hands go to my chin strap and she removes my helmet, dropping it into the dirt beside the bike. After, her hands come to my face where her thumbs smooth along my chin and she says, "Are we going to make out while we watch the sunset?"

Making out sounds nice and would keep in line with her silly thoughts that I'm a romantic. But time is running out, and I don't have the patience or fortitude to bear just kissing this woman.

"I was thinking about fucking you while we watched the sunset," I tell her as my eyes peer into hers.

Her mouth rounds in a little "O" of surprise, but her eyes fire hot, and I can tell she likes the idea very much. That knowledge starts my pulse hammering. Her eyes cut left and right, noting the only nod to getting caught is a winding dirt road that someone might come down. Otherwise, there's not a house or person in sight.

"Right here?" she asks as she nibbles on her lower lip. "Right now?"

"I'd need you to get those jeans and your underwear off first, but yeah… that's what I was thinking." I follow up with a push to her hips, grinding her down on my erection that started sprouting the minute she climbed onto my lap.

I expect Sloane to perhaps give this some serious consideration, or maybe even argue with me a bit.

Sometimes, she needs a little convincing, but that can be fun too.

Instead, she scrambles right back off my lap, almost losing her balance and ending ass down on the dirt road. But she catches herself, slapping a hand onto my shoulder to give herself leverage to kick her tennis shoes off.

She does that quickly, now standing in the dust in pristine white socks that won't remain white any longer. But she doesn't care. She undoes her jeans lightning fast, pushing them and her underwear down her smooth legs. I watch her almost in a daze, lust starting to drown me as I realize this woman just hopped off my lap in the middle of nowhere, perfectly willing to fuck me in the shadows of the Teton Mountains. I blink, try to get my bearings, and realize I have work to do as well.

As she's shedding her bottoms, I stand over the bike seat and pull my wallet out. I grab a condom, toss the billfold onto the road, hoping I remember to grab it later, and then pop my button fly with one hard pull.

"That's right," Sloane says huskily, and I shoot her a glance. She's completely naked from the waist down, and my knees almost buckle when I watch her slowly drag a hand down to press her fingers between her legs. "Get that cock out, Cain. I want to go for a ride."

I groan and push roughly at my jeans, just enough that my dick springs free, and I sit heavily on the bike seat again. My hand grabs onto my shaft, giving it a few relieving strokes while I watch mesmerized as Sloane fingers herself.

Standing on a dirty road in nothing but a t-shirt, a denim jacket, and white socks.

Not sure I've ever seen anything hotter in my life, and I've seen some stuff in my line of work.

I release my hold so I can get the condom out. My moves are practiced and efficient, and I'm suited up in no time flat. Holding my hand out to Sloane, I give her silent invitation to climb aboard.

She pulls her hand out from between her legs, fingers wet and slick as they curl around mine. Her other hand goes to my shoulder, and I haul her back onto my lap. She quickly tugs her hand free. Both hands now rest on my shoulders, and she starts to lower herself.

"Not yet," I say gruffly as I put a hand between her legs. "Let's get you loosened up a bit."

She moans as I slide two fingers inside her and god-damn, she's already dripping. I'm not sure if it's the bike ride that she found stimulating or just the fact I want to fuck her right now, but she's not going to need much more prep before she can take my big dick inside.

I've come to know her body very well, and I know exactly how to touch her to produce maximum pleasure. Working her clit fast and hard with my thumb, I keep two fingers deep inside her.

Sloane's head tilts back, her blonde hair falling away from her face. I stare at her slender neck and want to sink my teeth into it. She rotates her hips and starts to fuck my fingers in tandem with my own movements.

I get even harder as I listen to the tiny sounds of

pleasure and lust falling from her mouth, and then she's gasping, "I'm coming, Cain."

And she orgasms beautifully, her pussy gripping hard onto my fingers, sucking them in deeper. Her body shudders as I place my lips to the pulse at her throat. I stick my tongue against her skin, and it feels like hummingbird wings, it's beating so fast.

When her channel finally relaxes its hold on my fingers, I pull them free and put both hands to her hips. She tilts her head up, looking at me through post-orgasm haze, and says, "I'm going to fuck you now."

"No, baby," I tell her as I help to ease her down on my aching cock. "I'm going to fuck you. Just hang on, okay?"

She nods, too sated to argue, and then loops her arms around my shoulders for leverage. I use my hands on her hips and my boots pressed into the dirt road to thrust up and into her. A long and stuttered moan comes out of her throat, seemingly never ending as I fuck her from the bottom upward.

I heave up into her, seeking the deepest of contacts all while I try to suck in oxygen so I don't pass out because it feels so damn good.

I want to do this all night and all the next day and the day after that as well. I want to stay right here in this little private heaven with the sun setting behind the Tetons and the best pussy I've ever had plastered to my cock for eternity. I want to ignore my job and I want The Silo to burn to the ground because I hate it desperately at this very moment because it's ultimately going to tear this beautiful creature from my arms.

I wish I could tell her the truth.

I wish I could tell her that I have a job to do this Friday night, but it's nothing but a job.

In fact, I wish Sloane would just let me do this one job so I can fulfill my promise to Bridger and a customer, and then I'd stop doing any Silo work. I'd just maintain my job as head of security and I'd put my dick on lockdown so it only belonged to Sloane—or anyone else she'd choose to let us play with together as a couple.

I wish, I wish, I wish.

All pipe dreams.

As I fuck Sloane on my Harley, racing toward an even bigger and brighter orgasm than the last one she gave me this morning, I know I'm being an utterly hopeless fool who just happened to fall for the right girl at the wrong time.

Chapter 22

Sloane

C AIN PULLS ME to his body, kissing me again. His fingers go to the edge of the towel I have wrapped and tucked in between my breasts.

"One more time," he growls against my mouth.

"No," I say as I push back on his chest. "I just got out of the shower. I don't want you to dirty me back up again."

"I like dirtying you up."

True enough. We got home from our "bike ride" where our viewing of the sunset was eclipsed only by the fantastic orgasm he gave me while we fucked on his Harley. As soon as he got home, he pulled me into his bedroom and went at me again, except this time he pulled a "Bridger" on me.

Screwed me from behind with hard, brutal thrusts that I loved very much and then pulled out, whipped his condom off, and came all over my back. It was on shaky legs that I rolled out of bed and hit his shower up so I could get cleaned off.

Giving another push to his chest, I tell him, "Go get your shower or you're going to be late for work. I'm going to go cook up those pork chops so you can have something to eat before you leave."

His eyes go from hot, raging lust to warm tenderness. With lips curved up in a smile, he gives me a sweet kiss this time and says, "I like you taking care of me."

I give him a return smile, but if he could truly see the brightness inside of me when I hear something like that, he'd be completely dazzled. Cain Bonham has opened up to me in ways I never imagined the closed-off, scary, scarred guy ever would. It makes the narrow line I walk between him and my job more precarious as every day goes by. Yet, I can't let go.

I most definitely cannot walk away when there's still a chance I can figure out a way to save him, Callie, and my mother in one fell super-hero swoop.

Cain turns and steps into the shower I just vacated. I use the opportunity to go back to his room where I pull on a pair of old sweatpants and a long-sleeve Tennessee Volunteers t-shirt. As I pad down the short hallway, I take stock of my cooking knowledge. I'm not sure I've ever cooked pork chops before because I've always excelled at eating out. Growing up, we had a cook who catered to us, college was pizza and ramen noodles, and after college, I lived in D.C. where one simply didn't cook on their tiny gas stove in an overpriced hovel of an apartment. You went out, and you ate well.

As I enter the living room, I head over to Cain's laptop. I figure I'll Google how to cook the pork chops, because while I may not have the knowledge inside me, I can read and follow instructions very well. In fact, I once put together an entire entertainment unit that came in three large boxes with nothing but a set of instructions and a small Allen wrench.

Sitting down on his cold, plastic desk chair, I rub my hand over the track pad to pull the computer out of sleep mode. It flares bright and I instantly recognize Google mail on the screen, but I immediately start to move my finger to engage the cursor over the Firefox icon so I can access a browser. I start to tap on the pad to choose the icon when certain wording in the subject of an email penetrates my brain.

Can't Wait To See You Friday Night!

My eyes focus on the subject line, sent just this afternoon, not but three short hours ago. To the left of the subject line is the name Amy Mason.

An immediate buzzing fills my head, and my entire body prickles with apprehension. My heartbeat starts to pound as my body seems to recognize some type of dangerous intent with this email.

Can't wait to see you Friday night?

Jealousy floods my body, and I think back to just this morning when Cain and I were lying in bed, discussing future plans.

"Are you working this weekend?" I had asked, as our naked bodies lay entwined.

"Yeah," he said gruffly, his hand idly stroking my lower back.

"Want me to stay here?" It was an innocent-enough question, seeing as how he's wanted me to stay the last few nights.

He didn't answer at first, but then coughed to clear his throat. "Not this weekend. Woolf's asked me to work out on the ranch, and I have to be up really early. I'm actually going to stay in one of the ranch bunkhouses so I can get up and just get to work."

It sounded plausible. I never doubted his word.

Now I'm thinking I know why he didn't want me to stay here Friday night.

I don't hesitate a moment.

I don't question the wrongness of my actions.

I don't respect a single bit of Cain's privacy.

I double click on the email, and I read.

Cain,

My address is 3424 Fur Trap Road. I'll leave the door unlocked, but every other aspect should resemble a nefarious intention on your part to break into my house and take me hard. You said you wanted details, so here they are.

I fully expect you at my house no later than 10PM.

I expect you to pull me out of a sound sleep with a gun to my head and your hand between my legs. I kind of like what we did the last time, so put me on my knees and make me suck your cock. I also expect you to stay all night, having your way with me repetitively, so feel free to unload down my throat. We'll have plenty of time for you to fuck me hard after.

Please note that ropes or handcuffs are completely acceptable, as well as blindfolds and ball gags. Damn… I'm getting horny just thinking about all the things your big cock will do to me.

Hope this is sufficient to bring you inspiration and give you the protection you need. This is something I'm requesting and you're giving me. I'm doing this completely of my own free will.

XOXO,
Amy

P.S. I'll have plenty of your favorite beer for you!

The buzzing in my ears got incrementally louder with every word I read, so as of now, I feel like a swarm of bees is taking up residence in my gray matter. My skin flushed hot, then hotter, so as of now, it feels like an inferno. My stomach is coiled with tension, filled with nausea.

My eyes drop from the screen, and even though the glutton for punishment in me wants to read it again, I simply can't bear it. The knowledge that Cain has made plans to be with another woman this week is simply unfathomable to me. After what we've done together, I thought I could trust him.

Christ, after what I let him do to me with three other men… I totally fucking trusted him.

And then it hits me.

What I did that night with him and his buddies wasn't something that women who wanted to keep a man for the long term did. Cain is looking at me as just another great lay. His next great adventure. There's no way he's going to commit to monogamy with a woman who fucks multiple men in front of his face.

A surge of nausea rises in me, and I suck in a deep breath to keep it at bay.

"Sloane?" I hear from behind me, and I slowly turn my head to look at Cain over my right shoulder. He's dressed, his hair wet, and he's looking at me blandly. "What are you doing?"

"I was searching for a pork chop recipe," I say softly.

It's then I notice his shoulders relax.

So I add on, "I found the email from Amy Mason instead."

"Fuck," he mutters and takes a step toward me.

I shoot out of the chair and hold both my hands up. "Don't," I hiss at him. "Don't you fucking come near me."

"Sloane, it's not what you—"

"Fuck off," I scream as I try to bolt past him down the hallway, intent on grabbing my shoes and my bag. If I hurry, I can be in my car and on the road in twenty seconds.

Cain's arm shoots out, and he catches me around the waist. "Just wait a minute and let me explain."

I start thrashing in his arms, kicking my legs out. One heel catches him in the shin, but it hurts me more than him. "Let me go, you stupid motherfucker."

"Will you calm the fuck down?" he yells at me. "Let me explain what that is."

"I don't need your explanation," I say, my voice quavering now with emotion. Now that the initial burst of anger has been released, I start filling up with sadness and rejection. "I'm nothing but a cheap thrill for you and your boys. Certainly not important enough for you to keep your promise not to fuck around."

"That is not what's going on," he says with frustration as I continue to twist in his arms so he'll release me. "Let me explain—"

"Let. Me. Go," I scream at the top of my lungs.

"Fuck this shit," Cain mutters and he picks me up, hauling me over his shoulder. He spins so fast that my stomach flops. I hear him grab his keys off the counter, and then he spins again for the door. An acute case of vertigo hits me, and before I can recover, he's bounding down the steps of his porch, my lower ribs banging painfully on his shoulder. He takes me around to the driver's side of his truck, opens the door, and tosses me in.

I immediately scramble across the cab seat, intent on flinging myself out the passenger door, but his hand on my shoulder stops me as he climbs right into the driver's seat. He reaches down under the front seat, I hear something rattle, and then he slams a pair of handcuffs over my left wrist.

I start to shriek in outrage but only stunned disbelief squeaks out when he slams the other end onto his right wrist.

Cain then jams the key in the ignition, cranks the engine, and spits dirt and gravel from under his tires as he peels out of his driveway.

"What the hell are you doing?" I finally manage to grit out as he drives with my hand cuffed to his. I tentatively give a tug to make sure the cuffs are secure, but they are.

"Don't do that," he snaps as he turns angry eyes at me. "Unless you want us to wreck."

Cain is driving at a breakneck speed as he pulls out onto 191 and starts heading in the opposite direction of Jackson.

"Where are you taking me?" I ask, my blood still boiling with rage and my heart still battered from the betrayal.

"To The Wicked Horse," he says quietly. "I have to show you something, and then I can explain what's going on."

What in the fuck could he possibly show me at The Wicked Horse? Is Amy a waitress there or something?

And then it hits me.

He doesn't have anything at The Wicked Horse to show me.

He's going to show me The Silo.

MY MOUTH STAYS firmly shut the rest of the ride, and that's only because I have nothing to say at this point. I have nothing to say because my brain is too busy trying to process everything. I'm not sure what it is about this email that's prompting this impromptu trip, but Cain just may be getting ready to lay all the evidence I need at my doorstep.

The inner child in me... the one who's betrayed... hopes I can use whatever I'm about to see to bring Cain down hard. But the part of me that's been hurt... that's the part of me who wants to beg Cain not to take me there, but come up with some other rational explanation for what I saw.

Because I know whatever is within that round building that looks like a real silo is going to change everything that I've come to figure out up to this point.

Cain pulls into The Wicked Horse and rather than take his customary spot at the part of the lot bordering the road, he drives alongside the building and parks near the rear... forty feet from The Silo.

Wordlessly, he reaches into the clean ashtray and pulls out a key that he uses on the cuff. He releases the shackles and exits the truck. Coming around to my side, he opens the door and holds his hand out to me to help me down.

I look down at the gravel parking lot and say dumbly, "I don't have any shoes."

Like he's a knight in shining armor, Cain gallantly pulls me from the seat and cradles me in his arms. The irony of thinking of him as gallant is not lost on me. He bumps the door shut with his hip and carries me over to a slate path that is lined with solar lighting, leading right up to the silo.

When we get to the door, he drops me gently until

my feet are resting on the concrete threshold and fishes in his pocket for a small, black fob he pulls out. He looks at the digital screen, and then punches in a long number into the panel by the door. I hear a distinctive snicking sound indicating it's been unlocked.

Cain puts his hand on the doorknob but before he opens it, he turns to look at me and says, "That email you saw. That was a job. One that was scheduled before I ever met you. It's just a job."

"I don't understand," I say, because now I'm confused. I don't understand how that rendezvous being scheduled is a job to him. Surely he's not saying…

"Just come inside and it will all be clear," he says quietly… in a voice that sounds utterly defeated and which makes me want to comfort him for some stupid reason.

Insane really.

This guy is planning to fuck some woman in just a few days, and he wasn't going to tell me about it.

"You were going to cheat on me," I say in a small voice, my eyes lowering to the ground. "You promised me you wouldn't."

"And I didn't break that promise," he says firmly. "I was going to break things off with you before Friday."

My heart plummets and I didn't think it could hurt any more than it did, but I was wrong.

It feels like it's been stabbed with a rusty, dull knife.

Cain pulls the door open and motions me inside.

"Come on," he says softly. "Let me show you my world.

Chapter 23

Cain

I CURSE MYSELF for the hundredth time in the last twenty minutes for ever getting involved with Sloane Meyers. It was a stupid path I put myself on. One that was destined for nothing but pain in the end, and yet, I still gladly took all I could from her while it was available.

The low strains of some classical shit filters through the room. I much prefer something sexier when I'm doing my silo fucking, but some of the patrons wanted something more sophisticated.

As if that could make what we're doing more stylishly acceptable.

I lead Sloane down the hall and into the open, round room at the center. When we break free of the concrete walls of the hallway, the classical music is muted by two other distinct sounds.

The first is the chatter of about thirty people. It's sort of dead in here tonight, but that's normal for a Sunday evening.

The second is the moaning of people in the throes of ecstasy.

I look down at Sloane and find her eyes sweeping the room. Taking in the people mingling with cocktails, the bar at the center of the room, and then her gaze finally sweeps left and she takes in the windowed rooms of The Silo.

A small gasp of surprise escapes her lips, and her eyebrows shoot straight up. I follow her gaze and look at the first room. It's holds nothing but a raised dais with a black, silk-covered mattress. Four people occupy the room, three men filling up one woman three different ways.

Sloane takes a few steps past the window and looks into the next room. This is where she gets an eyeful.

The room is completely bare of any furnishings or implements other than a large, wooden stockade that I happen to know Bridger built himself a few weeks ago. He'd wanted to showcase it and apparently, tonight was the night.

Within the confines of the stockade is a woman.

Catherine actually, who is a regular in the club. She's a young, rich trophy wife to a decrepit billionaire who's on death's door. He gave her this membership so that she could get her rocks off. Although he's long since lost the ability to get his dick up, he loves to watch her work.

Catherine is also a woman who loves a good gang bang, and I'm talking about exactly the type of fucking that Sloane could have never imagined in her dirtiest multiple fantasy.

With her head and wrists securely locked in the

wooden frame, Catherine is gloriously naked and just as gloriously getting defiled by multiple men. There have to be at least seven guys in the room. Some completely naked, some standing around fully clothed and just watching as Catherine gets fucked.

One guy is pumping furiously into Catherine from behind, causing her shoulders to jam into the frame secured around her neck. Her tits sway back and forth with the motion.

Another guy stands to Catherine's side and has his hand between her legs, working at her clit. I know it feels good because her eyes are practically rolled into the back of her head, but she can't utter a sound because another guy has his cock shoved down her throat from the front of the stockade.

The man fucking Catherine suddenly grips onto her hips hard, slams in to the hilt, and throws his head back as he starts to come. He grinds against her, unloads a little bit more, and then stumbles backward completely spent. Another guy steps up, pulls his cock out of his dress pants, and rams it unceremoniously into her.

Again, Catherine can't moan from the invasion because she's in the process of deep throating someone's dick.

Normally, watching this would turn me the fuck on. I'd be in that room with the other guys, waiting to get my crack at a woman who likes being used roughly and with little respect. Either I'd fuck her pussy, her mouth, or even her ass, and I'd do so with no regard other than busting a nut and then letting my next buddy have a chance.

The thought of Sloane doing something like that makes me sick.

"Why did you bring me here?" Sloane asks in such a small, hurt voice that I wince. When I turn to look at her, she asks, "Did you want me to do that?"

Her gaze cuts over to Catherine.

"God, no," I say in horror as I take her by the hand and lead her back to the hallway. "I'd never want you to do that."

"What is this place?"

Sighing, I turn her so her back is against the wall and lean in closer so I can talk in a lower voice. While we're away from the main crowd, this is private and I don't want to be overheard.

"Sloane… this place is called The Silo. It's a sex club. Bridger owns it, and it's a place people can come to enjoy a safe and private atmosphere to indulge in their fantasies."

"Bridger owns it alone?" she asks, and I think that's an odd question.

"Yeah… he's the sole owner."

"You pay to get in?"

"A flat fee membership of $50,000 per year."

"And that woman?" she asks with a nod back to the main room.

"She's a regular. Her husband comes with her," I tell her, but now that I think about it, I didn't see the old geezer out there. He's always confined to a wheelchair, sucking down oxygen while he watches his wife indulge.

"So those rooms in there," she asks, her voice sounding a little stronger and not as broken with hurt. "People can just go in there and…"

I nod. "Yes. Some rooms are themed, but some are just places you can go in and have sex while others watch. Really… you can do anything you want here as long as your partner is willing."

Her eyes drop to the floor, and she chews on her lower lip. When she finally looks back up, she asks, "Are you a paid prostitute?"

"What?" I ask in astonishment. "No. Why would you ever ask that?"

"You said that woman Amy was a job. What else was I to assume?"

Good point. I take in a breath, let it out, and lean closer. Placing my hand on the wall near her head, I say, "Sloane… I'm the head of security for The Wicked Horse. That's my main job. But I am also a member of this sex club. Sometimes, I'm requested to be what's called a Fantasy Maker. I'll indulge someone in a fantasy to their specification. That's what the thing was for Friday night with Amy."

"A fantasy?" she asks dubiously.

"A rape fantasy," I confirm for her, because no sense in beating around the bush. "Amy likes that. Normally her husband participates."

"Her husband?" she exclaims with wide eyes.

"Yes. A lot of the members here are in committed, monogamous relationships."

She nods, as if that all makes sense to her now. "And you were going to break things off with me before Friday?"

"So I wouldn't be breaking my promise to you," I add on.

"I get it."

"Do you?" I ask as I put my fingers under her chin and push up until she's looking at me. "Do you get it's a job and it's something I have to do? I don't want to do it, but I committed. And while I don't get paid for these things, my bonuses are based on how often I'm requested. It's a way for me to make good money and get my debt paid down. If I didn't have that on my back, I wouldn't feel so obligated."

"I get it," she says again, this time with understanding. "You don't have to tell me anymore."

Pushing off the wall, I step back from her and take a deep breath as I look out into the main room. I'm at a crossroads, and now that this is all out in the open, I search in vain for a way to make this still work with her.

Turning back to Sloane, I ask, "Would you give me a pass on this Friday? Would you let me fulfill this fantasy, knowing it's just a job for me?"

Sloane's eyes turn sad and her lips flatten. She gives a shake of her head and says, "I can't. I can't separate it out. I know you can do that, but I just don't have it in me to know you're with another woman. I know that seems like a double standard, but I just… can't."

My shoulders sag, but I didn't truly expect a different reaction from her. I had hoped, but I didn't give it much chance. Holding my hand out to her, I say, "Come on. Let's me take you back to my house. You can get your stuff and—"

"I want to go back in there with you," Sloane says, and my body goes stiff with tension. She points back to the main room and adds on, "I want us to go use one of those rooms… right now."

"Why in the ever-loving fuck would you want to—?"

"Cain," Sloane says softly as she steps into me. She places a hand over my heart and says, "You explained what's going on. As of this moment, you haven't broken your promise to me. We have four more nights together, so let's make the best of them. And since this place is a part of who you are… a part of the way you are… I want to experience it with you."

I just blink at her, completely dumbfounded about this turn around. She's gone from enraged hellcat to calm acceptance of my unusual proclivities and job duties. She's giving me more than I could hope for… four more nights.

She's keeping a firm boundary, telling me we're over the minute I take on this job with Amy Mason.

My choices are to just cut her loose now, or take advantage of what she's offering.

And I'd be a fool to pass up Sloane Meyers in her bare feet and baggy sweatpants, with her hair still damp from her shower in a deviant sex club.

"Then let's go," I say as I grab her hand and lead her back into the main room.

AS SOON AS we step out of the hallway, I see Bridger by the bar. I pull Sloane along with me, weaving my way among the scattered patrons that are still socializing and watching the action within the rooms. Bridger's eyebrows rise when he sees us, his gaze raking over Sloane's unruly appearance.

"Hey man," I say as we get within earshot. "I'm going to be a little late on the job."

Bridger just gives me a shit-eating grin and then turns to Sloane. "Going to take a walk on the wild side tonight, darling?"

"Just for tonight," Sloane says in a matter-of-fact tone. "Tomorrow, it's back to plain old missionary."

I want to laugh at that, because Sloane may be sweet and inexperienced compared to me, but she is not a "missionary" girl. In fact, she's gotten quite bold under my tutelage the last several days, and she's graduated up to a nice-sized ass plug and is still begging for more.

"Well, enjoy," Bridger says.

"We will," I tell him, and then throw a thumb over my shoulder at the room holding the stockade. "That turned out fantastic. Looks like Catherine's having a blast."

Bridger's eyes turn a little sad, and he says, "Her husband died a few days ago."

"What?" I ask in astonishment, and Sloane gives a tiny gasp of sympathy.

"Died in his sleep apparently. She's broken up about it, I think."

"Huh," I say with a bit of skepticism. There never seemed to be any love between those two. I just assumed she was a trophy wife, and he was a rich ticket out of a bad life for her.

But whatever.

I have more important things to worry about.

Turning to Sloane, I ask her, "Which room do you want to go in?"

Chapter 24

Sloane

CAN'T BELIEVE I'm getting ready to do this.

It's probably a mistake, and I'm doing this for all the wrong reasons, but I'm still going to do it.

It's odd, how you can barely know someone but still share such intense experiences with them that you develop a deep connection. That most certainly happened with us.

But the truth is, we've been together a little less than two weeks, and I probably had no right to trust him. I had no business to take stock in the way he seemed to want me exclusively, and I should have never believed his promise to not fuck around while we were doing a whole lot of fucking.

But he breached that, and while I logically get that to him it's just a job, and that he was going to break it off with me and not really betray me at all, my heart still feels shredded to pieces.

He's made it clear that, ultimately, his job is more important to him than I am, which goes back to my theory that letting him give me my fantasy probably diluted any long-term respect he had for me.

As for the sex club and his role, I think this is a way Cain makes good money and digs out of his debt. Sure, he'll orgasm and enjoy himself, but I'm pretty sure these little fantasies he fulfills are nothing but employment for him.

Still, I also understand that this sex club is part of Cain's life. He said he's a member, so that means before I came along, and after I'm gone, he's going to enjoy the benefits of it. This is the part that hurts, because there's clearly no room for me here.

Except for tonight.

Tonight, I'm going to allow myself to be a part of Cain's kinky world. I'm going to experience a sexual high most people will never even imagine, and then I'm going to memorialize every sordid detail for my article for *Revealed* magazine. Cain's loyalties aren't to me, so mine can't be to him.

This means I can stop worrying about what my job might do to him.

Of course, I'll have to swallow down the bitterness of throwing Callie under the bus along the way, but I can't worry about her now. With Cain out of the picture, there's no life for me here. That means no friendship with Callie.

It's done, even though the sordidness of what I'm doing feels like a jagged razor cutting into my very soul.

I look among the rooms, taking into consideration where I want to go. There's a room with a woman tied to a large cross, getting flogged by another woman. The room with the one woman and three men going at each other, of course, and the room with the woman in the stockade. I watch as the guy getting his dick sucked pulls out of her mouth and comes on her face—another guy stepping in and taking his place. I grimace, because Cain was absolutely right. I wasn't built for that type of gang bang, but she seems to be enjoying it for sure.

There's another room with a woman strapped onto what looks like a medical examination table with stirrups, her feet secured in them and legs spread wide. An enormous guy dressed head to toe in leather, including a black leather mask that covers his face, stands in between her legs. He holds a machine with an electrical cord that's plugged into an outlet. The other end of the machine has a giant dildo on the end that's attached to some type of mechanism that causes it to pump in and out of her vagina like a jackhammer. She thrashes and moans on the table, and then her back arches up as she orgasms.

A cramp of desire hits me hard between my legs. I realize I've been turned on from the minute I got here, but I've only now had the freedom to appreciate it.

My eyes slide over to the next room, filled with various pieces of furniture and three couples in there fucking. That would be an easy enough choice, but I hesitate. None of it seems right.

None of it seems like it makes a statement to the man who I want to understand fully that I have the ability to satisfy him in all counts if he'd only just stay committed to my body alone.

So I turn to Cain and say, "Any rule against us fucking right here?"

Cain jerks and Bridger, who's still standing right beside us, laughs darkly. "You got a wild one there."

Cain doesn't even bother to acknowledge Bridger, but looks left and then right at the people all around us. Many of them are watching the action in the rooms, but others are just enjoying quiet drinks as they mingle close by.

"Right here?" he asks incredulously.

"Sure," I say with a shrug. "What's the difference except a piece of glass separating us and maybe some useful furniture?"

And to prove my point, I turn to one of the swivel stools sitting at the circular bar behind Bridger and pat my hand on it. "You could bend me over this and just go to town."

Cain shakes his head. "Yeah, that's not going to happen—"

I give a startled yip when Bridger's hands go to my waist. He easily picks me up, sits my ass down on the black, lacquered bar, and motions his hand toward me. "There you go, Cain. Your girl wants to get fucked right here."

I expect Cain to argue and pull me down, because I can tell I've thrown him off his game tremendously. It makes me feel good to know I can fluster the great sex machine and master, Cain Bonham.

But instead, his eyes narrow at me and then spark with an almost evil intent. He steps up to the bar, in between my legs that are dangling over the edge, and puts his hands on my knees.

Giving them a squeeze, he asks, "Right here?"

"Right now," I whisper in affirmation.

"Suit yourself," he says with a wicked laugh. His hands quickly pull my sweatpants free of my legs. I have to slap my hands on the bar for leverage as he practically pulls me right off the top along with my pants. His hands go back to hips, and then my underwear is being whipped free.

I take a moment and look around. Bridger putting me up on the bar caught everyone's attention that was sitting to the left and right. A few nearby couples watch with interest, and my head turns to Bridger, who is just standing casually next to me, his elbow resting on the bar near my thigh. He gives me a wink and says, "Enjoy, Sloane."

Cain bends over, presses his face right in between my legs, and runs his tongue up my center. A hoarse bark of surprise pops out of my mouth and I lean to one side to put weight on that arm, my other hand coming to Cain's head to hold him to me. With nothing but the power of his tongue and the movement of his face side to side, he starts working against my clit in a determined fashion.

"That's hot," Bridger says, and my eyes flutter closed without even looking at him. This is way hotter than what I imagined fucking in any of those rooms would be like. While the view is just as unobstructed, I guess there is some security in that wall of glass that separates the fuckers from the watchers.

Pain bursts in my right nipple. My eyes fly open to see Bridger's head at chest level, my t-shirt and nipple in between straight, white teeth. He then sucks at it through the material, licking to alleviate the sting. He pulls away and winks at me again, then turns his back on Cain and me, as if he's totally uninterested, which makes what he just did all that more wicked.

Cain works his tongue against me furiously, moaning his approval over my taste and scent. He flutters hard, growls against me, and my orgasm catches me off guard.

"Fuck," I cry out shrilly, my fingers digging into his scalp.

He laughs, kisses my pussy, and then stands up straight. Reaching over onto the bar, he grabs a napkin off a stack and wipes his mouth. He crudely balls it up and tosses it on the top right by my hip.

"Was that what you wanted?" he asks me soberly. "Did you like everyone watch you get your pussy tongue fucked?"

I swallow hard because I hear anger in his voice, and I don't get it. Isn't this what he wanted too? I mean, this is his fucking life. He's a member of this club, and I just tried to show him I can be as down and dirty as any of these people.

Plus, there's the added benefit of me getting a story.

Before I can say a word, Cain is pulling me off the

bar and throwing me back over his shoulder.

I protest with a "Hey, what the hell—" but he reaches his hand up, slides it up the back of my thigh, and presses a finger into my pussy from the back of me. I buck against the sensation, but his strong shoulder bears the burden. I'm upside down, but he spins away from the bar and starts walking away from the hallway that leads outside.

I have no clue where we're going until I hear a door open, the sound of a light being turned on, and then the door closing again. Cain bends over and puts me down, steadying me by my shoulders as I straighten up.

I get only a moment to sweep my gaze left and right, immediately realizing we're in some type of supply room. Floor-to-ceiling metal shelves lined with boxes, bottles, tubes, and bags filled with sexual paraphernalia.

"Why are we—?"

My words are cut off as Cain slams his mouth against mine, giving me a deep and bruising kiss. When he pulls away, he simply says, "No talking, Sloane."

His hands come to my t-shirt and he whips it over my head, leaving me completely naked before his lips are on me again. Cain's hands come to my ass and he hauls me up, wrapping my legs around his waist. He walks back five paces until I'm pressed up against a cold, concrete wall.

Cain then kisses me so soundly and thoroughly, my head starts to get fuzzy. He possesses me with his lips and tongue, and he seems to be trying to communicate something to me in the ferocity of his touch. My heart reacts, my arms winding around his neck, and I start to kiss him back.

I kiss Cain right there in a dismally lit storage room. The way his tongue strokes and rolls over mine is of a completely different nature. It seems to be full of apology and regret, and my answering kiss seems to tell him I understand even though I'm still hurt. Without a single word being said between us, the kiss speaks volumes.

I'm barely cognizant of my surroundings, perhaps I notice the sound of Cain's zipper coming down, I'm not sure, but then he's thrusting inside of me. The initial burst of pleasure with the tiny stretching sting makes me gasp into his mouth.

"Fuck, that feels good," Cain groans against my lips, and his hips start hammering at me. He thrusts up into me, grinding my spine into the wall and groaning in lustful abandon.

I try to say his name… I think in praise for how wonderful this is… but he's pounding into me so hard I stutter, "Ca-ai-ai-ai-ai-n." He ignores me, fucking me harder and faster. My fingers dig into the back of his neck and I press my face into his shoulder, hanging on for the ride as he completely dominates me.

Cain pulls back and slams in, causing me to cry out, and then he goes still. I pull my face up and look at him. His face is flushed with a sheen of sweat, but his eyes reflect back a brokenness that causes my heart to cramp.

"I don't want to lose you, Sloane," he says gruffly,

and then because we can't ignore the way he's lodged in me, all of our nerves pulsing for release, he does a slow swivel of his hips and grinds into me again.

I moan, "Then don't."

Please, please don't.

He pulls back, sinks into me slowly. "I don't want anything but this pussy right here."

My muscles clutch reflexively over the yearning in his voice, squeezing onto his cock hard. He groans again, pulls out, and slams back in.

He does it again and again. He picks the pace back up, tunneling deep as if he's trying to crawl inside my body. A singular shudder of pleasure ripples up my spine, back down again, and then bursts wide open in a firestorm of release that catches me completely by surprise.

"Oh, Cain," I call out as my head falls back against the wall.

Cain drives deep, plants his feet so he can grind hard against me, and starts to fall apart. His face falls to my shoulder, his fingers dig into my hips, and his cock starts to pulse inside of me as he climaxes.

His breathing is harsh, his shoulders hunched.

His face remains hidden.

Cain draws in a deep, stuttering breath. When he lifts his forehead from my shoulder, he looks me dead in the eye. "I'm not going to do it. Friday… with Amy. I'm yours and yours alone if you'll have me."

My eyes flare with surprise as pure joy seems to burst within every molecule of my being. "Are you serious?"

"As a heart attack," he says gravely. "I want you so much, Sloane. I'll give the sex club up. I'll find some other way to earn money. If I come back here, it will be with you... only as a couple."

The only way I can answer him is by taking his face in my hands and kissing him hard. He barely gets his tongue in my mouth before I'm pulling back to look at him, still disbelieving of the sacrifice he's making for me. "You'd do that for me?"

"I think you're pretty amazing," he says with a smile. "I know it's only been a few weeks, but this is so different from anything I've had before. I want more of it, and I'll do what it takes to keep it."

I slam my chest against Cain's, wrap my arms around his neck, and press my face against his. My eyes get wet with emotion, and I whisper, "I can't believe this. It's more than I could have wanted."

He squeezes me affectionately and mumbles, "So we're cool?"

"We're cool," I say as I smile, and I know he can feel it from where my cheek lays against his.

Another squeeze to my waist and then Cain starts to lower me to the ground. His cock slips free and the minute it does, a stream of liquid runs down my inner thighs.

I look down as Cain steps backward.

He looks down, sees his semen trickling down, and curses, "Fuck."

Cain puts his hands on my shoulders, and I look up

at him.

"I am so sorry, Sloane," he says tritely. "Christ... I wanted in you so bad, I wasn't thinking. And then... I realized it, but then I wanted to come inside you, and I just couldn't fucking help it. But I promise to fucking God Almighty... I'm clean. I have to take health screenings routinely, and I always wear a rubber. I swear it."

"It's okay," I assure him, because I trust him on that issue. "I'm sure it's fine."

"Are you—?"

I nod. "—on birth control? Yes."

Cain sighs in relief, pressing his forehead against mine for a minute. When he pulls back, I also assure him, "I should be clean too. I mean... that's the first time I've had sex without a condom. But I can go get tested."

I could tell that issue hadn't crossed his mind, so he shrugs it off. "I'm sure it's fine. But how about we both get tested and since it's just you and me, we do away with wrapping my dick up, okay?"

I can't help but laugh. "Okay. I will have to say, it's way nicer that way."

"Oh, yeah." He chuckles. "That was the fucking bomb, I shit you not."

"You're a poet," I say drily.

"And this poet really needs to get you dressed, back to my place, and then back to work."

"Will you send Amy an email cancelling?" I hesitantly ask him.

"Even better... I'm going to tell Bridger right now as we're leaving. He can handle the cancellation with her, and besides... I'm sure he can find some other guys to handle it."

"Like Logan or Rand? I assume they're members?"

"Or any number of other horny members," he points out with an affirming nod. "The club has almost one-hundred and fifty members. She's not going to be suffering from lack of attention."

"Okay, then," I say with a relieved breath. It seems like in the blink of an eye, things have changed drastically for Cain and me. It causes hope and happiness to fizz within me like a fine champagne.

"And Sloane," Cain says as he tucks himself into his pants. "You can't tell anyone about this club, okay?"

A flash of pain stabs into me, seems to tear my guts up as my little happy bubble is burst. Reality filters in, and I realize this line between truth and lies is impossible to walk anymore.

"Yeah... of course," I tell him soberly. "I understand it's a secret."

Chapter 25

Cain

I SIT IN my truck and look up at my small house. It's never seemed like anything but a house before to me, but knowing Sloane is sitting inside right now sort of changes the dynamic. I could see her staying there permanently with me, making a home with me.

One day.

It's something I haven't had since I moved out of my mom and Walt's house when I went into the Marine Corps at eighteen.

Certainly never had it with Rachel.

I glance at my watch and see it's almost 9:30 PM. I'm more than an hour and a half late to start my shift at The Wicked Horse, but then again, I didn't imagine tonight would ever go down the way it did.

When I saw Sloane sitting at my computer a little more than two hours ago, I could tell by her posture that something was seriously wrong. Although, it never occurred to me that she would have seen Amy's email. Hell, I hadn't even seen it at that point as I hadn't looked at my computer all day. I immediately just assumed she must have gotten some bad news about her mother or something, so when she threw out Amy's name to me, my heart just seized in my chest as I came to the quick understanding that Sloane was lost to me.

My reaction was impulsive, no doubt.

Picking her up, cuffing her to me, and taking her to The Silo was stupid and dangerous. I had no business revealing that to her, and it's something that could have turned out very badly. Could have even cost me my job.

But I had to make her see that yes, it's a sex club, but it's also part of my job. It was the only way I could truly explain to her why I had plans with Amy on Friday night.

What I didn't expect was for Sloane to react in a way I could have never anticipated. I thought she might understand once she saw, but I never expected her to want to partake in the sinfulness there. I expected her to take it all in and then tell me to go to hell.

I most certainly didn't foresee me eating her pussy on the bar in front of everyone, and that was indeed hot.

But when I was done and observing the flush on her face from her orgasm, I had an intense desire to keep our sex private from other eyes. Call it a primal caveman response, or maybe it was my soul recognizing its mate, I don't fucking know, but I had her back over my shoulder and my cock deep inside of her within the confines of the supply closet in seconds.

While I was fucking her, deep as can be, I kept thinking it would be the last time. She was lost to me. I'd never have anything as great as what was in my arms at that moment, and an epiphany rang as clear as church bells on Sunday.

Sloane Meyers was it for me.

She was more important than continuing on with meaningless sex within The Silo, or earning good bonuses from my fantasy making duties. My priorities clarified. I looked with clear eyes upon the woman who I believe was meant for me and for whom I was falling for hard and fast.

That caused me to lose it deep inside of her. I came so ridiculously hard, I almost wept against her shoulder.

I look back at the house. After I drove Sloane home, I walked with her inside. Led her straight back to my bedroom and watched as she crawled onto my bed, shoving her legs under the covers. I kissed her on her forehead and bade her goodnight, with a promise we'd talk more in the morning about what this all meant for us going forward. And though working at The Wicked Horse tonight is the last thing in the world I want to do, I headed back out the door.

My hand goes to the ignition and I start to turn it, eyeballing my house... wait, my home now, one more time.

"Fuck it," I say into the darkness of the truck's cab, pulling the key out.

I grab my phone and send a quick text to Bridger.

I'm taking the night off. Let Mikey know to take charge of the security crew.

I didn't ask Bridger. I just told him, hoping that didn't earn me a firing. But damn... I never take time off from work, always work extra shifts, and have always been at Bridger's beck and call when he needed me. I don't think one night off would be a problem.

Bridger texts back immediately, and apparently, all is good. *Not surprised. Have fun.*

I smile and open the truck door. He may be hard and scary a good chunk of the time, but I suspect Bridger might have a little bit of softness in the very center of his heart. Maybe not for himself, but he definitely likes those around him to be happy and fulfilled.

Making my way back to the house, I silently fit the key in the lock and enter quietly. I can still see that my bedroom door is open, as the light spills out into the darkened hallway. I imagine Sloane laying there in my bed, maybe just getting ready to turn out the light to go to sleep. I suspect she's worn out, but I hope not too bad. I have an insatiable need brewing inside of me again to have her, and I know she won't deny me.

Maybe it's time to even take that ass tonight, which would be an incredible way to cement the new bond we developed.

I creep down the hallway, glad of the worn but soft carpet to hide my footsteps. As I get closer, I hear her voice in a low murmur. I stop just outside the door, not wanting to interrupt if perhaps she's talking to her mom again. I consider even turning around and waiting in the kitchen, when I hear, "Brant... I've got an update."

I freeze, my curiosity piqued, and I tilt my head to continue listening.

"I've done some major digging with Callie Hayes, and I've also been inside the club. It's all locked down tight, and Callie's lips are secured. I've got nothing."

My breath goes stale within my lungs and my stomach seems to be filled with a ball of lead. There's silence, and then a long-suffering sigh. Her voice sounds worn when she says, "There's nothing there. No story. You need to let it go."

What the fuck?

Any thoughts of surreptitiously spying on Sloane evaporate, and I step into the room. She's still in my bed, her knees pulled up almost to her chin, with her back slumped against the headboard. The only sign I've surprised her by my appearance is a heavy sadness that fills her eyes as she realizes I've heard what she's just said.

Keeping her eyes locked on me, she says into the phone, "I was hoping I could persuade you differently."

My anger starts rising as I realize Sloane isn't who I thought she was at all. I've heard enough to know she's been planted here to find something on The Silo, and by the sounds of it, something about Callie.

Which means Woolf must be targeted as well.

But why?

"Brant… you do what you need to do, but there's nothing here on my end. Run the story if you have to. I'm afraid this will serve as my notice too. I quit."

Sloane then winces as whoever is on the other line

must be issuing a string of vulgarities. She listens for only a few seconds before disconnecting the call. She stares at the phone for a moment, seemingly lost in deep thought, and then drags her eyes back up to me.

"I'm sorry," is all she says.

"Who the fuck are you?" I grit out, my hands clenching into fists.

Sloane rolls out of the bed, dropping her phone on the mattress. When she walks up to me, her eyes are apologetic but pleading with me for understanding. She goes to lay a hand on my chest but I step out of her reach, my fists still balled tight.

The sadness in her eyes intensifies at my reaction.

"My name is Sloane Preston. Meyers is my mom's maiden name. I work for—well, used to work for a political magazine in D.C. I was sent here to find out about The Silo and to try to connect it to Governor Hayes."

My breath hisses out through my teeth as my rage intensifies.

"When I couldn't find a link to the governor," she continues on in a shame-filled voice, "I was ordered to try to find some dirt on Callie. They wanted me to write a sordid piece on her, and they'd connect the governor with a very weak political spin so they could publish it. They wanted sales and ratings."

"And what the fuck was my part in all of this?"

She swallows hard but doesn't drop her gaze. "You were my way into the club."

"Son of a fucking bitch," I roar as it suddenly hits me that everything I had with this woman was a fucking lie. My hand shoots out and grabs her by the upper arm. She gasps in pain, but I don't care. I drag her to the bed, picking up her phone with my free hand and throwing it in her purse on the nightstand. Then I grab the purse, shoving it into her chest, where she makes an awkward grab at it.

I immediately start dragging her out of my bedroom. "You fucking bitch," I hiss at her.

"Wait, Cain," she cries out, trying to dig her bare feet into the carpet. "I couldn't go through with it…"

"Yeah, I heard that part," I sneer at her as I pull on her hard. She stumbles, goes to her knees, and I drag her down the hallway. "Convenient how you said that only after I walked into the room and you knew you were busted."

"That's not true," she blurts out and I stop, yank her to her feet, and start pulling her across my living room. "I had planned to quit when I made that call."

"Don't fucking lie to make this easier on your conscience. I'm not buying it."

"Just wait," she yells at me, trying to jerk her arm free. Just as I reach the front door, she manages to rip away from me and take two steps back.

I turn on her, my breath coming in shallow bursts. My fury burns hotter as I take in the deceitful woman who turned out to be no better than Rachel was.

Actually, worse since my feelings were deeper.

"I was going to quit before then," she says hurriedly as she reaches into her purse. She looks in, shuffles through something, and pulls out an envelope. Her hand reaches out, attempting to hand it to me. "I wrote this letter to you explaining everything. I was going to leave tonight… leave this with you… telling you the truth of everything. And I thought… if you could forgive me, then maybe we could—"

I lunge at her, dismissing everything that comes out of her mouth, knowing I'll never trust her or another woman again as long as I live. I take her arm again, yanking her roughly to the door. She tries to pull against me, but I'm having none of it. I know my grip is so hard on her that it will leave bruises on her skin.

So fucking what. They'll match the bruises on my heart.

I jerk the door open, shoving her through it onto my front porch. She stumbles but catches herself before she goes down. Sloane spins quickly to look at me, her hair flying and covering a portion of her face. Tears are streaming down her face, and I have to wonder why in the fuck she's crying.

She hands the envelope toward me again. "Please, will you just read it?"

Glancing down to the envelope, I look back up to her. I narrow my gaze at her and put every bit of emotion into my words when I say, "Get the fuck off my property and don't ever come here again. You so much as come after Callie or anyone involved in The Silo, and I will end you. There won't be anywhere you can hide from me."

Sloane gives a tiny sob and nods at me in understanding, tears pouring so hard from her eyes that they drip off her chin onto my porch. "I understand. And don't worry. I won't do anything to hurt you, Callie, or anyone. That was never my intention."

I watch as she bends over, drops the envelope on the porch, and turns around to trot down the steps. She hustles into her car, and I watch until I can no longer see her taillights in the dark.

I look down at the envelope one more time, then turn around and walk back into my house.

Chapter 26

Sloane

I PULL OUT onto 191 and head toward Jackson, but my eyes are so blurred with tears that I can't see the road. Slamming on brakes, I pull over onto the shoulder, feeling the crunch of gravel and wild sagebrush under my tires.

Placing my hands at the top of my steering wheel, I lay my forehead on them and just go ahead and let the sobs out. I let myself purge all the pain and heartbreak I'm feeling, because I still have important things to do and I have to let this go sooner rather than later.

Oh, God... I didn't realize it would hurt this bad when Cain found out the truth. I didn't realize how badly it would clearly hurt him, and his reaction very much hurt me. The mere fact he wouldn't listen to my explanation... wouldn't even touch my letter explaining it all... it leaves me so empty feeling I'm not sure how I can ever reconcile this all within my conscience.

Cain has no reason to believe me based on what he overheard with Brant, but I had made the decision to tell Brant to go fuck himself yesterday after Callie and I had lunch. I thought of the connection I had with her, and the amazing relationship I was developing with Cain, and I weighed it against my abhorrence over hurting two people I came to care about and admire in a short time. I realized I couldn't go through with what Brant wanted of me, so I came back to my apartment and drafted my letters.

I wrote down exactly who I was and what I had set out to do.

The one I wrote to Cain lays on his front porch, where it will probably blow away and disintegrate from the elements.

The other I wrote to Callie.

I kept them in my purse, assured I would not hand them over until I had exhausted all efforts to get Brant to back off. I had no clue when or if that could happen. I know tonight was my first true attempt to get him to see reason. As soon as Cain dropped me off at his house and left to go back to work, I was filled with compulsion to make this all go away so I could try to make an honest effort at having something real with this man who had just willingly sacrificed a big part of his life to be with me.

In the matter of a few hours' time, I had gone from thinking Cain was all wrong for me to knowing he was the one. I was willing to leave D.C., relocate here permanently, and try to figure out a new path in life. I was at peace with that decision, knowing that in the end, I'd get what was most important.

But fuck… when Cain walked into that room and I

saw the condemnation tinged with hate in his eyes, I knew time was up. I had to cut my ties with Brant. He was screaming at me that he was bringing my mother and me down when I hung up, but I couldn't worry about that right now. I had to start making amends to the immediate people who were going to be hurt, and that was namely Cain and Callie.

Cain's a bust. He's not listening, nor does it appear he has room in his heart to forgive my betrayal. And honestly, I don't expect him to. What I did was too deceitful to even expect him to consider listening to a damn thing I have to say.

But maybe Callie will, and since she was the one I targeted, it's just as important to me that she understands I couldn't go through with it. I know Cain doesn't believe that was my intention all along, but perhaps she will.

Reaching with a shaky hand into my purse, I grab my phone. I know it's late, but I still pull Callie up in my contacts and hit her number.

She answers on the third ring and sounds fairly chipper despite the late hour. "What's up, buttercup?" she says.

My heart squeezes, because that's probably the last time I'll hear a friendly tone in her voice. "Callie…"

"What's wrong?" she butts in with concern heavy in her voice. She can hear the quaver in mine.

"I need to see you… tonight," I whisper, my throat clogging up with emotion.

"I'll come to you," she says quickly. "Where are you?"

Clearing my throat, I say, "No. I'd like to meet you at The Wicked Horse. And I need Woolf and Bridger there too. I know it's late, but it's important."

"Woolf and I are on our way," she says, not even questioning why I want to meet her at the bar. "We'll call Bridger and have him there. Just have the guy at the door show you to his office."

"Okay," I say and have to choke down another sob. "And Callie?"

"Yeah, babe?"

"I'm really sorry," I say morosely.

"For what?" she asks, and I hear a tinge of fear in her voice now.

"For everything," I say before hanging up.

ALL THREE STAND in Bridger's office as I requested, looking concerned over my appearance.

Tearstained face, wrinkled clothes, and dirty, bare feet. My shoes and bag of overnight clothes are still at Cain's house.

"Thanks for meeting me," I whisper as I reach into my purse, pulling out the envelope for Callie. I hand it to her. "I'd like all three of you to read it. I was going to give this to you eventually, once I had worked a few things out, but unfortunately, it has to be tonight."

Bridger looks intrigued, Callie looks worried for me, and Woolf looks at me skeptically. "Where's Cain?" he asks.

"At his house," I say calmly and don't elaborate.

Callie takes the envelope and breaks the seal. Hers is a little thicker than Cain's. Why is immediately revealed when she pulls out the letter I wrote plus a small, digital recorder. Her head snaps up, and she looks at me with confused eyes.

"The letter," I say in a raspy voice. "It explains everything."

Bridger and Woolf step into Callie's sides, and they start to read it over her shoulder after she unfolds it. I watch their faces and can tell by their expressions exactly how they're feeling.

Bewildered.

Betrayed.

Angry.

Sad.

It tells them everything. What my intentions were, what I found out, and most importantly, that I wasn't going through with it. That I was going to leave town and quit my job, but that I wanted Callie to know what I had done in the hopes she'd at least forgive me. I even signed it with my real name… Sloane Preston.

Callie finishes first, handing the letter to Bridger. She steps toward me, and Bridger and Woolf close ranks to finish reading. She steps up to me and takes my hands. I can't bear to meet her gaze, so she says, "Sloane… look at me."

I tilt my head, drag my eyes up to hers, and almost reel backward from the keen disappointment. "What's on the digital recorder?"

"Our conversation at The Merry Piglets. I didn't copy it. That's the one and only recording. I didn't turn anything over to my editor," I hastily tell her. "Everything I learned is in my head, and I'm not telling another soul. You have nothing to worry about from me."

"Does your editor have anything that ties me to The Silo?" she asks, her brows furrowed with concern.

"Absolutely nothing other than an anonymous tipster," I assure her.

"Colton Stokes," Bridger says confidently as he takes the letter and throws it down on his desk.

"I can't reveal that source," I say carefully, but then hopefully reassure them when I add on, "but I do believe that source is dried up and has no intentions of opening his or her mouth again."

"You do realize the risk you put us all at," Woolf growls at me, and I can see... he's just as pissed as Cain.

Callie reaches back and touches her fingers to his wrist. "Leave it, baby. Sloane wasn't going to do anything to hurt us."

"At first she was," Woolf says as he pulls his hand away and stomps over to the couch. He throws himself down on it, glaring at me.

"Just so I'm sure I understand everything," Bridger says as he leans his butt on his desk and crosses his arms over his chest. "According to your letter, you came here to flush out a story about Governor Hayes' ties to The Silo. You quickly found out he had no knowledge of it, then you were ordered to try to tie Callie and possibly Woolf to it, so they could publish a "guilt by association" type of story about the governor?"

"Yes, although Woolf wasn't really on my radar," I admit.

Bridge waves a hand at me. "That's because he sold out all his interest to me last month."

"For fuck's sake, Bridger," Woolf snarls from the couch. "Just tell her everything, why don't you?"

"She's not going to tell anyone," Bridger says with all confidence.

"I'm not," I assure him. "I swear it. I couldn't. And I am so damn sorry I did this to the three of you. You'll never know how sickened I am with myself."

Woolf gives a snort of disbelief and rolls his eyes.

"What I don't understand is..." Callie says softly, and my gaze slides to hers. "Why didn't you just drop it the minute you realized there wasn't much there?"

"I wanted to, tried to really, but Brant threatened my mom," I murmur. "I didn't put that in the letter because I didn't want you to think it was an excuse. I wanted you to know I took responsibility for my actions, and I wanted you to know before I left town that this was all on me."

"Threatened your mom how?" Bridger asks, his head tilted in curiosity.

"My father is Jared Preston," I say simply, and Callie gasps.

"Who the fuck is that?" Woolf asks.

"A United States senator from Tennessee," Callie says as she turns to look at her husband. "Forced out of office about five years ago after using federal funds to perpetuate an affair he was having with an Argentinian woman, I think."

"Brazilian," I clarify.

Callie gives me an apologetic smile and continues, "It was a huge scandal. There were impeachment hearings, and he left in disgrace. And if I recall, he left his wife, son, and daughter, married the Brazilian woman, and now lives life as a beach bum with new twin daughters, right?"

"That's the gist of it," I say bitterly.

"But what's the connection to your mom?" Bridger asks.

"Everything I told you about my mom was true. The surgery, the painkillers, the suicide attempt. She's been in and out of mental hospitals since then. What my dad did destroyed her. Her first attempt at suicide was when she found out about the affair. It hit the news channels."

"Fuck," Woolf says, and the sympathy in his voice is clear.

"Brant tried to blackmail me. He said if I didn't produce the story, he was going to run a follow-up piece to the Senator Preston scandal and focus on my mom's most recent hospitalization, which coincided with the anniversary of their divorce."

"Fucking prick," Woolf growls as he shoots off the couch.

"Oh, Sloane," Callie says as she reaches out to take my hands again. "That's terrible."

I pull my hands quickly away and step back from her. "Don't," I say forcefully. "Don't you dare feel sorry for me. I made my bed and now I'm lying in it. Yes, he was blackmailing me and I eventually didn't cave to it, but I considered caving. I could have told him to kiss my ass days ago, and I didn't."

"Because you were trying to figure out a way to protect everyone," Bridger says, his tone matter-of-fact.

"Doesn't matter," I say as I fold my arms across my chest. "I just wanted to explain everything. I'm going to catch a flight out of here tomorrow."

"What about Cain?" Bridger asks.

The tears well up in my eyes again, and I blink hard to make them go away. "Let's just say Cain didn't want to listen to my explanations."

Everyone is silent, not sure what to say. Finally, Bridger clears his throat and stands up from his desk. "Callie… Woolf. Why don't you two head home? It's late, and I want to talk to Sloane for a bit."

Callie looks like she wants to argue, but Woolf puts his arm around her shoulders, intent on ushering her to the door. She pulls free and throws her arms around me. Giving me a fierce hug, she whispers, "I forgive you and thank you for telling me the truth. It was very brave."

"Thank you," I choke out, the tears now breaking free. I squeeze her back briefly, and then Woolf is pulling her out the door. He gives me a curt nod of his head, and then they're gone.

I'm really going to miss her.

I turn to face Bridger and it occurs to me that I hadn't considered being intimidated by him at all this evening, but now that I'm in the room alone with the big man, I'm feeling slightly overwhelmed.

"Want something to drink?" he asks.

"No thank you," I say almost primly. "I'm tired and need to get to my apartment. I want to get an early start tomorrow."

"Don't leave," he says as he takes a few steps toward me. I resist the urge to back away from him, because although he's seemed to accept my story and apology, he hasn't quite said those words. For all I know, he wants to pound me into the ground. Hell, maybe he had Callie and Woolf leave so he can kill me and dispose of my body in secret.

Plausible deniability.

"Don't leave?" I ask as he takes another step toward me.

"Don't leave," he says simply and stops. "Give Cain a chance to cool down. Did you write a letter explaining everything?"

I nod.

"Then give him a chance to read it."

"He didn't want it," I say adamantly, because I'm

afraid to believe there's still a chance with Cain. If I believe, then I hope. If I hope, then I hurt when he snubs me again.

"Look," Bridger says softly. "You two clearly have something deep. It's new, but it's tangible. I could fucking see it a mile away. So stay and give it a chance."

I refuse to hope. "I don't think that's a good idea. Besides, I'm not sure I want to be with someone who wouldn't even give me the courtesy of listening. You, Callie, and Woolf listened, but he couldn't?"

"You're on the verge of falling in love with him," Bridger says so confidently, I almost believe him. I hadn't thought of the "L" word when it comes to Cain before, so I refuse to give it credence now when I have one foot on my way out the door.

"I am most certainly not falling in love with him. He's too closeminded and stubborn. In fact, I'm lucky I'm rid of someone like him." All lies, but Bridger doesn't know that.

"You truly don't have feelings for Cain?" he asks skeptically.

"Not really," I say, the words tasting bitter. "He was a good time and I became fond of him, but that's about as deep as it got."

He takes one last step so he's almost toe to toe with me. His hand comes up, and it curls around the back of my neck. When he pulls gently, my body falls into his and his other hand wraps around my back, pressing me in tighter.

"Then stay with me," he says in a low, seductive voice. He bends his head, putting his lips near my ear. "I loved fucking you that night and since you don't care about Cain, stay here and be with me."

My entire body tightens with refusal and I jerk away from him, taking two large steps backward. He is not the one I want.

Bridger just gives a husky laugh and cocks an eyebrow at me. "Don't tell me you weren't just now thinking to yourself that Cain's the only man you could want."

Clearly, he was just trying to make a point to me, but I don't want to accept it. I start sputtering. "Well… that's… the point is… I mean…"

"Sloane," Bridger says, cutting me off. "Stay and try to work things out with him. If your feelings are that deep, then do something about it and don't give up. He's a stubborn fuck, but he'll cool down eventually."

"I can't," I say automatically, but I'll admit… Bridger now has me hoping. "I just lost my job. My savings aren't all that great, and Stephenson doesn't pay me enough to cover my bills. I'm going to head home to Tennessee and I have about enough in savings for a plane ticket."

"Have you ever bartended before?" he asks bluntly.

"Um… yeah. A lot actually while in college."

"Then you can start tomorrow at The Wicked Horse. That will be a prime opportunity to put yourself in Cain's line of sight. Remind him why he's being pigheaded."

My head spins with the possibility. Should I do that? Is it even possible for him to forgive that type of transgression, especially as the other woman he loved betrayed him so badly?

Then a thought strikes me.

I narrow my eyes at him and ask, "Why do you believe me? Why did you so willingly accept my apology?"

"Because you were remorseful," he says simply, as if it was the dumbest question ever. "Anyone could see the truth in that. And you took full responsibility. Didn't even try to pin it on the blackmail until you were asked about it. It takes a lot of guts and fortitude to do that."

"But you don't know me," I argue, because I just can't believe that this is happening to me. The man I tried to screw over by outing his secret sex club is offering me a job.

"But I do," Bridger says with a knowing smile. "You are driven by a sense of justice, I'm guessing because of what your father did. In fact, I bet you probably had some lame-ass degree planned in college, but changed over to journalism so you could have a vehicle to expose corrupt politicians. Probably had all these altruistic ideas about bringing scumbags like your dad to justice and helping to clean up our system of the frauds. You came here with a fire in your belly to nail your first big target to the wall, and then you ran into trouble when your heart of gold got in the way. You ended up attaching yourself to a good man who showed you there's more to life than vengeance, and you realized wonderful women like Callie Hayes exist in this world. Even with your mother threatened, you ultimately did what's right, so that tells me your moral compass needs no fine tuning. And let's be honest... I know how fucking good your pussy feels, so I know without a doubt that Cain is probably already thinking twice about his decision to cut you loose so fast."

I stare at him, jaw dropped and mouth wide open. "You're... um... really weird."

"I'm intuitive and that freaks people out sometimes."

"If I work for you, you don't have any expectations that you and I will..."

"Relax, darling," Bridger says with a chuckle. "I just expect you to be a good bartender."

"Then I accept," I say, suddenly filled back up with a renewed passion to make things right. I'm going to get Cain Bonham back, no matter how long it takes.

"Be here tomorrow at noon," he says with a nod as he turns back toward his desk. "I'll have someone ready to train you."

"Thank you, Bridger," I say softly as I turn toward his office door.

"And Sloane?" he calls out.

I stop with my hand on the doorknob, turning to look at him over my shoulder. "Yes?"

"I'll still most gladly fuck you any time you and Cain want to invite me into your bed." He gives me a Cheshire Cat grin, and I feel something tingle between my legs.

That man is serious trouble, but I can't think about him now.

My mind is on another man who is far more troublesome at this minute.

Chapter 27

Cain

I OPEN THE door to my truck and step out, right into a fucking mud puddle.

Figures.

I'm surprised it isn't a pile of shit the way my life has been going the past… I look down at my watch… oh, twenty-one and a half hours, give or take a few minutes.

Slamming the door angrily, I step out of the puddle onto dryer gravel and trudge my way toward the front doors. The last thing I want is to be here. I'd much rather sit at my house and polish off a fifth of booze, preferring to numb my mind to thoughts of Sloane and all the ways in which she betrayed me.

My mood is black as I walk toward the nightclub. It's been black since last night when I walked in on Sloane talking to God knows who on the phone about… I'm still not even sure what the fuck she was doing. My rage was so consuming that I'm not sure I understand what she was telling me, but I got the general idea.

I got the important parts.

Undercover reporter.

Using me to find dirt on Callie and her father.

Fucking bitch was using me to get into The Silo. I think about her dirty fantasy I made come true and realize I was being played right from the start. Every single time I made her come, and every single soft touch or sweet word she gave me... all fucking calculated to lead me by the short hairs down a very defined path.

And when I think about the fact that just last night, I had made the willing and conscious decision to change my life so I could be with her, my black mood gets darker and colder. I nearly gave up everything for a woman who was using me.

I nearly lost my heart, but at least that's now firmly back under lock and key.

Stomping onto the long, wooden walkway that borders the front of the club, I about jerk the doors off the hinges as my fury is projected into my actions. The club is just about deserted at this early hour, usually late stragglers who just came in for a few drinks or some pub food after work. The music is turned down low, and I can hear the chatter of some of the bartenders and waitresses as they prepare for the bustle to start in about an hour.

"What's up, man?" Tank Godwin says from his perch on the end of the bar. He's one of the Double J hands, and I've known him for going on forever.

Giving him a curt nod, I head toward the back of the club. I need to check in with Bridger and let him know what's going on. While I'm guessing Sloane Meyers or Preston or whatever the fuck her name is, is probably long gone if I can believe what she was saying—and I probably can't—I need to give him a heads up about the breach. That makes my black mood start to burn within my veins like acid… knowing I inadvertently put Bridger and this club at risk simply by trusting the wrong person.

Just as I hit the hallway that leads to the back exit as well as Bridger's office, I'm brought up short when his office door opens. I fully expect one of the waitresses to walk out with a satisfied smile on her face, but my knees nearly buckle when I see Sloane step into the hall.

Bridger comes out behind her, murmurs something that I can't hear, and then gives her shoulder an affectionate squeeze. My eyes take in the fact she's wearing a pair of skintight jeans, black boots with neon blue spurs, and a black Wicked Horse t-shirt with the logo over the left breast.

I take all of that in, and yet my mind doesn't process what it means. Instead, my rage, which had been on a low simmer all day, fires up and bubbles, frothing to a point that my vision almost goes red. In three long strides, I'm on her.

My hand goes around the back of her neck, and because it's so slender, my fingers curl all the way around in a hard grip. She gives a terrified yip as I turn her toward me, pulling up so she goes to her tiptoes. Leaning down, I get my face in hers and snarl, "What in the fuck are you doing here?"

"I work here," she squeaks at me, her eyes round and fearful. I suppose my fingers digging into her neck aren't helping.

"Like hell you do," I growl at her.

"Let her go," Bridger says in a deadly calm voice.

Ordinarily, I jump to do Bridger's bidding. He is, after all, my boss. He's the leader of our kinky pack when it comes to the sex club, and I usually fuck the way he tells me to fuck when I'm in a group.

But right now, at this moment, I rebel against his order and tighten my hold on Sloane's neck. "I think you need to know what this bitch has done—"

"I'm well aware of what she's done," Bridger says, his voice just as calm but with a deeper rumble of authority. "Now let her go."

My hand falls away from Sloane, and she actually falls forward into my chest. Her hands come out and inadvertently balance against my chest. It feels like I've been burned. My body instantly becomes attracted to her touch. At the same time, it's being repulsed by it. I practically jump backward, slamming my back against the wall.

Sloane straightens herself and takes a step backward as well, eyeing me with a mixture of sadness and fear.

My head swivels to Bridger, and I try to maintain some level of respect. "You know she was working as an undercover reporter to expose The Silo, right? Was targeting Callie... probably fucking Woolf too. She's a snake in the grass and can't be trusted, so I assume you're going to fire her ass now that you know all of this, right?"

"I knew it all when I hired her," Bridger says, and then slides his gaze to Sloane. "Go ahead and find Francine behind the main bar. You'll shadow her tonight."

My eyes narrow as I watch Sloane give an unsure nod. She drops her face so as not to look at me and scurries past. My fingers itch to grab onto her again.

To throw her out of here.

Or maybe pull her to me and kiss the hell out of her.

Or maybe, just a good hard fucking, then I can toss her aside.

My head is so fucked at this moment that I don't know what I'd do, so it's a good thing she's gone.

"In my office," Bridger says and turns to walk back in there. I follow him in dutifully.

Once I close the door behind me, I say, "Come on, man… you cannot seriously think to give her a job here after she tried to screw you over."

"You'd be wrong about that," Bridger says as he walks around his desk and sits down in his chair. "I did give her a job, and you're also wrong. She didn't try to screw me over."

"I overheard her talking to someone about the club… and Callie. She admitted to me she works for a magazine."

"All true and she told me the same," Bridger says, his voice level and matter of fact. "But she did not try to screw me over. She didn't try to screw you or Callie over, for that matter. She did the right thing and dumped the story, turned over all the evidence she had to Callie to destroy, and she quit her job. Seems to me, she's the one who got screwed over."

"But her intent was—"

"And furthermore," Bridger says, talking right over me. "You have no right to judge her until you know all the facts. I assume you haven't bothered to read the letter she wrote you."

That stupid fucking letter.

I left it laying on the porch last night.

I thought about it all night.

Obsessed about it really, but I refused to read it. I left it there and I hoped it would blow away, just as I hoped these terrible feelings would go by the wayside. I stayed in my house all day today, not having anywhere I needed to be and preferring to sulk alone in my misery. When I stepped out on my porch to head to work, my eyes were helplessly drawn down to where the envelope had been when Sloane left last night.

And it was gone.

For a brief moment, a stab of regret pulsed within me. It was followed immediately by a sense of final loss… my last true tie to Sloane was gone. My eyes roved the area, figuring the wind took it since we had a rainstorm in the early morning hours. I saw it immediately about ten feet off the side of my porch on a patch of damn grass.

My relief was intense, and just as quickly, I cursed at myself for my weakness.

I called myself a motherfucking dumb motherfucking moron for even having a care in the world for that stupid letter. Really, what could it possibly say? How in the world could it ever excuse or make better what she did? What carefully thought out words by a known liar would ease the anger I had?

"What difference would it make?" I say bitterly. "She used me."

"That may have been her original intent," he says with a careless shrug. "But I guarantee you that's not what she was doing in the end."

"What the fuck ever, dude," I sneer as I cross my arms over my chest. "She's bad fucking news. You cannot let her work here."

"But I am," Bridger says simply.

I just blink at him, refusing to believe he would do that. Where's his goddamn loyalty to me?

"Look, Cain," Bridger says in a softer tone. "She was wrong and she knows it. She made it right in the end. And for what it's worth, I believe the reason she made it right was solely because of her feelings for you and Callie. She just couldn't hurt you."

"I heard her on the phone telling someone she worked for about the club and Callie. She admitted she used me to get to the club."

"Again," Bridger says in an even tone. "At first, yeah... that's what she was doing. But it tore her up, and she ultimately sacrificed that job to protect this club and Callie. It's all in the letter."

I give a snort, not wanting to believe a word he says. It's much easier to hold on to my hate and anger. It's definitely easier to be able to put her from my mind and pretend this never happened. I can't fucking do that with her in my line of sight here.

"You need to fire her," I say adamantly. "I won't work here with her."

"Then I suggest you get in your truck and go home," he responds.

My eyebrows shoot straight up. "Are you serious?"

"Dead serious."

"Suit yourself," I say, figuring either I'm going home on an unplanned vacation day, or that was just Bridger terminating my services. I don't bother to ask for clarification as I turn on my heel and head for the door.

"The letter, Cain," Bridger calls out to me. "Do yourself a favor and read the damn thing."

I ignore him and stomp out, fully intending to stay away until he cans her ass.

I SIT IN my recliner, mindlessly flipping the channel on the TV. Nothing is holding my attention, but then again... I'm not a big TV watcher. Never have the time actually, so it's no surprise now that it's not giving me a single ounce of numbness.

I glance at the clock.

Almost ten PM, and I think about the letter for

about the hundredth time since I left Bridger's office this evening. It's still laying in my side yard, and this I know because I walked to the end of my porch when I got home and saw it there in the moonlight. I stared at it, warring with myself about whether to read it, but I left it alone.

It's like a damn homing beacon, calling out to me, *Read me. Read me, Cain.*

Christ… I can't get it out of my head.

"Fuck it," I mutter to myself and turn the TV off. I launch up out of the recliner, the springs groaning, and before I can talk myself out of it, head outside.

The envelope is damp when I pick it up off the ground, and I have a small measure of relief as I think the words will possibly be smeared from the rain. But truthfully, I don't know if it was even in the rain. It could have blown off long after the storm had passed through last night.

I carry it inside, head to the refrigerator, and pull out a beer. Opening it, I take a few pulls and then sit at my small kitchen table, staring at the thing.

My name is written in neat, cursive letters on the outside, barely smudged from the wet.

Before I can talk myself out of it, I put the beer bottle down and open the envelope.

Inside are two sheets written in the same blue ink as my name on the outside, dated three days ago. I take a deep breath, and I read.

Dear Cain,

By the time you read this letter, and if all goes according to plan, I will be on a plane headed back home to Tennessee. While it would have been very easy for me to disappear without a word, I felt I owed you the truth so you could perhaps garner some small measure of comfort after you find out what I did.

First... my name is Sloane Preston. Meyers is my mom's maiden name, and I used a fake name because I came to Jackson as an undercover reporter working for Revealed *magazine in Washington, DC. My job was to follow up on an anonymous tip made to my employer about a sex club that had ties to Governor Hayes.*

While my actions sicken me now, I feel I have to honestly tell you everything. I first targeted you in the hopes that you would gain me access into the club. That first night we were together... I tried to orchestrate that. I punched that guy on the dance floor, hoping you'd find me interesting. I hoped you would want to know more about me, and it apparently worked. I had set the hook, and you took it.

I'm sorry to hurt you that way. I wish I could avoid causing you pain, but it's more important for me to be honest with you, so I can hopefully find some redemption within myself.

Here's something else I'm being honest with you about. After that very first night with you, I knew down deep in my gut that it was a mistake of mas-

sive proportions to get involved with you. Every day… every moment we spent together, I found my connection to you growing stronger, and my feelings for you growing deeper.

Please don't ever doubt my feelings. While I was indeed trying to find a story, my real efforts went into building something with you. Every day, my own self-esteem and pride took a battering as I continued to lead a double life, and yet I couldn't bring myself to cut you loose. You started to become necessary to me, and in a very selfish move, I tried to figure out how to have it all.

I figured out early on there wasn't a story there. I swear to you I tried to convey to the magazine time and time again that there was nothing there. I was met with resistance and firm orders to dig deeper. This past week, I wracked my brain trying to figure out a way from this mess. How I could salvage my job and my relationship with you. How I could look myself in the mirror and not be ashamed of what was looking back at me.

Even when things were at their darkest for me, you ended up being my one shining light in this debacle. Ultimately, no matter what my employer wanted me to do, I realized I just couldn't hurt you. I couldn't hurt Callie. My job simply wasn't that important. It was my hope I could get them to back off, but I was fully prepared to quit if that didn't work. In fact, the purpose of me writing this letter is so you know that when you finally find out the *truth about me, my intent at the end was to do whatever was necessary to protect you, Callie, Bridger, and the club. If you're reading this letter, it means the magazine is not accepting my inability to manufacture a story, and I'm going to have to quit.*

Once that happens, I'm going to have to go home to Tennessee.

I really hope it doesn't come to that, but if you are reading this letter, it means I couldn't save everything. Just the things that mattered most.

I wish you so much joy and happiness in life. My heart will be forever broken over losing you, but I hope to God that you find a way to make peace with this and move on. I care about you so much, Cain, and it kills me to know how much you're going to be hurt by this. I only hope you can find it in your heart to forgive me and ultimately find someone who is good to you.

Love,
Sloane

I set the letter down and stare at it. My fingers curl around the beer bottle, and I grip it tight. I'm not sure how I feel about what she's said. I do have to admit, it seems like her intent for the most part was to protect Callie, the club, and me. I'm not sure why she couldn't just tell me what was going on, but it doesn't seem she was out to hurt us.

It also seems that maybe she did have feelings for me. If only I could truly, deep down, believe that.

Chapter 28

Sloane

I WONDER IF there will ever come a time that I'll see Cain for the first time in any given day, and not have my entire body just sigh with pleasure over the magnificence of this man.

He opens the door to The Wicked Horse and strides in with confidence. I pause my efforts in wiping the bar down and admire the tight fit of his black BDU pants and the t-shirt that proudly proclaims him as head of security. He's recently had a haircut but he didn't shave tonight, and I remember with yearning the feel of that scratchy beard against my legs.

Cain didn't stay away from The Wicked Horse long. Only a day, as a matter of fact. Bridger had told me the first night I worked that Cain demanded I be fired, and that he wouldn't work here with me. I was stunned when Bridger told me that he sent Cain home, but he didn't seem surprised when he came in to work the next evening.

And as he's done every night for the past three nights, his eyes sweep the interior until he's confident he knows where every single person is. He always saves the bar for last, because he knows I'm there.

He always glares at me, as he does now. His brows furrow inward and his eyes narrow, the expression fierce and his scar looking angry. Then his gaze moves on, and he barely looks at me again for the rest of the evening.

Hell, last night, he stood five feet from me while a customer leaned over the bar and tried to grab my boob. One of the other bouncers across the room saw it and moved in to take action. When I cut my gaze over to Cain, he just stared at me a moment with hard eyes and turned his back on me, clearly giving me the message he didn't even care enough about me to do his job.

Cain walks down the length of the bar, nodding at a few other patrons, and disappears in the back kitchen area. That's also been his pattern the last three nights, as he routinely shows up at work at least ten minutes early and then hides from me until his shift starts. With a sigh, I finish wiping down the bar and check with the existing customers to see if they need refills. It's early yet and only three people sit at the main bar, but in about an hour, it will start to fill up.

"That is one sexy ass man," Tina says behind me. She's new here too, although she's been here a few weeks longer than I have. Her eyes stay pinned on the door that Cain just went through. "I wonder what it would take to catch his attention."

"Punch a guy in the face," I mutter under my breath.
"What?"

"Nothing," I say with a smile. "I think he's gay. At

least that's the rumor I heard."

Tina's face falls with disappointment, but then her eyes flick over my shoulder and light back up. "Or what about him? I've heard rumors from some of the other waitresses that he's a beast."

I turn around and see Bridger walking out of his office. Yeah… he's a beast alright, but I'm not going to let her know. Besides, I have a feeling that the only ones who get to play with Bridger are the ones he chooses and not vice versa.

He walks to the end of the bar and jerks his chin at me, indicating he wants a word. Tina sighs loudly and I leave her behind, making my way down to him.

"What's up?" I ask him.

"Just checking in to see how things are going," he says as he leans both elbows on the bar. "Haven't had a chance to talk since you started."

"I'm really enjoying the work," I tell him honestly. "Thanks again for the job."

"Yeah, no problem," he says with a wave of his hand. "But I was talking about Cain."

I look at the swing-through kitchen door over my shoulder and sigh. "Well… it seems he glared at me for maybe two seconds less than yesterday, so that's improvement, right?"

Bridger cocks an eyebrow at me. "Well… what does he have to say?"

"Say?"

"Yeah… you've talked to him, right?"

SAWYER BENNETT

"No," I say, blinking at him stupidly. "He doesn't want to talk to me."

"Well, no shit, Sherlock. You're going to have to press the issue with him. He's not just going to wake up and everything will be fine."

I don't like his pissy attitude, especially since this has been tough on me. Watching the man who has my heart in a chokehold look at me with nothing but distaste, living in a strange place with no friends, and worrying myself sick about what hell my actions will bring down on my mom is hard. Not a day goes by that I don't consider packing it up and heading home to Tennessee.

It's what my mom would like even if she doesn't come right out and say so. I told her pretty much what had happened as I had to prepare her for the article if Brant chooses to run it. So far, he hasn't, but I'm just waiting for it to hit any day now. And I really should be home with her if that happens.

But I also told my mom about Cain and my feelings for him, and she's been supportive of me staying here a bit to see if I can make amends.

"When am I supposed to have this big talk with him?" I sarcastically ask Bridger. "It's not like this place is conducive to a serious talk, and I'm pretty sure he'll shoot me if I come on his property."

"It's pretty quiet in here right now," Bridger says while giving me a pointed look.

"Right now?"

"Do I need to repeat it?"

"But I'm working," I say.

"Then take a fucking break, Sloane. It's not rocket science."

I roll my eyes and say, "At the risk of getting fired, you are one complicated man."

"Lucky for you, I'm a fucking romantic at heart."

"Yeah... you are no more a romantic than my ex-boyfriend who thought the act of bringing me a six-pack before a date would earn him brownie points, but I appreciate your zeal for others to find happiness."

Bridger just cocks an eyebrow at me.

"Fine," I say as I throw the towel on the counter below the bar. "I'll take a break. But if I'm not back in ten minutes, you better send a posse out to dig for my body."

"Good girl," he murmurs and pushes away from the bar to head back to his office, but not before giving a jerk of his chin toward Tina. Apparently, he's decided to play with her, and since there are two other bartenders to watch over things, Tina scurries out from behind the countertop and follows him back to his office.

Taking a deep breath, I head for the kitchen.

When I walk through the swinging door, my gaze sweeps the room for Cain. I don't see him and ask Frank, one of the cooks, "Seen Cain around?"

"Went out the side door a few minutes ago," he says, nodding his head toward the emergency exit.

I square my shoulders and head that way.

As soon as I push the door open, the cool August air

hits me and I cross my arms to ward off the chill. August evenings in Tennessee are warm and humid, but it gets chilly here at this time of year.

My head immediately swivels to the right where I see Cain leaning up against the wall, looking at something on his phone. His head snaps up with a semi-friendly expression, but when he sees it's me, his lips flatten out.

"What do you want?" he mutters.

"To talk to you," I say.

"Don't want to hear anything you have to say," he retorts.

"Well, tough shit. Man up and put your listening ears on."

Cain pushes off the wall and takes a step to move past me, so I blurt out, "I saw your mom today."

Cain stops, straightens to his full height, and squares his shoulders at me. "What?"

"I saw your mom. Went in for a manicure. While I couldn't tell her details, I told her that I hurt you and I was very sorry for it. I apologized for hurting her son."

He stares at me with his mouth slightly agape, gives a small shake of his head, and goes to move past me. So I tell him, "You walk away from me, I'll just follow you through the bar and continue to talk. Then everyone will know our business."

Spinning on me, he growls, "You and I have no business together. You are nothing but a bad memory."

Okay, that really hurts, and I involuntarily rub my knuckles across my sternum to alleviate the ache.

"Okay… I deserve that. But I also deserve to have you hear me out."

"You don't deserve it."

"Callie, Bridger, Woolf, and your mom seemed to think I did."

Cain snorts. "Just because they did doesn't mean I'm stupid."

"Come on, Cain," I plead with him. "You owe me."

"Why would you think that?" he asks incredulously.

"Because I sacrificed a lot for you," I snap at him.

"You sacrificed for me?" he scoffs.

"Yes," I say firmly. "I put my family at risk, and I lost a good job because of you. In the end, I gave up everything for you and Callie. The least you can do is listen to what I have to say."

For a fraction of a second, I think he's going to roll his eyes and stomp past me, but then he crosses his arms over his chest and watches me with silent but skeptical eyes. It's enough of a reprieve that I take a quick breath and push forward while I have his attention.

"I'm really sorry for what I did. My intentions were never to hurt anyone—only to gain the truth. But once I found out there wasn't a truth, I realized I had to do the right thing. From very early on, I was constantly trying to figure a way out that would protect everyone."

"Your letter said that," he says flatly and takes a step toward the door. "Anything else?"

"Yes," I whisper. "I really care for you. I miss you."

His eyes flicker back and forth between my own, and

I can tell he's actually considering my words. But then his irises lighten to a cool green, and he dismisses me while reaching for the door. "Wish I could say the same."

The stab that pierces my heart this time brings a prickle of tears to my eyes. He takes notice of the sheen, locks his jaw tight, and turns away from me as he pulls the door open.

"I'm not giving up," I desperately tell his retreating back. "I'm sticking around until you forgive me."

He doesn't respond, and the door closes in my face. I wait a few minutes, blinking my eyes to dry them. Sucking in a quavering breath, I let it out slowly. That so did not go how I'd hoped, and went worse than I could have imagined. The futility of trying to chip through the concrete surrounding his heart hits me hard, exhaustion permeating my very core.

With fatigue of the soul threatening an impending breakdown, I walk back into the kitchen, back through the service door, and hang a left toward Bridger's office. I'm just... done.

Cain is nowhere to be seen, but that's not important. I tried, and I failed, and it's time to cut loose Jackson, Wyoming.

Just as I reach Bridger's office door, it opens and Tina walks out with a glazed look in her eyes, dabbing at the corners of her mouth. I see Bridger just behind her fastening his buckle. His eyes lock on mine, and he gives me a mischievous grin.

I stand to the side and let Tina pass, then look back

to Bridger for permission to come in. He gives me a smile and heads behind his desk.

"That was fast," he observes, noting my conversation with Cain lasted no more than ten minutes.

"You too," I throw back at him.

"What can I say… Tina's got a mouth on her."

I roll my eyes, because I do not need to imagine Bridger getting a quick blow job from my co-worker. I most certainly don't feel like listening to her talk about it tonight.

"So what happened?" he asks as he kicks his feet on top of his desk.

"I apologized, told him I cared about him. He told me he didn't feel the same."

"Ouch," Bridger says as he winces.

"Yeah… and I'm tired of my heart hurting over him, so I'm cutting my losses and heading home. I'll continue to work until you can find a replacement for me."

Bridger waves a dismissive hand. "I could replace you in ten minutes if I needed, but you're not leaving yet."

"Yes, I am, Bridger," I say tiredly, my voice cracking. "It's no use. He's not going to forgive me, and even if he did, he's never going to look at me the same. I've ruined it, and there's no redemption for me."

"Well, you're clearly not seeing what I'm seeing," he says with a knowing look.

I roll my eyes, refusing to believe that the all-knowing, all-seeing Bridger has something for me to pin my hope on.

"That man can't take his eyes off you these last few nights."

"He never looks at me," I argue.

"When you're busy and your attention isn't on him, he's watching you like a hawk. And his gaze is hungry and regretful and wistful. Trust me, I know."

I shake my head in denial. "Then figure a way for him to get over this. Because clearly, my words aren't doing anything."

"Something more than words is needed," Bridger ponders as he flips his feet off the desk and opens a side drawer. He rifles through a folder and pulls out a single sheet of paper. "I offer to certain employees a silver membership to The Silo. I'm giving you one now, and you'll need to sign this non-disclosure agreement."

"What?" I ask in disbelief. "I don't want a membership there."

"Yes, you do," he says firmly. "Cain needs something to prompt him to action, and seeing you in there will work. Trust me."

"You want me to go there and have sex with someone else?" I ask in astonishment.

"No, darling," he replies in a dry voice and as if I said something completely stupid. "You just need to act like that's what you're going to do."

"Trick him?" I ask dubiously.

"Prompt him," he counter argues.

"It won't work." But God... what if it does? What if that's just what's needed? A faint glimmer of hope flares within me, and I take a step toward his desk as he hands out a pen for me to sign the document.

I take it from him, bend over the desk, and start to read the agreement. But then I raise my eyes to Bridger's and whisper, "Has he been... you know... to The Silo since we broke up?"

Bridger's eyes go soft with sympathy, and he gives me an assured smile. "No. Only to walk through on his normal shifts here each night. He didn't even ask to take the rape fantasy with Amy back."

I let out a huge gust of relieved air and hastily scribble my name to the document without reading it. I don't need to know what it says, as I'd never reveal the club to anyone. Not even at the risk of my mother.

"Alright," he says with a devious grin. "Operation Slap Cain Upside the Head will commence tomorrow evening. Take the night off and be at The Silo at ten PM. I'll meet you there to give you the security fob to get you in."

"Okay," I say shakily. I can do this. I know I can.

"And Sloane," Bridger says ominously.

"Yeah?"

"Dress in your sexiest outfit. Preferably no underwear. You're going to need everything in your arsenal to get this hardheaded cuss to bend."

I grin at him in wicked delight. "That, I can do."

Chapter 29

Cain

TAKING A DEEP breath, I pull the door open to The Wicked Horse. I steel myself for the fourth night in a row that I'll have to watch Sloane all night, wondering what could have been and how I could have been so easily fooled. I would think my decision to keep my walls up would make it easier, but it isn't. Every night that I can catch the smallest of glimpses of her behind the bar tears my insides up. I want her so fucking bad on a physical level that I'm constantly walking around with a half-hard dick. I've jacked off several times, all to her memory… almost swearing I can smell her shampoo when I come all over my hand.

When I'm not obsessing about having sex with her, I'm replaying every single moment we spent together.

Every conversation, trying to see what I was missing.

Every touch she put upon me to try to figure out if there was truth or facade in the action.

It's driving me fucking bonkers.

Callie is also driving me fucking bonkers.

She called me last night, wanting to check in and see how I was doing. My voice was flat when I told her I was fine. She said, "Bullshit," and then proceeded to lay into me for not giving Sloane a chance. I listened to her for about thirty seconds, and then I hung up. She called me back, but I ignored her.

She then sent me a single text that said, *Asshole.*

Yup... that's me.

My eyes sweep the interior of The Wicked Horse, and with a sense of excitement that I actually hate about myself, I look to the bar to take in the beauty of Sloane Preston.

Except she's not there.

I swivel my head back and forth, checking out the club again, but I don't see her. Walking up to the bar, I tap my hand on the counter and ask the other new bartender, Tina, "Where's Sloane?"

"Hey boyfriend," she says in a singsong voice. *What the fuck?* Does she think I'm gay? "She's got tonight off."

"Oh," I say, and it's not lost on me the keen sense of disappointment I feel. Shaking my head, I push away from the bar and head toward the kitchen, intent on trying to just do my job tonight and hopefully go more than two minutes without thinking about the not-so-sweet-and-innocent Sloane Preston.

IT'S ABOUT 10:30 PM, and the club is packed. The nightly wet t-shirt contest just finished and yeah... I enjoyed watching that. In fact, it makes me start thinking

I need to get back in the saddle. It's time to start fucking Sloane out of my memory, and I should actually have Bridger put me back on the fantasy list. If I can't have Sloane and all the things that seemed to promise a new life of happiness, might as well get back to doing what I do best.

Speaking of Bridger, my attention is caught by the back exit door opening that leads out to The Silo. He steps through. Pulling it firmly shut, he starts to head toward his office. I step away from my post, knowing my guys will cover, and make my way toward him.

Just as he's punching in the code, he catches my movement and looks at me with a smile. "What's up, dude?"

Bridger opens the door, and I follow him in. "Not much. Everything's pretty tame tonight."

"That's good," he says and then proceeds to sit behind his desk, leaning forward to look at his laptop. "Need something?"

"Yeah," I say as I scratch at the back of my neck. *Just say it. Just tell him.* "I want to get back on the fantasy maker list."

Bridger's head snaps up, and he gives me a smile. "Sure thing. Plenty of people will be happy about that."

Then why don't I feel happy about it?

"Okay, cool," I say, hedging for a bit of time. Bridger's attention goes back to the laptop.

I shift my weight from foot to foot, and he looks back up at me. "You need something else?"

"Um… just wondering how Sloane's working out," I say lamely. Internally wincing, I hope I don't sound like a fucking moron.

Bridger's eyes light up, and he nods at me. "She's doing great. A real whiz behind the bar. It was a good decision to hire her."

"Think she'll stick around?"

Bridger shrugs. "Maybe. She's a hard worker and dedicated. It's why I insisted she take a night off."

"Oh," I say, not sure what that means. But then he enlightens me.

"In fact," Bridger says slyly, "I gave her a silver membership as sort of a bonus. Thanks to you inviting me to your little fantasy with her, I knew she'd appreciate something like that."

"You did what?" I bark at him as I straighten my spine, my hands curling into fists.

"Yeah… she seemed a little unsure of it, but she's a feisty girl. She's over there now; I think psyching herself up to walk on the wild side. Rand and Logan are over there, fawning all over her."

What the ever-loving fuck was he thinking?

"Are you okay?" Bridger asks with an innocent look on his face.

"No, I'm not fucking okay," I snap as I turn on my heel and stomp out of his office.

It takes my long legs no time at all to eat up the distance from Bridger's office to The Silo. I pull out my fob, read the number, and then punch in the security code so hard that one of the buttons jams, but I don't give it a second thought. I fling the door open and storm inside, prepared to... what?

I have no fucking clue.

When I enter the open interior, my eyes scan the crowd, which is very busy this Friday night, and immediately see Sloane sitting at the bar. And for fuck's sake, she looks like a Wanted Poster for Sin on a Stick.

Cherry-red dress that is painted onto her body, strapless and barely covering her tits. It rides up high on her thighs as she sits at the bar, one leg crossed over the other. Matching red, high-heeled sandals with red ribbons that wind up her legs, and bright red lipstick that I'd love to have smeared all over my cock and her face after a hardcore mouth-fucking.

Rand stands to one side of Sloane as she sips at a drink, and his hand strokes her bare shoulder. Logan stands on her other side, elbow on the bar and his lips near her ear, whispering something utterly fucking dirty I bet.

Rage clouds my vision as I push my way through the crowd, not being nice if someone gets in my way. Logan sees me first, his eyebrows rising up and a shit-eating grin on his face. He says something, and Rand turns his head toward me, also with the same smirk. His hand drops from Sloane's shoulder, and he takes a step back from her.

Smart guy.

Sloane must sense me because her spine stiffens, and

she turns on the stool to face me. Her eyes rake down my body, and her eyes give me a shy smile of welcome.

Not buying it.

My hand shoots out and grabs her upper arm. I pull her from the stool and she wobbles on those high heels, Rand's own hand going out to steady her.

"Touch her and I'll cut it off," I growl without even looking at him. The fucker snickers, but his arm drops to his side.

I lean my face down near hers, my eyes pinning her with fury. "Do you want it so bad you'll just jump in the next guy's bed?"

She shakes her head emphatically, those blonde curls flying back and forth. "No… I only want you."

I give a bark of a skeptical laugh and start pulling her away from the bar, through the crowd and out the exit door. When the night air hits us, I hiss at her, "You're getting in your car and going home."

Sloane steps off the slate paver outside the door and digs those heels into the dirt. Her arm jerks free, and she says, "I'm not going home."

"Well, you're not going back in there," I flatly tell her.

"Then take me out here," she whispers.

Every cell in my body swells with lust, even as a fissure of anger ripples through me. "You'd like that, wouldn't you?" I sneer at her, trying to shame her for her wanton ways, but Christ… I want her so damn bad.

"With you," she says earnestly. "Only you."

I take a deep breath, and I have to ask, "Is this a set-up?"

In the glow of the light outside the Silo door, I can see her cheeks turn red. But she looks me straight in the eye, "Yes. Bridger's idea to spur you into action. I went along with it."

"Fuck," I mutter as I look back toward The Wicked Horse.

That asshole. Putting temptation right in front of me, knowing damn well I'll let my cock speak its own mind.

"So, you want me to just fuck you out here?" I put enough of a shaming sneer in my words to have her blushing again.

"I'd prefer you take me back to your house, but if all I can get of you is out here, then yes. Wherever you want. However you want it."

I might have been good had she said something different. I might have even had the balls to walk away from her sexy body and yearning eyes.

But however I want it?

Unfortunately, I want it hard and fast, and I want it right this fucking minute. My options are limited, and I quickly weigh them.

Back into The Silo where I can pull her into the supply room again.

Or even better to possibly shame her, right into one of the rooms so I can fuck her for the entire club to see, and then walk away from her.

But no, those aren't right either.

Because the way in which I'm about to sacrifice my principals demands privacy.

So I take Sloane's hand and lead her around the side of The Silo. I walk her halfway around the circular outer structure, until we are in absolute darkness with nothing around us.

Turning her from me, I have her face the concrete building. Grabbing both of her hands, I place the palms against the staves. I step into her backside, press my lips to her ear, and whisper, "I can have you any way I want?"

She takes in a shaky breath and nods. "Yes."

Dropping my hands, I take the edge of her skirt and pull it over her hips where it hugs her waist and stays out of my way thanks to the miracle of spandex. I tilt my head to the right and look at her in the glow of the moonlight.

No fucking underwear.

Goddamn perfect.

I drop my hand to that sweetly rounded ass, push my middle finger down in between her cheeks, and rub my finger along the seam. She moans and jerks against me.

"Can I have your ass tonight? Would you give that to me, sweet Sloane?"

She chokes out a half sob, half moan and murmurs, "If that's what you want?"

My cruel, black heart… the one that's still hurt and betrayed, gives a soft laugh that borders on evil. "Nah… that was something special we might have had, but I'm just not that interested in it anymore."

Which is a fucking lie. If I had some lube, I'd so take her ass, but without it, I don't want to risk hurting her. And besides… that would take time and I don't have that luxury. This is going to be a hard, fast, impersonal fucking so I can give some relief to my balls, which have been squashed into knots since first locking eyes on her tonight.

I pull my head back and angle it further to the side so I can look at Sloane's face. She has her cheek pressed up against the side of the wall and there are unshed tears pooling.

And damn if I don't feel guilty that I just hurt her feelings.

"Shhh," I shush her gently, dropping my right hand and bringing it around the front of her body. I slide my fingers between her legs, letting them brush back and forth lightly against her pussy, which is slick and inviting. "Don't cry, Sloane. I'll make this good for you."

She blinks, and a single tear spills. I can't fucking stand it, so I sink a finger into her and she moans sweetly.

"Yeah… that feels good, right?" I murmur.

My left hand goes to her strapless top. Pushing it down, I free her breasts and palm one. I rub the pad of my index finger over a nipple while my finger below presses into her deeper.

"What do you want Sloane?" I ask her nicely, imagining all the ways in which I could fuck her right now.

"Tell me what you want and I'll give it to you."

She takes in a shuddering breath, lifts her cheek away from the wall, and cranes her neck to look at me. Her eyes still shining with wet, she says, "I want you to forgive me."

My cock leaps in response to those words, or perhaps just at the thought of getting inside that tight wetness, but the asshole in me comes through. I prepare to tell her that's never going to happen, but then she takes the wind out of my sails.

"Please," she begs. "Please forgive me."

With her nipple pinched between my forefinger and thumb and my finger lodged deep inside her, I think for a desperate moment.

Perhaps I should forgive her.

But the words are jammed deep in my throat.

So instead, I kiss her.

Chapter 30

Sloane

WHEN HIS MOUTH claims mine, I sigh deeply and melt in relief. He didn't say the words I needed, but surely... this kiss... it means something, right?

His tongue rolls deeply in my mouth, my neck straining to keep the perfect angle so that he doesn't break away. I push my hips back, seeking more contact with his body, and he groans when my ass rubs up against his erection.

Pulling his mouth away, breathing hard, Cain's hands go to my hips. He takes a step back, pulling me along with him just a fraction. One strong hand goes to the middle of my back.

"Bend over," he rasps out.

My lips still tingling from that kiss, and my blood racing through my veins, I do as he commands, knowing that the deeper I bend over, the more my ass is tipped just right to him. I brace my hands hard against the concrete wall.

For a moment, his hands are gone and I hear the unmistakable sound of his zipper coming down. I take in a deep breath and push it out roughly when I feel the head of his cock at my entrance. He pushes in slightly, curses under his breath, and his hands are back at my hips.

My fingertips dig into the concrete wall, and I close my eyes tight.

With a roll of his hips, he slowly pushes into me. He doesn't stop and slides in deep until his pelvis is pressed against my ass and the zipper to his jeans digs into my skin.

"Oh, Christ… Sloane," he mutters, his breath huffing out over my upper back.

He feels so good.

So very right.

"Cain," I murmur, hopefully conveying with that single word what this moment means to me.

Holding me steady at my hips, Cain pulls back and sinks back into me, his cock dragging against every sensitive nerve I have and producing a full-body shudder.

"You like that?" he asks gruffly.

"God, yes," I say on a moan. "Do it again."

"Greedy," he mutters, but I can actually hear a smile on those words.

Pulling out, he slides back in with exquisite care. He does it again, and again, not seeming to be in a hurry. I'm not in a rush either, wanting to savor every single moment of him being locked inside me. This may be my last chance, and I don't want to forget anything.

Cain pulls out. With a rough jerk against my hips, he slams in, the slapping of our skin breaking the quiet night.

"Fuck yeah," he groans and picks up the pace. I drop my face and stare at the ground, the tips of my red heels peeking up at me and my breasts swaying with the motion of his increased thrusting.

I rotate my hips, try to draw him in deeper. My breathing becomes shallow and labored, my body tightening as I race closer to orgasm. And then Cain hunches his body over me. He slides one hand around my front, going between my legs. His fingers pluck at my clit while he tunnels in and out of me. The other hand comes up, circles around my neck, and he pulls me up slightly.

Placing his lips near my ear, without ever missing a beat of his pumping cock, he murmurs. "Not going to lie, Sloane. I missed fucking this pussy."

While his voice rumbles richly, the words are designed to let me know that the sex is the only thing he's interested in about me. That cuts deep, yet I can't seem to find my own voice to deny it. I want to call him a liar and tell him we had so much more, but every time he hits me deep, my brain starts to get fuzzier and fuzzier.

He keeps talking, a weird mix of sexual heat and frozen taunts.

Not sure I'll find better than this, but one can hope.

I'm going to come in you so deep, you'll be feeling me for the rest of your life.

And my absolute favorite, *I'll hate myself for it, but I'll jack off to this memory of tonight for some time to come.*

Finally, he shuts up, and it's a good thing too because I want to slap him for ruining this. His bitter feelings and acerbic words are starting to cause darkness to well up inside of me. I almost have the fortitude to pull away, but then his finger presses roughly against my clit and he slams into me hard.

His voice breaks when he says, "Christ... you fucking destroy me, Sloane."

My orgasm tears free, refusing to be quelled, and it explodes out in homage to the explosive passion between us, no matter how much hurt resides there. Cain pulls out, pushes back in roughly, and then starts to shudder as he comes. His forehead comes to rest on the back of my head, he grinds his pelvis against me, and he whispers, "Fucking destroyed."

My tears well back up again. I blink once and they fall down my cheeks, stream past my jaw, and drip onto his hand. I suck in a breath and tell him, "I'm destroyed too."

Cain's body tightens, and he breathes out a regretful sigh. Placing his lips at the back of my head, he gives me a soft kiss. I feel hope start to swell within me.

Releasing his hold on my throat and pulling his other hand out from between my legs, Cain straightens and slides free from me. I immediately feel his semen start to run out of me, a poignant reminder that we once again shared a deep intimacy by having unprotected sex.

I straighten up, awkwardly pushing my skirt down and then pulling the stretchy material over my breasts.

When I turn to face him, I find him tucking his dick back in his pants and zipping up.

Finally, he raises his gaze and looks at me with sad eyes. "I forgive you, Sloane. I understand you were doing a job and that you ultimately sacrificed it."

A smile breaks out on my face, and I take a wobbly step toward him. His hands come up, palms out to hold me off, and he takes a step back from me.

Shaking his head, his eyes turn hard. "But there's nothing else between us."

"No," I say immediately. "That's not true. Didn't you feel it?"

"I felt an amazing fucking orgasm," he says, his bitterness evident. "But that's all. God help me, Sloane, I trust what your body can do for me. That was never in question. But it's the only part of you I trust, and that's just not enough for me."

"But—"

"I have to get back to work," he says, giving me a nod of farewell. "Take care of yourself."

"Cain," I say desperately, tears now falling freely again. "Please… give us a chance."

He doesn't respond, just melts into the darkness.

THE NEXT SEVEN hours are a blur.

I make my way on shaky legs from the back of The Silo to the parking lot, twisting my ankle no less than three times on the uneven gravel playing havoc with my four-inch heels. The pain is barely noticeable as the intense squeeze of heartbreak has my full attention.

It takes me just a little over thirty minutes to drive to my apartment. Another five online and I have a ticket booked out of Jackson leaving at 7:31 AM, connecting through Denver and then on to Nashville.

It takes me twenty minutes to shower, dry my hair, and put on my pajamas.

Another hour and I have my measly possessions packed.

Four hours of tossing and turning in bed with fits of tears that I refuse to let fall but which keep my throat clogged with emotion.

Red eyes and exhaustion making people do a double take as I walk through the small, rustic airport toward security.

A quick text to Callie, because she's the only one who will truly care, and besides… other than Cain, I don't have anyone else's phone number. *I'm getting ready to board a plane. Going home. I'm sorry again for everything. Will you let Bridger know? I didn't know how to get up with him this early in the morning.*

Callie… ever the early riser, texted back within moments. *Why? What happened? I can come there, and we can talk.*

My text back. *No, it's okay. This is the right thing to do. Take care of yourself. I'm sorry again.*

I turned my phone off before she could text back.

The plane boarded, and I slept all the way to Denver.

Drank three cups of coffee while I waited for my layover and had an extreme case of the jitters on the flight to Nashville.

Called my mom when I landed, cried, and told her I'd be home soon. She cried too. I refused to look at my text messages and turned my phone back off.

Rented a car and drove the hour and a half to my mom's house in Sewanee.

Made it home by four PM, and by five, I was on the couch with my mom, telling her everything that happened.

We cried together.

Chapter 31

Cain

I STRUT INTO The Silo, a man on a mission.

This is the only way to get Sloane out of my mind. I need to make a complete break, and that means giving up the last vestige of a tie with her. That means I need to fuck someone else, so I can get back to being me.

Once I fuck someone else, I can stop replaying in my mind every tiny detail of what happened last night. The weird feeling I had when I didn't see her behind the bar when I walked into The Wicked Horse. The astonishment when Bridger told me she was in The Silo. The rage seeing Logan and Rand look at her with hunger. The look of happiness on her face when she saw me.

The fucking way she told me she only wanted me.

And the way she felt so fucking right with my world when I sank into her.

Yeah, all of that shit has to go. Time to vacate it out of my mind and get back to living life.

The crack of a whip catches my immediate attention as I step into the common circular area. My head swivels in the direction of the sound and I see Bridger in one of the rooms, working a woman over with a four-foot single tail whip while she's mounted to a St. Andrew's cross. He's wearing nothing but a pair of jeans and a sheen of sweat as he lands another precise strike on her ass, which is crosshatched with red stripes. She's stoically silent when the leather strikes, but her back arches in pain.

Bridger is an artist with his implements, and I've watched him make people come with just a few well-placed lashes to their delicate skin. I don't understand people who need pain to get off, but there's no denying… it's erotic as hell to watch.

I turn my back on the show, vaguely hearing two more cracks before I get up to the bar. I order a Hoback Hefeweizen, take a seat on a stool, and turn out toward the common area to take stock of the pickings.

Catherine is here, wearing a romantic-looking dress made of white silk and lace, baring her shoulders. Her dark hair is long, wavy, and she's wearing a single white daisy tucked behind her ear. My dick twitches a tiny bit as I realize she's going for the sweet, innocent look tonight, meaning she wants to get sullied up good by whoever fucks her.

Maybe.

But then again, I should stay away from sweet and innocent reminders tonight. Too much like Sloane.

A scream echoes out from the room where Bridger is working the woman over, and I see her entire body shaking as she moans in ecstasy. Bridger drops the whip to the floor, walks over to her, and removes the restraints at her wrists and ankles. She sinks down to the floor, smiling up at him in gratitude, and he gives her a curt nod. That's about as touchy feely as Bridger gets when he's doling out his kink.

I watch as he walks over to a bench, picks up a black t-shirt, and pulls it over his head, straightening it down over the flocks of blackbirds on his torso. He walks out of the room without a backward glance, disappears a moment as he traverses the back hall, and then appears from the exit hallway.

He makes eye contact with me immediately, and his lips tip upward in silent welcome.

See… even he knows that I need to get back in the saddle so to speak.

Bridger walks across the room, completely oblivious to the hungry stares that follow after him by men and women alike. But most will never have him because he's choosy and he's expensive. While most acts of debauchery that occur within these rounded walls are part of the membership fee, those who want a crack at Bridger have to pay big bucks. And that's not prostitution because he doesn't have sex with those paying customers. Nope, he just reddens their skin, sometimes drawing blood if that's what they require, and they happily hand over their hard-earned bucks for a momentous orgasm brought on by the sting of leather.

"Nice to see you join us," Bridger says drily as he takes a seat next to me. I spin my stool back around, so we're both facing the interior of the round bar. Bridger nods at one of the bartenders, who knows to bring him a bottle of sparkling water, his preferred drink after working up a sweat.

"It's time," I say simply and take a sip of my beer. At least that's what my brain says, but my dick might be saying something else. While it might have given a tiny twitch at thinking of Catherine a moment ago, I think that was more of a reaction to her similarity to Sloane in that moment than anything. And even watching Bridger play is usually guaranteed to get me half-hard, but I'm as soft as a goose-down pillow right now.

No worries though. I'm in no rush to get my rocks off tonight. In fact, I plan on taking my time about it, making sure it counts. Making sure it finally obliterates all of these awful feelings swirling inside of me, especially when I think of Sloane crying last night.

And Christ... even though the words felt right, why did it hurt so much to walk away from her? Why did I feel like I was leaving something important behind? Something that felt a little bit like myself.

I take a longer pull on my beer, swallow it, and then take another. Maybe I need to just get drunk instead.

"Charles Mason is back from his work trip," Bridger says offhandedly, as if it's just another day at the office discussing business. "Wanted to know if you wanted to get together with him and Amy this week. In one of the fantasy cabins."

"Yeah, sure," I say distractedly, and then take another mouthful of beer. I swallow hard and set the glass down. "Whatever."

"Well, try not to be so excited," he says blandly.

I blink at him in surprise and try to put on my best high school cheerleader voice while I clasp my hands in front of my chest. "Well, yay... of course I'd just love too, Mr. Payne."

"Smartass," he grumbles with a smirk.

"Welcome back, dickweed," I hear as two hands slap onto my shoulders. I turn slightly and see Rand behind me, his fingers digging into my muscles briefly before releasing his hold. Logan comes up on the other side of Bridger and takes a seat.

"Assume no hard feelings?" Logan asks as he gives me a sly grin. "It looks like things worked out well for you last night, right?"

"What happened last night?" Bridger asks with mild curiosity as he looks at Logan.

"Miss Bonham here got his panties in a twist when he caught us flirting with Sloane last night," Rand says with a mocking laugh from my left.

Bridger's head swings the other way to look at him briefly before cutting to me. "That right?"

I refuse to answer because I don't want these guys ragging on me about my overt display of jealous proprie-ty last night. It's something I prefer not to dwell on, especially since it was so out of character for me in normal circumstances, and just completely fucking weird given the fact I couldn't stand Sloane.

Well, yeah... I can stand her. Hunger for her actual-ly. But I was furious with her and wanted nothing to do with her. So it was just fucking weird last night.

"Oh, yeah," Rand tells Bridger whose eyes slide past me to listen. "Came in here, dragged her out all caveman style. Never came back so I assume Little Bonham saw some hot action last night and Miss Sloane had a satisfied smile on her face today."

I don't miss the change of emotion on Bridger's face, because he goes from mild interest to outright anger. He turns that gaze back on me and says, "What the fuck did you do to her?"

I rear backward slightly from the menace he projects, but I stand my ground. "What the fuck does that mean? And what's with the 'tude?"

"I wasn't sure what the hell happened, but now it's clear... you must have done something to send her scurrying," Bridger says with ice practically falling off his tongue.

"Scurrying?" I say dumbly, having no idea what in the hell he's talking about.

"Back home... to Tennessee. She texted Callie this morning from the airport that she was leaving. Callie and Woolf went by her apartment, and it's empty."

"She's gone?" I murmur, my tongue feeling numb as it says the words.

"Yeah, she's gone," Bridger mutters. "And I'd like to know what the fuck you did to send her running."

My mind spins and fuck... I feel a little dizzy. Now, whether I would have actually gone through with fucking someone tonight is beyond me at this point, but I do know one thing as I sit here contemplating what I've just learned. I never in a million years thought Sloane would be gone. I just assumed she would stick around and continue to work on me. I can't say as I hated what happened between us last night.

Oh, who the fuck am I kidding? I fucking loved every nut-blowing moment of what we did. So much so, I think subconsciously I was sort of banking on it happening again, maybe even secretly hoping that my walls would get chipped away with every orgasm we wrung out of each other.

Yeah... no way in hell am I'm ready to fuck someone else tonight, I think with total clarity.

"Cain," Bridger barks and I startle, raising my eyes from my beer to him.

"I didn't do anything," I grit out. "I fucked her... she enjoyed it. I left."

"Try again," he commands.

"I told her I forgave her, but that there wasn't anything between us anymore. I left right after...went back to work."

"Well, no wonder she fucking left," Rand says quietly.

"You're kind of a prick," Logan adds on. "She's a sweet girl too. Wouldn't have minded—"

"Say another fucking word of that thought," I growl at Logan, "and I'll rip your tonsils out."

Logan's mouth snaps shut, and he glares at me.

"And why the fuck are you all taking her side?" I

grumble, my eyes coming to rest on each of their faces in turn. "She's a snake in the grass. A liar. A betrayer."

"Dude, you have got to get ahold of your tender sensibilities," Bridger mocks me. "That girl came to Jackson with a serious agenda—an insatiable fire lighting her sense of justice. You ended up tilting her world in just a matter of a few days. In just that short period of time, she gave up vengeance and justice all for you and Callie. She apologized. She made it right. And if I know Sloane, and I'm betting I do, that girl probably poured her heart out to you in an effort to have you care for her again, and you left her standing in a puddle of tears. She's got a soul made of pure gold, and you're a fucking moron who chased it away."

Vengeance? Justice? What the hell is he talking about?

But I can't think about that now because guilt overwhelms me. That's exactly what happened, and while I might have felt a twinge of it last night, it's oppressive to me now. Still, I'm not ready to go down without a clean fight, and I need one of them to at least admit to me that I have a right to feel betrayed and angry about this.

It would really help if one of my fucking friends had my back just a tiny bit.

So I try to explain myself better. "I get that she was in a bad situation, and I get that she pretty quickly realized what she was doing was wrong. I even understand that ultimately, she made everything right, and for that, I forgive her. But I'm sorry... she should have come clean sooner, especially when I… when she… when we started having feelings. If she would have just cut the deception a little sooner, it would have been easier to bear."

"She couldn't," Bridger says. "She had no choice."

I can't help the half-scoff, half-snort that comes out of my mouth and nose. It's not a pleasant sound, but it makes a point. Because she most certainly had a choice, and she chose badly. That's what I can't let go of.

"She was being blackmailed." The flat anger in Bridger's voice punches deep into my gut, and I don't doubt his words for a minute.

"Blackmailed?" I say incredulously.

"Yeah… her editor threatened to write a lurid article about her mom's most recent hospitalization and her past suicide attempts."

Again, I go dizzy and my confusion is like a thick puddle of goo within me. "Why in the fuck would her editor care about her mom's suicide attempts?"

"Because her mom was married to some senator who cheated on her and used government monies to fund his affair. The scandal destroyed her mom. It was the first time she tried to commit suicide. Her editor threatened to open the story back up if she didn't produce some type of evidence against Callie and the club."

Vengeance? Justice? It all makes sense now.

"Son of a bitch," I wheeze out, feeling like the air in my lungs went on hiatus. I press my fingers to my temples and squeeze my eyes shut. This is not fucking happening. "Why didn't she tell me?"

"She didn't want you to think she was making excuses. She thought just being honest about her mistake would be good enough."

"But she told you," I point out bitterly, opening my eyes and drilling Bridger with a heated look.

"True enough, but we'd pretty much made our peace with her before that," he says, and my guilt starts humming again.

"If she would have just said something…" I say, and my voice drifts off.

No, wait… that's not exactly right. If I look at this whole shit storm with an unjaundiced eye, it makes perfect sense Sloane didn't tell me. She's the type of person who owns up to her mistakes and she takes responsibility. I've always admired her integrity, and maybe that's why it hurt so much when I realized it might have been lacking. But yeah… I could see Sloane not bothering to tell me the entire situation, wanting me to forgive her on the merits of her personal remorsefulness for hurting me, not because someone was forcing her to do something bad.

"Christ," I mutter, pressing harder into my temples, my brain on overdrive. "Has that asshole editor run the story? Is that why she left to go home?"

"No, she left to go home because you're a moron who's a little slow on the uptake," Bridger says, his tone full of sarcasm. But then his eyes take on a wicked gleam, and he almost chortles when he says, "But that punk-ass won't be running it. I've managed to convince him otherwise."

I blink stupidly at Bridger. "How's that?"

"It's amazing what about five thousand will buy you in the way of a good investigator. Within two days of Sloane telling me about this prick, I'd found out that he had a secret young piece on the side and his wife had no clue."

"He was having an affair?" Rand asks with a laugh.

"With a man… a young congressional aide," Bridger says with glee. "I have the pictures to prove it, and what do you know? He backed right off Sloane."

That should make me happy. However, for some reason, it makes darkness well inside of me.

That Bridger was the one who protected her.

Saved her.

Believed in her.

Fuck… was everything I apparently was not, and it sickens me to my core over how stupid I've been.

I push up from the bar stool, pull my wallet out, and throw money on the bar for my beer and a tip. Bridger's eyebrows shoot up in a brief moment of surprise, which is odd because it's practically impossible to surprise him.

But then, he knowingly smiles at me and says, "Have a nice flight."

Chapter 32

Sloane

I PULL THE back of my hand across my forehead, wipe the sweat and layer of dust off, and huff out a hot breath. I'm not sure what possessed me to come up to my mom's attic and rummage through some of my old college boxes, but here I sit in my pajamas in a room that boasts at least a ninety-five-degree temperature and suffer while I work.

I suppose I'm filled with a displaced sense of nostalgia. Maybe a desire to look at things that took me back to a happier place in my life. That would be the summer between my sophomore and junior years at the University of Tennessee.

Before my dad got caught sticking his dick somewhere else.

Before our family got tied up in national scandal.

Before my mom tried to kill herself.

Those were the good days and so I'm reaching back out to them, desperately searching for some old photographs of my college buds and me, more than a few highlighting my skill at keg stands at various frat parties, but still... it was before my pure bubble of naivety and happiness was burst, and before I was set on a path that led me directly to Jackson, Wyoming and perhaps the biggest heartbreak of my life.

I also figured I'd pull out some old photos, maybe some knickknacks that provide good memories, and place them in the spare bedroom of my mom's house where I'm crashing for the moment. Of course, Mom has told me to stay as long as I want—well, her word was *forever* actually—but the point is… I have to figure out what to do with myself.

Don't get me wrong… I love Tennessee. It's my home state, and there is an innate level of comfort here. While this isn't my childhood home, this is where my mom has lived since she and my dad separated, and so it is now my home too. It would not be unrealistic of me to stay here, look for a job locally, and try to regroup.

But I love D.C. too. The hustle and bustle, the culture, a decent group of friends I made who weren't exactly besties but with whom I could go out and have a great time on the weekends. It was a good life. Granted, the career was apparently a shit decision, but I could see making D.C. my home. There's certainly more job opportunities there if I want to stay in journalism, although the notion of that is soured a bit for me. At this moment, I'm jaded enough to believe the media may actually be more evil than my father.

A sharp stab of longing courses through me as I regretfully consider Jackson, Wyoming. This past week, I had envisioned myself living there. Figured I'd quit

Revealed magazine, somehow salvage a relationship with Cain that was started on lies, and possibly get a job on the quaint local newspaper staff. There's no doubt Wyoming is the most beautiful place I've ever been, and I could totally see myself living there permanently. I mean… I wasn't completely sure about the winter, but figured it wouldn't be so bad being holed up with Cain during the cold and snowy times.

My pipe dreams were huge; my optimism unparalleled.

I was an idiot to think something so good that started with dishonesty could ever last. Why I even thought I should stay behind after my plot was exposed and try to "fix" things with Cain is beyond me. There's no way a man like Cain with his hard lines and bitter past would ever have let me back in. Not with someone like Rachel in his past who secretly aborted their baby and charged it off on an already overextended credit card, knowing that one day he'd learn the truth.

Evil, evil bitch and her actions were a big part of the reason I could never gain purchase with Cain after my betrayal.

The attic stairs creak and I can hear my mom climbing them. Her head pops up through the rectangular entrance in the floor, and she smiles at me. "What in the world are you doing?"

"Just going through some of my old college boxes," I tell her as I pull out a stack of old notebooks filled with scribbles commemorating boring lectures.

She climbs the rest of the way through, turns, and sits her butt on the wooden floor, legs dangling over the edge. My mom is a beautiful woman, and I'm not sure why my dad felt the need to go younger with bigger boobs. Maybe it was Fernanda's exotic accent or the fact she wears a belly button piercing, or maybe she just gives great head… who knows, but as much as I will admit my stepmom—and I gag when I think of her in that con-text—is a stunning woman, she just can't compare to my mother's graceful beauty. She's like a southern belle Grace Kelly with fine bone structure, luminescent blue eyes that I inherited, and a magnetism that always seemed to draw every person's gaze when she's in a crowded room. On the outside, she's funny, witty, charming, and bright. She can hold a conversation with any stranger, and her kindness and generosity knows no bounds.

On the inside, sure, she may be an emotional wreck, but unless she gets to her very dark place, you'd never know she has demons that randomly torture her. There's not a doubt in my mind that she was successful for the most part in keeping those demons at bay, but with the combination of the prescription pain pills, which she was using to self-medicate her emotional weaknesses, and my father's very public betrayal and subsequent scandal, she simply couldn't keep it together anymore. Now she has her good days and her bad, and I'm happy to say that since my return yesterday afternoon, her smile seems genuinely joyous and content.

Maybe I should just stay here and give life in a small, southern town a shot again.

"Feeling the need for a trip down memory lane?" she asks, leaning back on one arm and turning her body slightly to watch me. My mom is still in great shape, petite and luminescent. Maybe she'll find love again one day. Although, I hope she doesn't settle for it, hoping it will make her whole. That's no reason to be with someone.

I shrug. "Maybe just a few things that will help me remember a more peaceful time in my life."

"Ain't that the fucking truth?" she says with a grimace, and my eyes snap up from my notebook for a class I took called Crafting a Story in the Digital Market.

"Mom," I say in a drawled-out, admonishing tone.

She raises her eyebrows and looks at me innocently. "What?"

"You said the 'F' word."

"Fucking right I did," she says with a grin. "I'm an adult. I'm allowed to."

"But not to your daughter," I point out. "There are some things you just don't do as a mother."

"Oh, seriously, Sloane. Quit thinking of your mom as a prude," she says with a laugh. "Now… I'm going to go take a walk with Chester Cheetah. Want to come?"

Chester Cheetah is her three-pound Chihuahua. No clue where that name came from, but she loves that dog more than anything and spoils him just as much.

"I'm good," I tell her as I put the notebooks back in

the box, not finding anything that provides me with company. Just some now-wonky feelings about getting a degree that may be quite useless to me. "I think I'm going to go get a shower and maybe fix some eggs and bacon. Want some?"

She shakes her head. "I ate breakfast about seven hours ago. It will be dinner time soon."

"Yeah, well, I slept through that obviously," I say with a grin and push the box aside. "I had some catching up to do."

It's true. I slept until about three o'clock this afternoon. When I rolled out of bed, I felt a pressing need to hide myself away in the attic, searching for something to make me feel better.

I follow my mom back down the stairs, and she helps me fold the attic ladder back into place. She gives me a kiss on my dusty, sweat-covered cheek and heads back downstairs to take Chester for a walk. I head back into my bedroom, gather my clothes and toiletries out of my still-packed suitcase, and then take a much-needed shower.

My stomach rumbles as I take the effort and time to polish myself after my shower. That means drying my hair and even swiping on a bit of mascara, because no matter how crappy I feel on the outside, I always feel infinitely better if I can make myself slightly pretty on the outside.

Gathering up my clothes, I exit the bathroom and pad down the short hallway to the spare bedroom I'm occupying. While this house is nice, it's a lot smaller than our upscale house in Nashville that we lived in when my father wasn't in session. It definitely doesn't have the fine appointments of the townhome they had in Washington when he was in session. But still, it's perfect for my mom right now and she enjoys being back in her hometown.

Perhaps this is where I should be too. Maybe. It feels a little right, but that's probably the comfort of being with my mom. As I enter into my room, I think maybe it would help to even decorate this more to my tastes—

I give a piercing shriek as I realize there's someone sitting on my bed when I walk in. A hulking figure so large it depresses the mattress in at steep angles.

"Hello, Sloane," the deep voice says, and my heart refuses to stop its mad gallop when I realize it's Cain in my room. Blood racing like mad not only because he scared the shit out of me, but also because Cain is sitting in my room.

Cain.

Gorgeous, scarred, sexy Cain who, although he says he's forgiven me, still has no regard for what we had.

"What are you doing here?" I ask as I press a hand holding my panties to my breastbone, giving a rub to try to calm the unsteady beat underneath.

His eyes pierce into me as he sits hunched over, his elbows resting on his knees and his hands clasped between. Face so serious... somber, and quite possibly even apologetic. "You left without saying goodbye."

I turn from him, walk over to the closet, and throw

my dirty clothes on the floor. I'll need to go out and buy a laundry basket at some point. Keeping my back to him, I say, "I thought we said our goodbyes the night before last."

"No, I said goodbye," he points out. "You didn't seem quite willing to accept it, last I recall."

Spinning to face him, I let a little anger come through. Whoa… didn't know I was really all that angry until right this moment. "You fucked me against the wall of a sex club and told me quite clearly that I wasn't enough for you. Then you left. Why would I ever bother saying goodbye to you at that point?"

"I was wrong," he says ever so simply. Like that is the answer to all of our problems.

Is it?

"How do you figure?" I ask skeptically, because the one thing I've learned about Cain in our time together… he is brutally honest. He doesn't hold with punches, even when he knows they're going to hurt like a son of a bitch.

"Your mom seems really nice," he says, completely ignoring my question. "Granted… she was apparently on her way out to take some little rat-looking dog for a walk, but in the five minutes we spoke, I totally understand now."

"Understand what?" I'm thoroughly confused.

"That you were trying to protect her. Why the blackmail your editor held over your head was so powerful. I think about if that was my mom, and I would have done the same damn thing." He looks at me without judgment, his eyes sympathetic. He stands from the bed, towering tall, and walks to me. His hand comes out and he strokes his knuckles across my cheek, murmuring when he says, "You should have told me."

I close my eyes briefly, relishing his touch. When I open them back up, I tell him with naked honesty, "I didn't want you to think there was a valid excuse for my actions. That blackmail wasn't over my head at first. I came here and started things with you under very a dishonest and wrong purpose. The blackmail came later."

"True," he says, dropping his hand. I have to restrain myself from snatching it back to my face. He turns away from me and walks to the window that overlooks the street. "Yet you tried to make it right. Maybe you didn't go about it all in the correct order, but you were doing what you thought was best without intent to hurt. You were trying to save everyone in the end, and I have to respect that."

I hold my breath, afraid to even try to hope what this all means. He flew here... to see me.

To accept my apology.

Give me understanding.

"I was wrong in not giving you the benefit of the doubt," he says quietly as he looks out the window.

To apologize? He's apologizing to me?

"No, that's not true," I say quickly, clasping my hands in front of me. "You had a terrible experience in your past that was guiding you. The woman you loved betrayed you in a terrible way. I get why you couldn't so easily give me the benefit of the doubt."

Cain's head snaps to me, and his eyes narrow a bit. "I never loved Rachel."

"You didn't?"

How is that possible?

He turns his head back and looks out the window, pulling down on the wooden blind slat to get a better look. "I never felt for her what I feel for you."

My head spins. A kernel of hope-filled yearning forms, and then bursts open in my chest.

He tilts his head, his eyes scanning the street. "This is a nice neighborhood," he says casually, perplexing me greatly. "I could see us living here."

"What?" I ask, my voice clogged with confusion.

"If you won't come back to Jackson with me, I could move here." He turns from the window and looks at me, eyes naked with an honest offer.

"I don't understand," I squeak out.

I so don't fucking understand what's going on here.

Cain takes two long steps, and he's back in front of me. His hands come to my face and he pulls me in a few inches, bending his head closer to me. "Sloane... I don't know if I really understand what love is... but I'm feeling something inside of me for you that has to be something close to it. Maybe it is it. All I know is that I've been a fucking moron, according to Bridger, and I've come to the very late realization that I have to have you in my life. I seriously can't go another day without you, and I'm really sorry I didn't come to this brutal conclusion earlier. So I flew here with the hopes of talking you into coming back to Wyoming with me, but if you won't, I can relocate here. If you'll have me, that is. If you'll forgive me for being such a monumental prick to you, and give me another chance."

"Oh, wow," I breathe out, letting every bit of hopelessness and misery seep out. "Just… wow."

"Do you?" he gently asks. "Forgive me?"

"Yes," I whisper as I start to melt. My hands come to his chest to rest against the steady beat of his heart.

"Can you?" His head bends, brushing his lips against mine.

"Can I what?" My hands curl into his shirt, gripping hard as I feel my legs start to go weak.

"Can you love me?" Another whisper of his lips against mine.

"Yes," I say with a smile. "I can totally do that."

Then he kisses me deeply, holding my face so I don't think to pull away.

But I would never think to do that.

"Will you?" he says against my mouth, lips brushing back and forth. He leans his head away from me so he can look into my eyes.

"Will I what?"

His eyes are almost pleading. "Come back to Wyoming with me? Make a new life with me there?"

Chapter 33

Cain

"I 'M SO FUCKING horny right now, I'm pretty much guaranteed to attack you the minute we get in the house," I tell Sloane with all honesty.

"Why ever would that be?" she asks sarcastically as I pull into my driveway and shut off the engine to my truck.

"Because you've been squirming in that seat the entire ride from the airport. The way you're shifting around… little tiny groans that you're trying to suppress but I can hear all too clearly. My dick feels like it's going to break."

"Well, that's what you get when you insisted I wear this ass plug," she gripes at me, but she has a tiny smile on her face so I know she's not hating it all that much.

It's true… I'm horny as fuck because I know she's a hot, squirming mess with that plug wedged in deep. But that's what she gets for denying me the last two days we've been at her mom's house in Tennessee. While Sloane had no qualms about returning to Wyoming with me, and her mom was happy to see her happy, we stayed a few days so that Sloane could spend some time with her. It was my absolute pleasure to tell both women they didn't have to worry about an article from *Revealed* magazine, telling them all about Bridger's little talk with Sloane's editor.

So yeah… absolute torture the last two days sleeping in a bed with Sloane but not being able to fuck her. She said it was out of respect for her mom, and I got that, sure. But damn… my balls ache with need for her, especially after knowing that plug is getting her ready for me.

As soon as we got off the plane in Jackson, I pulled her over to the restrooms, reached into my carry-on suitcase, and pulled out the plug and a bottle of lube. I shoved it into her hand, and she almost dropped the items. She looked absolutely so stunned to see them in her palm. Glancing around like a crazy woman, she desperately closed both hands over the offending items, hoping no one was looking.

"Go in the bathroom and put that in," I told her gruffly, my cock already swollen and making an embar-rassing bulge in my jeans. "We're going to seal this deal by you giving me your cherry when we get to our house."

For a brief moment, there were all kinds of fight and denial in her eyes, but apparently, she was so touched by the words "our house" that she gave me a red-cheeked nod and scrambled off into the bathroom. I had to restrain myself from rubbing my crotch as I imagined her getting that thing in all by herself in the bathroom, which I know isn't easy but can definitely be done with enough determination.

The absolute persistence she must have had, because I did go up one size larger.

She came out of the bathroom with a flushed face and an awkward walk. I asked her how it felt, and she growled at me. My dick got harder.

I pull the key out of the ignition, and Sloane turns her head to look at me. I know she's feeling all kinds of uncomfortable right this minute, but she looks at me with pure adoration. "I'm glad you came after me."

"Welcome home," I murmur, leaning over to kiss her softly.

She sighs into me but I pull away, sweet romance done with for right now.

I pull Sloane into the house. We leave her bags in the back of my truck, and I'm not even sure I close the front door behind us. Drag her down the hall and into "our" bedroom, using rough hands to jerk her clothes off.

"Get on the bed," I tell her gruffly, pulling at my own shirt. Not very seductive but I've got a lifetime to show her all the ways I can be with her.

Sloane crawls onto the bed while I pull my shoes and pants off. I hastily dig through the drawer of my bedside table, standing up straight with a bottle of lube in my hand. When I turn to look at her, I groan and almost shoot my load right there.

She's on her knees, elbows to the mattress, and ass tipped up high in the air. Grinning at me with her cheek pressed to the pillow and a lock of hair over one of her brilliant blue eyes, she says. "Your ass awaits, sir."

I walk up to the bed and smooth a hand down her back, over the swell of her ass, where I give it a squeeze. "As much as I like you in that position, turn over on your back, baby. We're doing this face to face so I can watch your face when I pop that virgin ass."

She groans over my crudity but flips over on her back, her legs pressed primly together.

I walk to the end of the bed, throw the lube down by her hip, and pull her apart by the ankles. She has one hand lightly resting on her flat tummy, the other arm crooked by her head with her index finger trapped between her white teeth. She looks at me coyly, and it's the most beautiful thing I've ever seen.

It causes me to hesitate, just basking in the stunning creature before me that is all mine.

Forever.

Yup... forever.

I crawl onto the mattress between her legs and lower my weight onto her, causing her to pull her hand away from her stomach. Dipping my head, I bring my mouth to hers and give her a searing kiss. Her hands come to the back of my neck, and she arches up into me as she accepts my tongue.

Slipping one hand between her legs, I brush my fingers through her folds, not surprised in the least that they are dripping wet. I know the plug may have been a tad uncomfortable during the car ride home, but I also know it was causing skitters of pleasure within her the entire time. The fact that she's so wet tells me that I'm not just taking her gift, but she's also giving it to me with relish.

And while my ultimate goal is to take Sloane's last remaining virginal element, my cock wants inside her too desperately at the moment. I rotate my hips, she spreads her legs a little further, and I start to push my way inside her slick pussy.

"Mmmmm," Sloane murmurs against my tongue. "More."

I give her and myself more, because it feels so fucking good having that wet heat pull me in toward nirvana. I slide inch after inch of my cock in, deeper until I'm bottomed out and grinding against her. Every press of my pelvis against hers pushes her ass into the mattress and the plug gets jostled within her.

I have no game plan other than to make Sloane feel good. That will naturally make me feel good.

My hips start pumping, wet flesh smacking, moans filling the air. I slip a hand in between our bodies, find Sloane's clit, and start to rub against it while I fuck her harder. She pants into my mouth as I continue to kiss her, and I can feel her heart slamming against mine through the skin and bone separating them as our chests are mashed together.

"I'm... Cain... I'm going to come," she manages to mutter against my lips, and I slam into her harder.

Sloane's hips punch upward as her back arches off the bed. She gives a cry of ecstasy, a sob of relief, and her body starts to shudder. I pull my head up and watch as her eyes roll back under her lids as she orgasms. Pressing my knees into the mattress, I put a hand under her ass and raise it off the mattress. With my other hand, I reach behind her and grasp onto the plug, pulling it out slowly as her body shakes and trembles. Her eyes fly open as the plug is removed, and she lets out another hoarse cry, bucking against the sensation.

"Oh, God... Oh, God..." she mutters over and over again, her head thrashing left and right against the mattress.

Fucking sexy as hell.

I pull my cock out of Sloane's heat. She's so far gone in the throes of a never-ending orgasm that she doesn't seem to notice. I grab the lube, flipping the cap with my thumb. A steady stream pours onto her pussy. "Lift your legs, baby. Spread them apart for me."

Sloane raises her head from the mattress and looks at me with bleary eyes, but she complies. I stick my fingers under the stream of lube, catch a bit, and then toss the bottle aside. I smooth my slick fingers over her pussy, and she shudders again. I push my fingers down further, rub them over the tender skin from there to her tight hole, and gently massage in tiny circles.

"Feels good," she murmurs, rotating her hips and bringing her hands underneath her knees to help hold her legs open. It's wanton and filthy looking, and my cock weeps from the sight.

Speaking of cock... I fist it with lubed fingers, place one hand on the mattress, and lean forward. I guide the tip of my shaft right to her anus, rubbing all around it, and she mewls like a starved kitten.

"Deep breath, Sloane," I urge her. She sucks in a lungful, drawing my eyes briefly from my cock against her ass to those perfect tits with pebbled nipples. "Let it out slowly."

She does and my gaze drags back down to the erotic sight of my hard cock getting ready to plunder her ass.

I grit my teeth, push forward... right through her tight ring that was mercifully loosened a bit from the plug. My eyes shoot up, seeing Sloane with her brow glistening with sweat and her lower lip between her teeth. She has her head lifted off the pillow, and she's looking down between our legs with wide-eyed curiosity mixed with apprehension.

"Easy," I gentle her and push further in.

"Oh... wait... ow," she gasps out. I still, looking up at her while she adjusts. I've got no more than the fat head of my dick in her, but I know she's struggling.

"Want me to stop?" I whisper.

She shakes her head frantically. "No. Feels way better than it hurts. Give me more."

Oh, thank fuck... I don't think I can stop.

Sweat beads along one temple and slides down my jaw. I push in deeper, one, two, three more inches. Sloane chokes out a pleasured sob as my cock slides along her delicate nerve endings inside. She's past the point of pain, and I know this because she lifts her hips, trying to get me deeper.

I comply, and I slide completely in, bottoming out with a grunt of pleasure. "Oh, fuck, that feels good," I mutter as I drop the other hand to the mattress and just hold myself within her.

Sloane's eyes are fluttering, on the verge of closing in uncontrolled ecstasy. I'm going to lose her soon, I know, so I make sure she understands something very important.

"Sloane… baby," I say, and her eyes slowly open, eventually focusing on my own. "This ass is mine and no one else's. Ever."

Her brows draw inward. "What do you mean?"

"I mean… if you want us to play around again… with Bridger, Rand, Logan… I'm okay with that as long as no one ever touches this ass."

"You still want to… do that?" she asks in astonishment, and while I'm not one who normally likes to converse during my cherry ass fucking, this needs to be said.

"Maybe," I hedge. "We both have memberships to the club. I like kinky shit, and now I know you do too. I'm open to it."

Because yes, Bridger held Sloane's job at The Wicked Horse, and while I don't think she'll work there forever, it means I could pull her over there for a quick fuck on our break if I wanted to. That thought causes my cock to jerk inside of her a bit, sort of chomping on the bit to let loose.

And this is what she really needs to hear, because this

is the most important part and really doesn't have a damn thing to do with us playing with others. "I trust you. Implicitly. I can separate out the kink from the love, so if you want to try some stuff at The Silo, you just tell me what you want and I'll deliver."

Sloane's head comes further off the mattress as she peers at me, now seemingly oblivious that my cock is wedged deep in her ass. "Why do you trust me? How? After everything—"

I cut her off with a punch of my hips against her ass, reminding her there is a big dick filling her up. She groans, but I ignore it. "Because of everything you risked and sacrificed. You put me above your career, your mother… you wanted me after I was a prick. I love you and with that comes complete trust. If you want something that's out of the bounds of normalcy, and it makes you feel good, I'll always give it to you."

Sloane's eyes turn so tender that my heart actually starts thumping like a happy puppy's tail. She gives a slight shake of her head and says, "I think I'm going to pass on having any other men play with us. You're more than enough for me, but… I'm not averse to playing in the club with you."

And that is something I can happily live with.

"Sounds like a plan then," I tell her with a smile.

She lifts her head up further, and I meet her mouth with mine.

My life is complete.

Epilogue

Rand

I WALK THROUGH The Silo, turning the lights off behind me as I go. Normally, this would fall to Bridger or Cain, but neither one is around tonight. Bridger's attending some party out at the compound for the Mayhem's Mission motorcycle club, which translates into fucking some free pussy unassociated with The Silo. While this is Bridger's baby, sometimes I get the feeling that his "duties" here wear on him.

Sometimes, it seems he actually hates "servicing" some people, but maybe I'm trying to read something into the situation. Regardless, he's not here and neither is Cain.

He just flew back from Tennessee today and he's shacked up with Sloane, I'm sure still hammering out the necessary apologies that woman deserves from him.

Cute couple though. I figured out of all of us dudes, he'd be one of the last to drop given his history with Rachel, but what the fuck do I know? I'm definitely unlucky in love, but I'm okay if it never comes my way. I've got friends, a great job, and all the kinky fuckery I could ever imagine.

I snicker to myself, thinking about that.

Kinky fuckery.

Some chick said that the other night while Logan and I were both doing her, and we thought it was hilarious. She said she it was a term in one of her favorite books, but whatever.

It totally describes what happens within the walls of this circular building.

I make my way down the short hallway to the exit door, flipping down the switch of the sconce lighting and pushing the door open. The air is crisp and smells refreshing. Cleans the soul kind of good because sometimes when I walk out of The Silo, I feel like it's tainted by the things I do.

But again, whatever. I might feel dirty at times, but some of the shit I dip my wick into also feels fucking amazing.

I pull the door closed and ensure the lock is engaged. Security's become more important now than ever given that fuckwad Colton Stokes blabbing his mouth. Of course, on one hand, you could say it was a good thing because it brought Sloane Preston to our neck of the woods. Not only was she a fantastic fuck, and I hope Cain lets me in on that again, but it's also made my buddy super happy. So maybe Colton just deserved an ass whipping instead of the murder I'd like to dole out to him for threatening our existence.

The parking lot is nearly deserted, The Wicked Horse having closed nearly an hour ago. The Silo is technically open 24/7 for any members who want to get debauched, but the bartenders go off duty at the same time The Wicked Horse closes down at 2AM. I'm the last to leave after getting a last minute cock-suck from Carol, one of the lovely purveyors of fine drinks. She toddled out not but fifteen minutes ago with a tart goodbye. I should have returned the favor to her, but she owed me the blow job because she lost a bet last week on the Yankees game. She's a transplanted New Yorker and I hate the Yankees, so I always bet against them, no matter the price of the potential loss.

My eyes zero in on my Suburban parked up against The Wicked Horse in the space nearest the slate path that leads from the back door over to The Silo. I click the remote entry fob and the lights flash, indicating the doors are unlocked. I reach for the handle, pull it open, and just as I'm about to step in, my gaze falls on a white Mercedes coupe sitting two rows back and three spaces over. I start to turn away and then do a double-take as I realize it's Catherine's car.

I know she left The Silo probably about half an hour ago after giving everyone a show tonight. Since her husband died last week, she's been at The Silo every night, indulging in every wicked sex act you can imagine. Not that she didn't indulge before, but for some reason, since the old fart's death, she's seemed a bit more free-spirited in her pursuits. Maybe even doggedly determined to outdo herself every time.

Tonight, my tongue was hanging out of my mouth

while she occupied a room all to herself and played with a variety of electrical and mechanical toys that Bridger's been collecting. She got right up against the glass wall and made sure everyone could see what she was doing. I bet I watched her come at least six times before she finally fell into a heap on the floor, panting with sweat-soaked skin and drowsy eyes. After she collected herself, she got dressed and sauntered out the door, waving goodbye over her head. I was so fucking horny after that, it took no time at all for Carol to wrench an unbelievable orgasm out of me. And strangely… I was imagining Catherine sucking my cock at the time, which is a bit weird.

It's not like there's any mystery there. Catherine's deep throated me on a few occasions before, and I've fucked her on even more occasions than that. Didn't think she was really anything different from all the other sexual encounters I've had, but for some reason, it was her dark hair I imagined clenched in my fist rather than Carol's strawberry-blonde curls.

Perhaps Catherine left her car here and went home with someone else. That must be it and just as I start to turn my eyes back to my vehicle, I see movement within the darkness of the interior of her car. I peer harder, willing the light from the nearest security post to reveal the inside, and if I'm not mistaken, the seat is leaned back and she's lying down. Perhaps having just turned from one side to the other.

What the hell?

I close my door and walk quickly across the lot to her car, my head tilted in curiosity. As I get closer, I can see better, and it is indeed Catherine lying in the driver's seat reclined all the way back. She's on her side with her hands curled up by her face, her back to me. Those long, dark locks are spread out over her back and shoulder.

I tap gently on the window, knowing I'm going to startle her but not being able to help it. She jerks upright, looking at me with frightened eyes. When she recognizes me, I can see her give a sigh of relief. She raises the seat up and rolls the window down. It's then that I notice her car is running.

"Hey," she says, her eyes darting around the parking lot.

"What are you doing?" I ask, completely perplexed to find her sleeping in her car. I know she's not drunk because Catherine doesn't drink. At all.

She does some crazy shit in the club, and she doesn't want anyone to ever think it's not of her own free will. She owns her kinky fuckery… and owns it good. I don't think she does drugs, so it's very confusing to find her here like this.

"Um… I just…" Her voice trails off and her gaze falls down to her delicate fingers, which are intertwined tightly with one another.

"Catherine… were you going to spend the night out here?"

She lets out a huff of frustrated air. Looking back up to me with resignation in her eyes, she admits, "Yes."

Nothing more.

I cock an eyebrow at her. Catherine and her late hus-band reside in Vegas permanently, but he has a luxury cabin just outside of Jackson that they spent a lot of time at since he got her a membership at The Silo.

"Is your car broken down or something?"

She shakes her head and looks back down at her lap.

"Then what the fuck?" I ask, exasperated and also damn worn out from the night's activities. I want to get home and get some shut-eye. Work comes early and I cannot miss it. I have to open the tattoo shop I work for at ten in the morning, and I need the few hours of sleep I can squeeze in.

She's silent and I think she may refuse to answer me, but then her small voice reaches my ears and it stuns me. "I don't have anywhere else to stay."

"What do mean? You have a seven-thousand-square-foot home not thirty minutes away."

She shakes her head, that dark hair falling in a veil to hide her face. It's a gorgeous face, too. High cheekbones, exotic slant to her liquid brown eyes. It's a face that should be in movies or on magazines. A face beautiful enough that it landed her a wealthy husband on death's door and should have left her swimming in riches.

"Catherine," I prompt, pulling on the handle to her door. It's still locked so I reach my hand inside, find the lock, flip it, and then pull the door open. I step in, squat down, and place my hand on her thigh. "What is going on?"

She pulls in a shaky breath, lifts a hand to tuck her hair behind her ear, which exposes her face again, and then turns to look at me with bleak eyes. "He didn't leave me with anything. Just this car, which he had titled in my name."

"Excuse me?"

"Samuel left everything to his two children, which I get he would leave them with something. But he always promised me he'd take care of me. I'd always have a place to live. His attorney showed up at the Jackson house two days ago with an order that I had to vacate. I was allowed to pack up my clothes, and that was it."

My breath hisses out from between my teeth, and I wish that creepy fucker was still alive so I could pound his withered, crippled ass into the ground. That goddamn motherfucker.

I stand straight and hold a hand out to her. "Come on. You can crash at my place tonight. I'll help you figure something out."

"Seriously?" she asks, her eyes wide and her lips trembling. "I mean… we don't really know each other."

"I've been balls deep inside you a time or two, Catherine. I think I know you a little bit," I say with a teasing smile.

She blushes, and fuck… that's pretty. I've never seen Catherine blush, and she's done some things to make even the kinkiest of motherfuckers go red in the face.

"Are you sure?" she hesitantly asks.

"Positive," I say and push my hand toward her.

She turns the engine off before taking my hand. Swinging those long legs bared from the black leather mini skirt she wore tonight out, she says, "I'll be glad to pay you. You know… in sex or something. I've only got about fifty dollars in cash left to my name."

My cock leaps at the thought, because yeah… although I'm tired, I would not say no to fucking her tonight. But instead, I decide to be a gentleman. "You don't owe me anything. Let's get you to my place so you can get a good night's sleep. We'll talk about it more tomorrow and try to figure out how to take care of you."

She blushes again and stands from the car. Her hand goes to my chest and she leans up on tiptoes, I think maybe to give me a hot kiss, but instead, she brushes her lips across my cheek. "Thank you, Rand. You're a lifesaver."

Hmmmm… I like the sound of that.

If you enjoyed *Wicked Lust* as much as I enjoyed writing it, it would mean a lot for you to give me a review on your favorite retailer's website.

Connect with Sawyer online:

Website: www.sawyerbennett.com

Twitter: www.twitter.com/bennettbooks

Facebook: www.facebook.com/bennettbooks

Other Books by Sawyer Bennett

The Cold Fury Hockey Series
(Random House / Loveswept)

Alex

Garrett

Zack

Ryker

The Off Series

Off Sides

Off Limits

Off The Record

Off Course

Off Chance

Off Season

Off Duty

The Last Call Series

On The Rocks

Make It A Double

Sugar On The Edge

With A Twist

Shaken Not Stirred

The Legal Affairs Series
Objection

Stipulation

Violation

Mitigation

Reparation

Affirmation

Legal Affairs Serial Romance Boxed Set

Confessions of a Litigation God

Clash

Grind

Yield

Friction

The Wicked Horse Series
Wicked Fall

The Forever Land Chronicles
Forever Young

Stand Alone Titles
If I Return

Uncivilized

About the Author

New York Times and USA Today Bestselling Author, Sawyer Bennett is a snarky southern woman and re-formed trial lawyer who decided to finally start putting on paper all of the stories that were floating in her head. Her husband works for a Fortune 100 company which lets him fly all over the world while she stays at home with their daughter and three big, furry dogs who hog the bed. Sawyer would like to report she doesn't have many weaknesses but can be bribed with a nominal amount of milk chocolate.

Sawyer is the author of several contemporary romances including the popular Off Series, the Legal Affairs Series, The Carolina Cold Fury Hockey Series and the Last Call Series.

Printed in Great Britain
by Amazon.co.uk, Ltd.,
Marston Gate.